Keeper of Hearts

Crossings of Promise

Historical fiction with a touch of romance

Dianne Christner
Keeper of Hearts

Janice L. Dick
Calm Before the Storm

Hugh Alan Smith
When Lightning Strikes

Keeper of Hearts

DIANNE CHRISTNER

Herald
Press

Waterloo, Ontario
Scottdale, Pennsylvania

Library of Congress Cataloging-in-Publication Data

Christner, Dianne L., 1951-
    Keeper of hearts / Dianne Christner.
          p. cm.— (Crossings of Promise)
          ISBN 0-8361-9207-9 (pbk. : alk. paper)
    1. Anabaptists—Fiction. I. Title. II. Series
PS3603.H76 K44 2002
813′.54—dc21   2002000052

The paper used in this publication is recycled and meets the minimum
requirements of American National Standard for Information Sciences—
Permanence of Paper for Printed Library Materials, ANSI Z39.48-1984.

KEEPER OF HEARTS
Copyright © 2002 by Herald Press, Scottdale, Pa. 15683
    Published simultaneously in Canada by Herald Press, Waterloo, Ont.
    N2L 6H7. All rights reserved
Library of Congress Catalog Number: 2002000052
International Standard Book Number: 0-8361-9207-9
Printed in the United States of America
Inside design by Gwen M. Stamm
Cover art by Barbara Kiwak
Cover design by Sans Serif, Inc.

10 09 08 07 06 05 04 03 02 10 9 8 7 6 5 4 3 2 1

To order or request information, please call
1-800-759-4447 (individuals); 1-800-245-7894 (trade).
Website: www.mph.org

To Jim, Rachel, Mike, and Heather:
Thanks for your love and encouragement.
To S. David Garber and Mary Clemens Meyer,
Herald Press editors: Thanks for
your expertise and patience.

Wherefore let them that suffer according to the will of God commit the keeping of their souls to him in well doing, as unto a faithful Creator.

1 Peter 4:19

Prologue

In his Holy Roman Empire, A.D. 1544

My *kingdom is a rotting apple!* Charles V, Holy Roman Emperor, tilted his pointy nose upward to peer out the high arched window. Far beyond, many lands and lords joined together to form a vast kingdom. Its people were a diverse and contrary lot, and today he was tired of dealing with them. The emperor's gaze from the top of Coudenberg Hill swept across gothic peaks, the forested royal hunting reserve, and the beautiful palace grounds to rest upon a single apple tree dotted with pink blossoms.

. . . *a rotting apple bruised by the groping hands of the Turks and French. Everywhere, mushy-brown pulp. But the Germanic princes are the worms who rot the kingdom's core. For centuries, religion has kept the Holy Roman Empire united. No longer. Shouts of reformation fill the land. I must protect the church.*

Charles V turned away from the window. His vestments reflected the light, adding to his regal appearance. Walking to a high cupboard, he opened the drop door and pulled out an inner drawer decorated with precious stones. His eyes rested on a parchment scroll. Picking it up, he pointed it at one of those worm-princes, Duke Wilhelm.

The duke ruled over one of the largest realms in the kingdom. His lands encompassed Cleves, Julich, and Berg and ran along some of the emperor's own hereditary possessions. The emperor assessed the younger man. *Duke Wilhelm does well to veil his hatred toward me.*

It was less than a year since Charles had sent troops to wrestle back the piece of land, Geldern-Zutphen, that bridged his own possessions from north to south. When Duke Wilhelm was forced to relinquish Geldern-Zutphen, he had also reluctantly agreed to dissolve all alliance with the emperor's enemies and give up religious reformation.

The emperor thoughtfully traced one of his long, lean fingers along the cupboard's ebony and tortoiseshell veneer. "We have another fire to extinguish. The banks of the river Rhine are aflame with Anabaptists."

It was as if a corpse stood before him, so still was the duke. The emperor jutted out his bearded chin. "Menno Simons, the heretic, is in your land. It shouldn't be hard to find him, for I hear that everywhere his foot touches, converts spring up. What will you do about this matter?"

"I will find him, milord. I will stop him," Duke Wilhelm said.

The emperor nodded, his eyes falling on an ornate hour-glass. How long would it take the cadaverous duke to stop Menno Simons, the heretic? The princes were often reluctant to carry out the sentence of death the law required for radicals that did not conform to the church.

In the small village of Visserswert, within the German duchy of Cleves-Julich

Miles van Vissers pulled off his knee-high boots and set them by the hearth. Taking a small, leather knapsack from his pocket, he placed it on the trestle table among the river rushes his wife, Mariel, had dried for weaving. "I fear 'tis my fault our daughter is spoiled and headstrong," he said to her.

She sighed deeply. "Nay, 'tis both our faults. My own childhood was so lonely I have only wanted to love her. 'Tis easy to give in to our only daughter."

"Aye. When she looks at me with those eyes the color of sea and sky, the ones so like your own, I grow tender toward her. But just now, when she demanded to visit her friend

Esther, I saw something in her eyes that was not so sweet. I knew then," he said, as his finger shot into the air, "and not for the first time, I had been too easy on her."

"She is fearless when it comes to getting her own way. Even her brothers coddle her. I was pleased when you did not give in to her just now."

Mariel's words encouraged Miles to approach a delicate matter. He cleared his throat and ventured, "I've an idea. Perhaps this idea is of God, for it has been sailing around in my mind for several days past and does not care to leave."

"Pray, tell me." Mariel placed a hand on Miles' doublet and felt his quickening heartbeat.

"On my last voyage, I learned of a great need. The merchant Palmken has a failing wife. He has a business to run and a house full of children, and his servants are barely managing. I had the notion to send Anna to help the family, to nurse the woman and tend to their children."

Mariel withdrew her hand and gasped. "Anna, leave us?"

"Our daughter has seen sixteen summers and winters. 'Tis time she learned to take her eyes off herself."

"How far away is this place?"

" 'Tis only down the river Maas and along the coast of the North Sea."

"Is it a safe place?"

"She will be in the Lord's care."

"And you believe this thing is of God?"

"Aye."

Mariel nodded. "I wish I had your faith, Miles."

"Open the knapsack."

Mariel pushed aside some rushes, loosened the leather strap on the knapsack, and shook out its contents. Three beautiful seashells dropped onto the table. They shone like pearls as they reflected the light from an open-shuttered window.

"Oh." Mariel's eyes lit up, and she flashed Miles a warm look.

"They caught my eye when I was on the docks today. I thought you and Anna might like them."

She examined the shells with pleasure. "They have the colors of a sunset."

Visserswert, One Year Later

Anna van Vissers tipped her face upward into the breeze that blew across the North Sea, over the bow of her papa's ship, *de Lowlander*. Her hair billowed free and wild. She was eager to put many waters between her and her recent sorrow.

It was four seasons ago she had left the green and heather fields of Visserswert, her head filled with fanciful ideas of what the world was all about. Anna knew nothing of suffering then. Oh, she had tried to help, but there had been nothing she could do. The woman had shriveled up and died, leaving five children that Anna felt helpless to comfort.

How she missed her family! When her feet touched ground again, she would run straight into Mam's loving arms, and give her papa a kiss. They would stroll along the river dock, where the air reeked of salt and fish, and visit the shops with nets and barrels that enticed Papa. The men would slap him on the back and tease Anna until she blushed. She was longing to see her brother, Willem, and her friend, Esther.

Papa would pray, and they would go to the Eelene parish church across the river Maas. She had attended services all her life in this church that proudly adhered to the traditions of God—the God who kept them from harm and evil.

The world of the past four seasons had left a foul taste in her mouth. She relished the old flavors—memories of her own dear village—where her life could return to normal.

"But, Grandfather . . ."

"Nay, Peter. I must do this thing before my time comes." Jarvis Cremer's large, withered hand gripped the silver hilt of a dagger.

Peter Cremer sucked in his breath reverently as the old man placed the prized possession in his open palm. He couldn't remember a time when his grandfather had not worn the dagger against his right hip.

"You remember the meaning of my name, lad?"

"Aye, Grandfather. Jarvis, 'keen with a spear.' "

" 'Tis a *baselard*. You know its origin?"

Peter whispered over the lump in his throat. "Basel."

Jarvis nodded. "Wear it in memory of all the brave men that came before."

"I will wear it to honor you."

"That you will—I am sure of it. And your name means 'rock.' Perhaps the dagger will help you become that man. If my eyes were not planted skyward in your grandmother's direction . . ." His voice trailed off.

Peter could only nod.

A *few weeks later*

Trouble was brewing. When the Duke of Cleves-Julich stopped one reformer, two more popped up like dandelions in his place. It was more than a year since the duke had stood before the emperor in his royal chambers, and the emperor's impatience had intensified. New reports of the elusive Menno Simons tickled the Duke of Cleves-Julich's ears, and he could think of nothing but routing out the heretic and appeasing the emperor.

The duke's bailiff, his nose bent toward gain, had followed a scent and questioned a healer woman who confessed that she had given Menno's wife herbs. When the bailiff arrested her, she claimed she didn't know where Menno and his wife could be found, but she gave the bailiff the name of a Visserswert man, Miles van Vissers. Miles, she said, knew where the preacher Menno laid his head to rest each night.

PART ONE
Visserswert

Chapter 1

Anna van Vissers' body ached from its cramped position. Only that morning, she had hidden between the canvas implement sack and the wooden water barrel in her brother's wagon. It was a hasty decision, conceived from fear and love.

Anna's insides still quaked every time she remembered the angry beadles who had apprehended her papa. Since then, weeks had passed, and hope of Papa's release grew slim. She had just recovered from her heart-rending experience at the Palmkens'. She could not survive another loss, not of one so dear as Papa.

Now her fellow travelers, still unaware of her presence, were busy setting up camp. *If I can just stay awake until they sleep, I can help myself to some rations and sneak out of the wagon to relieve myself.* Anna eased her creaky bones into a more comfortable position, then froze at the sound of her brother's voice and footsteps.

"I will get our bedclothes before it gets dark," Willem said, as he stood beside the wagon.

Anna sucked in her breath and waited. A hand brushed against her thigh. Suddenly, the blankets were peeled backward, and a draft of cold air enveloped her. There was a long silence.

"Anna?" Her brother's surprise quickly turned to anger. "What is the meaning of this?"

She exhaled and raised herself on her elbow. Willem was

scowling. Well, she was not pleased either. "You do not need to use that tone with me, Willem."

The others, Horst Cremer the stonecutter and his son Peter, ventured toward the wagon. Anna could see their startled eyes peering at her over the sideboard. Horst's wits returned first, and he offered a hand. "Come down."

Untangling her skirt with a quick jerk, Anna tried to obey his request. Her knees buckled painfully, and she fell backward onto the heap of discarded blankets.

"Ach! My legs are numb."

Horst's eyes softened briefly, but his voice remained stern. "Take the time you need." The stonecutter turned his back to wait, but Peter and Willem continued to frown disapprovingly at Anna from across the sideboard.

"Must you stare?" she asked. Peter and Willem jerked their gaze away and turned their backs. She could see by Willem's red neck that he was deeply angry.

He had strictly forbidden her to accompany them to Valkenburg, though she had begged him. In her estimation, he had been unreasonable. She wanted to help Papa, too.

Briskly she rubbed her legs, which stung like fire, and considered the circumstances. The Duke of Cleves-Julich was obsessed with ferreting out a heretic named Menno Simons, the leader of a group the Church called Anabaptists. The duke hoped that by imprisoning her papa, Miles van Vissers, he could force a confession that would lead him to Menno Simons.

Anna was her papa's treasure. He had made a game of addressing her as some rare jewel—a pearl when he knew she was hiding something, an Antwerp diamond when she was bright and cheery, a ruby when she was moved by the heart. Surely she could persuade him to cooperate with the duke. Papa *must* listen to her. His life depended on it.

"Ahem." The stonecutter cleared his throat.

It was time for reckoning. Anna tapped his shoulder.

Horst's hands encircled her small waist and lifted her down from the high wagon. When she touched the ground, he released her and limped backward several steps. "Now, I will repeat your brother's question," he said, unconsciously rubbing his leg, lame from earlier years of soldiering. "What is the meaning of this?"

"I had to come. I have to talk to Papa."

"Talk to Papa!" Willem roared back. "That is foolishness. You should have stayed home with Mam. Now we have to worry about your safety as well as Papa's."

Anna shrank from his wild, gesturing arms and pulled her cloak tight, but the coldness pierced from within rather than without. It seeped from the deepest, most private part of her soul. Guiltily, she wondered if Willem was right. She could feel her determination dwindling.

Her mother did have a hoarse cough, but the stonecutter's wife, Freda, was with her in Visserswert. Surely she would see to Mam's needs, wouldn't she? The dull ache inside Anna's head intensified. She rubbed her temples to soothe the throbbing and pinched her eyes shut. She would sooner be sick than give way to tears in front of the men.

The ground swayed. A set of strong hands gripped her shoulders. "Anna?"

Dimly, she heard Horst's voice. "Peter, fetch Anna something to drink, and I will fix her some food."

Anna struggled to right herself. "I am sorry, Willem," she managed to say.

"Hush, Anna. I am not done with you." Willem swept her up into his arms easily. "But for now, let's get you close to the fire."

By the time Anna was growing warm from the crackling blaze, Peter arrived with a vessel of water. The coolness refreshed her throat, and she drank greedily. "Could I have more?" she asked.

Peter looked troubled as he took the tankard and hurried off.

"Thank you, Peter," she said, when he brought her the water. "I thought I would die of thirst today." At last she was satisfied, and said, "I know I deserved my discomforts, disobeying the way I did."

She shifted her gaze from Peter to her brother. "But I had to come. Please let me stay."

"I don't have much choice now, do I?" said Willem. "Time is something we cannot waste."

"But she cannot come!" Peter paced before the campfire. "I could take her home on Father's mount."

Willem seemed to consider it, but Anna realized too that time was their worst enemy. Their eldest brother Skylar needed time to appeal to Archbishop Herman von Wied. The softhearted archbishop might agree to help, but he was in Bonn, and the journey was a day and a half east and another day up the Rhine. Their journey to Valkenburg was a shorter one, and they had traveled only one day, but Anna knew there could be no turning back.

Before they could discuss it further, Horst limped toward them with food he had prepared. "Eat this, Anna." She took it and ate hungrily. He waited until she was finished, then said, "You have been foolish to go against your brother's wishes. Now, if you are wise, you will agree to do as you are bidden for the rest of this journey." She felt his light touch upon her arm. "We want only what is best for your own safety and for your papa's. Do you understand?"

Anna nodded, but she did not understand. Why should she do nothing to save her papa?

"We have your word then?" Horst asked.

She stared mutely into the fire. How could she give her word when she had no idea what it would take to free her papa? She must choose her words carefully.

"Anna?"

She stopped nibbling at her lip. "I trust we will not be at odds again."

His look was stern. "I trust not."

Soon the camp talk turned to Anna's papa. "Papa knew the risks," Willem said. "We all know the risks."

"This is true," Horst answered.

Anna heeded every word. In the weeks since her papa was apprehended, she had hungered for every scrap of information. Willem had tried to protect her and Mam from the details of Papa's fate.

"If we can just stall the magistrates until word comes from Skylar," Willem went on.

"The brethren in Valkenburg may be able to help us, too," Peter suggested.

Anna knew they had forgotten her presence. She dared not move, lest she draw their attention again. Peter was hidden from her view, but as he spoke she could envision his features. His lean face would be set, under his shoulder-length brown hair, his square jaws clenched in calm determination. His brown eyes, like always, would be warm and attentive.

During their conversation, no one referred to the wagon and the preparations they had laid. Should Anna's father be executed for heresy, they hoped to bring his body home for burial. Anna squeezed her eyes shut, blotting out the hypnotic flames of the campfire. Papa had not resisted much when Cleves-Julich's man, the bailiff from the territory of Valkenburg, had barged into their home.

If only Papa had denied his acquaintance with the despicable Menno Simons, she thought. *Should a deed so kind and innocent as giving the man a ride down the river Maas to the village of Roermond be deserving of death?* Her papa, a boatman by livelihood, was a generous man. Was that cause to die?

A burst of crackling sparks startled her eyes open. "I will take the first watch," Peter said. His hand involuntarily touched the dagger at his side.

"And I the second," Willem offered.

Eventually, all the beds were laid. As Anna settled in, Peter passed close by and, not faltering in his gait, bent close to whisper, "Sleep easy, Anna. Never fear about highwaymen or wild beasts while I am on guard."

In the darkness, she could imagine Peter's teasing grin, yet Anna knew his words rang true. The stonecutter's family had been close friends with her family, and sometime over the years, Peter had appointed himself her protector.

A westerly wind churned the countryside's creaky windmills. Mist blew off the river Maas. Anna shivered and tugged her blanket tight over her head. She hated this helpless feeling. *Oh, Papa.*

Chapter 2

Willem reined in the team, then pointed a sturdy forefinger above Anna's hood. "Look."

In the distance, through the haze, rose the mighty defense towers of the Kasteel of Valkenburg, high and round like giant scrolls. The marlstone walls shone with a golden tint.

A tremor ran through Anna's body. There was never anything so magnificent or daunting in their hamlet of Visserswert. This fortress towered well above the rolling, green cow pastures and walled-in farming village below. Anna felt a small tug on her hair and looked at Willem, who gave her a reassuring smile.

"Let me see to this," Horst cautioned. His mount kicked up a splatter of mud as he galloped away.

Anna watched the conversation between Horst and the gatekeeper. Horst gestured. The gatekeeper cocked his head to the side and stretched his neck to get a better look at them. Soon the gatekeeper motioned them forward with a sweep of his sword, and she felt the brusque bump of Willem's shoulder.

"Ga'op!"

When they passed through the gate, Anna averted her face until they were well out of sight of the gatekeeper and safe within the village of steep gabled roofs, white timbered houses, and narrow cobbled streets.

Then she turned to Peter, in the back of the wagon. "How did your papa get us past the gatekeeper?"

"Father told him we are visiting a family in the village."

"But we are not . . . " she began to protest.

"Menno Simons gave us the name of a family."

"That heretic? Why, he is the cause of Papa's ill treatment!"

"Hush, Anna." Willem cast a wary glance over his shoulder at Peter. " 'Tis better not to mention him or the believers to Anna. She detests them."

Anna drew her mouth into a grim line. She must act more wisely.

A cheery blaze on the hearth warmed the lower chambers of the Welkom Huis. In the upper story, a small fire also flared—Anna's temper. She planted her hands on her hips. "But I want to go with you. I did not come to stay shackled inside some tavern!"

"It is a respectable inn. And I will not be drawn into an argument with you. Come," Willem said.

Rolling her eyes, Anna brushed past Peter and Horst to follow Willem down a row of closed doors and into the room they would share. Anna felt more cheerful when she saw the window and the bedside table with a basin of water and a tin lamp. She had never spent the night in an inn.

Nodding toward the bed against the far wall, Willem pleaded, "Rest now while you can. I must see how things fare. You will be safe here."

"My safety is of no consequence."

Willem guided her toward the bed. When she resisted, his face grew red with emotion. "You shall stay, Anna!" He thrust out his hand to dramatize his point and accidentally whacked the oil lamp. The tin bonged loudly.

Glaring at Willem, Anna reached out to steady it.

He jerked back his hand and strode across the room. Then he turned to say, "We will not be gone long."

"Whetstone!" Anna muttered at the closed door. Her

brother was just like a grindstone, honing her nerves. And presiding over her like some lord!

Several hours passed before a rap at the door wakened her. Anna shuffled across the room and drew open the door. When she recognized Willem, she snatched at his sleeve. "Come in." Horst and Peter trailed into the room behind him, their faces crestfallen.

"Papa is in the kasteel donjon," Willem blurted.

She dropped her arms limply to her side. "How did you find out?" Though she had expected it, the news enveloped her with terror.

"Never mind that now. While there is still daylight, Horst and I are going to the kasteel."

"Indeed not! You cannot leave me again."

"Peter will stay and take you to supper."

Peter's wink poorly masked his disappointment, and she felt a twinge of shame that Peter must be burdened with her keeping. "Very well," she said.

That evening, Peter and Anna lingered over their supper of pork pie and cider in the common room, near the hearth. A serving girl moved in and out among the narrow plank tables, the ragged hem of her skirt sweeping the floor. Anna spent most of her time observing the activities of the inn. Still, throughout the meal, she had noticed an underlying mirth in Peter's expression.

Finally she asked, "Why do you keep smirking at me, Peter?"

He placed his elbows on the table and leaned forward. "I cannot disregard the memory of your saucy retort when Willem first discovered you in the back of the wagon." He mimicked, " 'You do not need to use that tone with me, Willem.' "

"Oh, that." Anna grinned. "I was stalling."

Peter slapped his hands on the table and laughed heartily. The serving girl's round hip bumped a table as she peered over her shoulder, but he paid her no heed. "You almost convinced me that Willem was the one caught in the act of wrongdoing."

Anna smiled sympathetically at the inquisitive serving girl, then cocked her head, and asked, "Truly?"

"Almost."

A moment of silence passed, then Anna asked, "Do you wish you were at the kasteel with the others?"

Peter hesitated, then replied in a soft voice. "I have enjoyed your company. I missed you while I lived with Grandfather."

Anna pulled a skeptical face and leaned forward. "Let us go after them. I have noticed your dagger . . ."

"Whoa!" Peter raised his hand. "Do not even think such things. Not while you are in my care."

"Willem does not understand. I must see Papa."

"And I hope you shall."

At times, Peter could be as unyielding and stubborn as her two brothers. Tonight the look in his eyes warned her that he would not disobey Willem's wishes.

Peter watched Anna pout. Even in the low light of sparsely placed beeswax candles and tin lamps mounted to the wall, her eyes fascinated him. When she was angry, they froze like an icy river—deep blue with glints of silver. When she was happy, they warmed like a sunny sky. Right now they resembled the mischievous North Sea her papa navigated in his merchant ship. Perhaps that was why he felt the need to protect her.

Anna blinked and gazed at him inquisitively. "Did your world change while you were gone?"

Peter had spent two years in the northern area of Krefeld

living with his grandparents because his grandfather had been too weak to care for his failing wife. After the death of Peter's grandmother, he and his grandfather had returned to Visserswert.

"Aye. Much has changed," Peter nodded. A few curls had worked themselves free from Anna's coiled braids, and he remembered how she had looked when they discovered her in the back of the wagon. Her hair had been free and wild—darker than wheat, and like leather, only softer.

Peter reined in his thoughts. Since his return to Visserswert, Anna had affected him differently. He was not sure why or even if he liked the change.

He frowned and pushed back his chair. "It has been a long day for you. Perhaps it is time to retire."

She shrugged. "Very well."

As they left the room, the serving girl leaned on a broom by the hearth. She gave Anna a wistful glance, then strolled toward the table where they had been seated. When Anna and Peter had climbed the stairs and reached Anna's door, he turned to her and put his hand on her sleeve.

"Give me your word that you will not do anything foolhardy," he said, seriously.

"How do I know what seems foolish in your eyes?"

"You will stay in your room?"

"I would not venture out into the darkness of such an evil city alone."

Peter was not entirely convinced. He studied her a moment longer, his hand lingering on her arm.

She tilted her head and gave him a saucy smile. "Peter, I do not even have the lay of the land yet. I will stay."

When he had her word, his hand slipped away. "I trust you will sleep well then. Good night."

"And you."

Peter returned to his room and lit the solitary tin lamp. He looked at the gloomy shadows and wished there were something he could do to help his friends. Anna had been close to the truth. Now that she was tucked safely in her bedchamber, he did wish to be with the others at the kasteel or wherever they were.

Horst limped up the steps of the village house and gave the door a few firm raps. Beside him, Willem softly cleared his throat. They were surrounded by thick blackness. It was a bad time to venture onto unfamiliar streets, where robbers lurked ready to take advantage of the unsuspecting or careless. The two men were relieved when the door swung open and a pleasant-faced man appeared.

"We heard you might be able to help us, that you are believers, and that we can trust you," Horst said.

The man's expression changed. "Such talk. And from strangers."

"We are from Visserswert. My good friend, this lad's father," Horst gestured toward Willem, "is imprisoned in the kasteel donjon. Please, believe us."

The man inside the house studied them, then cast a searching glance behind them, and nodded. The door opened wider. "Come in."

Horst and Willem slipped inside.

The sounds of laughter and conversation that drifted up from the lower level of the Welkom Huis had long ceased by the time Peter heard Willem's and Horst's footsteps on the wood-plank floor. As they lingered in the corridor whispering, Peter hurried across the room and cracked open the door.

"How did you fare?"

"We could not get into the kasteel, but we spoke with some of the city's brethren," Willem whispered, wiping sweaty strands of blond hair from his face.

"Aye?"

"They spread the word even now," Horst added. "There is a good chance they can get us in to see Miles. One of the brethren's sons is a knight at the kasteel."

"Excellent!"

"Sh!" Willem pressed his finger to his lips and nodded toward Anna's room. "We must be careful. We don't want to endanger our new friends, and I don't want to raise Anna's hopes just yet."

The creak of the door roused Anna, and she shifted in the bed. "Willem? Is that you?"

"Aye."

"Where have you been all this time?" she asked in a sleepy voice.

Anna heard him moving about in the darkness. His voice sounded weary. "The donjon guards will not let us in. I guess it is up to Skylar."

"But Skylar is not here. Papa is depending upon us."

"Papa does not know we are here. He is depending upon God."

Willem's reply grated on Anna. In her opinion, Papa was testing God. He had participated in the religious meetings where Menno Simons preached about a believer's baptism. But arguing with Willem over spiritual matters would only increase his fervor to hide details and make him more close-mouthed. Anyway, she did believe in God and trust him to answer her prayers at the Eelene parish church.

"But of course. I am sorry."

In the darkness, she felt Willem's light touch on her shoulder. He wound a strand of her hair around his finger. "Don't worry, little sister. I will not give up until we see Papa. I will sleep on the floor."

"Thank you, Willem," she whispered.

A week passed, and each day Willem tried to get into the donjon. Every night he came back to the inn late, from where Anna did not know. Usually Peter, or Horst, with his hobbling gait, accompanied her on walks through the village during the day. She spent the long evenings in the Welkom Huis. There was still no sign of Skylar and no appeal from Archbishop Herman von Wied. Anna's impatience increased daily, especially with her tight-lipped brother.

Every time she left the inn, she watched for landmarks. She listened with a keen ear and acquired much information, including the routines of the kasteel guards who passed in and out of the gates and beyond the thick kasteel walls. A plan began to form in her mind. But it was as if her brother could see the spokes turning, for she found herself under even closer watch by Willem, Horst, or Peter.

A dream finally spurred Anna into action. Early one morning she dreamed her papa had given the duke the information he wanted about the Anabaptist heretic Menno Simons. But when she awoke, Papa remained a prisoner in the donjon.

Anna's mouth went dry, and she began to tremble. In recent years, hundreds had been executed for similar deeds—burned at the stake in Antwerp, drowned in the rivers, and killed by the sword in places like Amsterdam and Zurich.

She recalled the hate on the beadles' faces as they forced her papa out from their home. She would never forget how they had lifted their gleaming rapiers in warning as they threatened Willem. "And we'll be watching you!"

Suddenly, Anna panicked. Willem had already left for the morning. She must set her plan into motion before it was too late for Papa. She willed herself to calm down enough to dress. Then she stuffed her only extra gown beneath her cloak and went down to the common room, where the guests were dining. She hoped that Horst and his son were nowhere in sight. They were not, but she knew that it was only a matter of time. Without hesitating, she seated herself at a table to wait for the girl who had served them every day since their arrival.

She clasped and unclasped her hands, all the while straining her neck to catch a glimpse of the plump serving girl. Finally, the girl sauntered into the room.

Anna motioned her over. "I hope you can assist me in an urgent matter," she whispered.

The girl's breath smelled stale as she leaned close, and her cheek dimpled in a smile. "What matter might that be?"

"I would like to make a trade. Here." Anna pulled a bit of the dress's fabric from under her cloak. It was the only spare clothing she had brought when she stowed away in Willem's wagon, but it would be worth the sacrifice. "This dress for a beggar's dress. Could you find me one?"

The girl's eyebrows shot up. Anna knew that she instantly recognized the fine quality of the cloth, some that Anna's papa had purchased in his travels. The girl's probing eyes moved over Anna's trim but shapely figure. Anna felt embarrassed, until she saw the beginnings of a conspiratorial smile.

"I believe I might have that sort of thing."

Anna pulled the dress back beneath her cloak. "Good! I have the far chamber," Anna whispered. "Can you bring it there?"

The girl nodded.

"Thank you. But please hurry."

Anna paced the floor until she heard a soft knock. Rushing to the door, she pulled the girl inside. "Did anyone see you?"

"Nay, the hall is deserted."

"Good." Anna closed the door and crossed the room to fetch her own gown and held it up for inspection. She did not offer the undergarment, with the wide sleeves lined in fur, for it was her favorite.

The girl cast a yearning look across the full gathered skirt and square-necked bodice of the dress, edged with bluish gray. "It is lovely."

"And you will never mention this to anyone?"

"Nay."

"Let me see what you brought."

With deft, plump hands, the girl unbundled a drab gray, woolen shift. Anna took one look at the shapeless garment and squealed, "Perfect! Here." The two girls exchanged garments, and then Anna guided the servant toward the door. "Thank you. And remember," she cautioned, her finger to her lips, "nary a word."

"I shall remember," the girl vowed. With a partially concealed smile, she disappeared behind the closed door.

Anna swept across the room, her fingers already undoing the white bodice lacing of her dress. She halted when she heard a knock. Before the door could crack open, she lurched wildly toward the bed and shoved the serving girl's dress beneath the fur covering.

With her back to the door and her heart galloping, she called, "Enter."

Willem entered and strode across the room. "I see you are up. Good!"

"Why?" Anna's fingers fumbled, trying to retie her dress.

Willem lowered himself onto the edge of the bed, and she felt a surge of fear that he might notice the unsightly lump under the fur coverlet.

"We are going to see Papa," he said.

His words caught Anna off guard, and it took her a moment to recover. When she did, she reeled around. "At last! Oh Willem, can it truly be?"

"Aye. Hurry now, Anna. Arrangements have been made. We must go to the kasteel before the archers finish morning exercises."

Anna felt a rush of relief that she would not have to carry through with her plan. On its heels, she felt mounting excitement. "I am ready now."

"Good," he smiled.

Anna followed Willem from the room, then hung back. "Oh, just one moment. I forgot something."

Back in her chambers, Anna snatched the ugly woolen shift from beneath the covers and searched for a better hiding place. Where could she hide the smelly thing from Willem? *Ugh!* It did carry a stench. She tugged mightily at the straw mattress until she was able to stuff the dress under it. She bounced on the bed to smooth out the lump and grabbed her cloak on the way to the door. *I am going to see Papa.*

Chapter 3

Horst and Peter accompanied Anna and Willem as far as the kasteel *barbican*, the outer tower and fence with sharp-pointed stakes. Overhead, dark clouds hovered and a sudden clap of thunder rent the air. Peter glanced apprehensively at the sky, then at Anna and the kasteel that loomed before them.

"Are you sure you should take Anna along?" he asked Willem for the third time.

"Aye. He is sure." Anna gave Peter a black look and gripped her brother's arm.

"She has come this far. There will be no turning back for her," Willem said. Anna shot him an appreciative smile.

"We will wait for you here, then," Horst said.

Peter's expression remained glum. Anna was glad when Willem hurried her along to the drawbridge and across the moat. As they moved inside the gate they heard the zinging sound of bowstrings. Archers lined up in rows, taking aim on the practice grounds. They wore yellow doublets, belted in red, over black woolen hose. Anna could hear the thuds of arrows penetrating their targets. A man who was intently watching the training acknowledged them with a nod. They waited, as Willem had been instructed.

Soon the same man, dressed in the lambskin and fur of the knighthood, joined them. His eyes showed no emotion. "Follow me," he grunted.

Anna clung to Willem's arm as they hurried to keep up

with the knight. He motioned them past the chief porter, a frightening figure with his long dark hair and sinister, thin black mustache. Inside the bailey, people scurried about their duties in the stables, shops, barracks, and chapel. They paid no heed to Willem and Anna. Her gaze fastened on a guard stationed at the top of a tower. They passed through another gate and up a narrow stone stairway that led into the keep.

There the knight spoke again. "This will be your only visit. Keep it short."

Willem thanked him. The man's gruff attitude caused Anna to wonder if Willem had bought him with a fistful of guilders.

Once inside, they followed the knight past a magnificent coat of arms and into a narrow passageway that wound downward. In the thick darkness, Anna could not see where to place her feet on the slippery stone staircase. She clung to Willem's arm as the dreary corridor twisted downward. Her shoulder brushed against the damp, slimy stone wall.

Finally they stopped. Anna caught her breath and inhaled musty air. Their guide spoke in low tones to a jailer and said to them, "I will return soon."

The jailer immediately opened a heavy door on large, iron hinges and handed them a lamp. They stepped inside. The door clanged behind them.

"Papa!"

Anna felt the weak grip of her papa's hands. "My children. I cannot believe you are here."

"Hello, Papa." Willem's voice was husky.

In the cavernous depths of the donjon, the only other light came from a small, square window far overhead. A pitiful amount of straw in a corner was the only comfort in sight.

Anna was shocked by her father's weak state. He had always been a strong man, used to the heavy labor aboard ship. Now his face looked drawn and thin. When Willem held the lamp close, the light revealed a large yellow bruise.

"Please, sit down," Anna begged Papa, and she and Willem helped him lower himself before joining him on the floor. Several large roaches scurried away.

"We must get you out of here," said Anna.

"Nay. 'Tis not the will of God, child." Something in the certainty of his voice silenced her, though the familiar objections rose to choke her throat.

She listened as he explained. "I have been sentenced."

"What is the sentence, Papa?" Willem asked.

"Do not fear, children. It sounds terrible, but I am content." Miles breathed deeply, and his chest rattled. "Ready to meet my Savior. My eyes are fixed on my heavenly home. I am filled with unspeakable joy."

"The sentence?" Willem repeated, his voice softer this time.

Miles wheezed, "They can burn my body, but they can never destroy my spirit."

Anna pressed her fist against her mouth. *Execution by fire? This cannot be happening! I will not allow it. What is Papa thinking? I must change his mind.*

She clawed at her papa's sleeve. "We need you, Papa. Just tell them what they want to know. Then you can get out of here. Just look at you."

She had always been able to win her papa over with a look or a smile, but today he seemed as unmovable as the donjon's stone walls. He had changed so much in the past weeks that she hardly knew him.

"Two priests visit regularly." Miles took another labored breath. "The bailiff comes, too, to get information. But I will never lead them to Menno Simons. The Lord uses him in a mighty way. I do not regret my choice to be baptized. I only regret that they took my Bible away from me."

Anna wondered if, indeed, his mind had failed him. "But Papa, we love you. Think of us. Think of Mam."

"It breaks my heart to be parted from you, from Mariel."

Miles broke down with wretched sobs. He fought for control. "I must be faithful." He breathed heavily. "Set eyes on Christ . . . his love and . . . eternal home . . . together again . . ."

"Papa," Willem interrupted, "Skylar has gone to Archbishop Herman von Wied in the city of Bonn. Soon you will be delivered."

"Nay," Miles' eyes drooped, and he shook his head. "The emperor presses . . . the duke shan't let me go. I am his peace offering to the emperor . . . If he cannot have Menno Simons . . . My time is short."

"But, Papa," Anna tried to dissuade him.

"I have peace." Miles turned to Willem. "It is up to you and Skylar to teach the family the true way."

"What way?" Anna asked.

"Put aside sin as much as you are able, with Christ's help. Follow him alone. Believe and be baptized. The Holy Spirit will fill your heart with love."

Anna frowned while Willem nodded, accepting the responsibility. "I will."

With a sinking feeling, Anna realized that both her papa and Willem were snagged in Menno Simons' deadly claws. They were as long and sharp as those of the fierce black lion pictured on the duke's coat of arms. She had gleaned enough information to know that receiving baptism as an adult was one of the worst offenses to the church. So that was why Papa was here. Not only had he befriended Menno Simons, but he had been baptized.

"Take care of your mother." Miles looked at Anna. "And your sister. Tell your mam I love her."

"Aye, I shall."

Tears rolled down Papa's cheeks. "The Lord is faithful. They have not confiscated our property. Surely, it is an oversight. But no matter what happens, trust in God." He clutched Willem's sleeve. "Promise me!"

"I promise, Papa."

A scraping sound came from the metal latch of the heavy door behind them. Miles struggled to rise. Anna panicked as Willem helped her papa stand.

"Have faith, Papa," he choked. "God be with you."

"And God be with you both," said Miles. "We shall meet again." He pointed upward, then cupped his hands around each of their faces and kissed them.

Anna would forever remember the taste of her papa's tears and the feel of his once strong, now frail, hands on her cheeks.

Willem pulled her away, and the door slammed shut. He held her until her sobs subsided, then half-carried, half-led her up the steep, narrow staircase. Her heart felt as if it would explode from the sorrow she carried. They stepped out of the kasteel into a downpour of rain. Willem fumbled for her hood, threw it over her head, and grabbed her hand.

The execution took place five days later. Their brother Skylar had appeared, weary and dispirited, without the writ from the elector. The archbishop had been traveling, and there was nothing Skylar could do.

He was horrified to discover Anna was in Valkenburg. But even Skylar's protest could not change Anna's mind.

On the morning of the execution, she huddled with her brothers and the others from Visserswert. A crowd of onlookers pressed close—peasants, merchants, noblemen, and even children. They awaited the authorities who were to convey Miles from the kasteel. A giant bonfire already burned, warming the curious group of bystanders. Anna trembled. A dull ringing filled her head.

Finally, she saw Papa. The bailiff and two magistrates surrounded him. The procession stopped, and a priest approached her papa. Miles shook his head. The priest allowed him to pass. The bailiff and the magistrates led him to a ladder.

"Nay!" Anna screamed, lunging forward.

She did not feel Willem and Skylar grasp her arms. Two men tied Miles to the rungs. He refused a blindfold and searched the crowd until he saw his children. A smile lit his face. He began to sing praises to God, and the crowd hushed and listened.

Two soldiers hoisted the ladder above the bonfire. This caused another outburst from the crowd. Anna could not endure it. She struggled until she broke free from her brothers' grasp, ran frantically to the front of the crowd, and dropped to her knees.

"Nay! Nay! For the love of God, Papa, recant! Recant now, before it is too late!"

But her papa did not hear her through the jeers of the crowd and he did not look in her direction again. His dreamy eyes focused heavenward. His singing stopped. He coughed. Then his voice rang loud and clear. "The angels come! I see the Savior!"

"Nay! Nay!" Anna screamed. She could not bear it. Before the flames rose to engulf Papa's body, she stumbled to her feet. Peter reached over to steady her, but she jerked away and fled.

A man named Guido stood apart from the crowd. He was a stranger to Anna but was acquainted with Willem. When he saw what was happening, he felt compassion for her and followed. Peter and Willem also followed.

Bumping and pushing, Anna reached the fringes of the crowd. She ran on through narrow cobbled streets, blindly following the twisted, winding lanes. Finally, she reached a grim wall and sank to the ground, burying her face in the folds of her skirt.

For a long time, she crouched there. Sobbing uncontrollably, she was oblivious to her surroundings until she saw a pair of loose trousers and large buttoned boots. Strong arms gently lifted her. In her weakness, she pressed her face against the solid chest and continued sobbing.

Time passed. Peter's strained voice aroused her. "Is she all right?"

Then it was Willem talking, sounding winded. "Bless you, Guido," he panted.

The dullness lifted. It was not one of her brothers who carried her. It didn't matter. Nothing mattered. The stranger gently transferred her into Willem's protective arms.

"You have suffered enough. Please come to my house and rest," the stranger offered.

There was a long silence. Then Willem replied, "Nothing remains for us now." His voice broke. "We must take the news to Mama. Please . . ." Anna could feel Willem's stifled sobs as his chest heaved against her cheek. He choked out, "Give your family and friends our goodwill and thanks."

"Perhaps I will see you on my travels. God be with you, brothers," the man said.

Light dawned on Anna, as if she had surfaced from the depths of the sea. *Brothers?* A surge of anger pulsed through her. *That is what the heretics call themselves. This man is an Anabaptist, just like Menno Simons!* Now she understood where Willem had been spending his time.

Before the dark current could pull her under again, Anna struggled and broke free from Willem. She tumbled to the ground, then, fueled by hate, staggered to her feet again. She hurled herself at the huge stranger and battered his chest.

"You! You killed him. You killed my papa. I hate you!" she cried.

Peter lurched forward and restrained her. "Anna, stop!" He scooped her up in his arms and strode away.

"I am sorry, Guido," Willem choked. "She doesn't know what she's saying."

"Aye, I do!" Anna cried against Peter's scratchy cloak. "The cursed Anabaptists. They killed Papa."

Chapter 4

Two days passed. The waterwheels of Valkenburg looked small in the distance. The wagon's two large wheels swooshed over clay and grated across limestone, past cow pastures, rolling green hills, thick stands of willow and pine, fields of heather, and meandering streams.

But Anna gazed straight ahead, over the team of horses Willem had hired from the local stable in Visserswert. In her mind, she saw donjons and jailers, bailiffs and beadles, and porters with sinister black mustaches. She pictured guards dressed in the duke's black, red, and yellow—his coat of arms that depicted a vicious, black lion. She saw large bonfires and, mostly, she saw her papa.

We have left Papa behind. We are going home to Mam without him. Papa is gone. Ashes. How could his beliefs be more important than life? Bitter bile rose in Anna's throat.

The journey home was difficult for everyone. The sky even turned gloomy and a clap of thunder cracked.

Willem grimaced. "Peter! We've not much farther to go, but you had best get out the blankets."

The wind whipped up. A wayward strand of hair escaped Anna's hood and stung her eyes. In vain, she tried to push it away. Peter fished in the wagon for the woolen blankets.

Horst's and Skylar's mounts, skittish from the thunder, appeared alongside the wagon. "It is coming now for sure!" Horst yelled above the wind.

"Ride on," Willem gestured. "No need to stay and get drenched when we are this close to home."

"Nay, I will stay with you."

"We will stay," Skylar agreed.

"You can tell the family we are on our way." Willem urged them on to shelter.

Horst put his shoulder into the wind and rubbed his bad leg. "Nay. If the wagon gets stuck, you will need our help. We will stay." He pulled his cloak up over his neck and touched the brim of his hat. "We will fare fine," he said.

No sooner had he said it than huge drops pelted Anna's face. She gasped as Peter draped a blanket tent-style to protect them from the downpour. The road soon became slippery, and they could see little beyond the gray haze. Rivers of water streamed off the heavily muscled backs of the team. Then, abruptly, the house appeared.

Willem nudged Anna with his arm. "Hurry inside!"

She left the men to the chores of sheltering the horses and unloading supplies. The sopping wet blanket weighed her down as she tramped up to the sheltered entrance and shouldered open the door. It was dark inside the tiny white-timbered house.

"Mam!"

Puddles formed on the rushes at Anna's feet. She draped the blanket over a chair and hesitated. She could hear hurried footsteps approaching from a back room. She lurched forward, but faltered when Peter's mother appeared.

Freda Cremer smiled warmly. "I am so glad you are back, Anna."

Freda was Dutch, from the kingdom's northernmost lowlands, and wore her blond hair in two neat, braided coils, one above each ear. Her cheeks were always rosy, as if she had just labored over a hearth. Freda put her arms around Anna. She made no mention of Anna's stowing away to Valkenburg. Instead, she shivered and released her. "Brr-rr! Let us get you dry."

"Where is Mam?"

Freda's voice became strained. "She is sleeping. Your mother is ill. Dry off first before you see her, and I will fix you all a meal."

Disappointed, Anna did as Freda instructed. When she had changed her clothes, she peeked into the tiny, dark room that adjoined her own bedchamber. The room was still, except for a rattled, labored breathing. The bedcovers gently rose and fell. She tiptoed closer until she could see Mam's face. Her cheeks were flushed and her eyes closed. She looked almost lifeless. Anna quietly backed away from the bed and hurried from the room to find Freda.

The men's muddy boots lined the hearth in the big room, and their wet outer clothing was strewn about. They sat around the wooden trestle table, bundled in dry blankets. Anna's stomach growled at the hearty meat aroma.

As she stepped forward, conversation stopped. She looked at Freda and swallowed. "May I help?"

Freda's eyes shone sympathetically, and she handed her a knife. Anna began slicing a round loaf of brown bread.

"How does Mam fare?" Willem asked.

Anna paused in her slicing. "She looks very sick."

"Not well, I fear," Freda added. Her concern-filled eyes moved from Willem to Anna. Taking the platter of bread, she said, "Sit, now."

Anna nodded and seated herself. Guiltily, she recalled the hoarse cough Mam had when they left.

Freda explained, "She has gradually worsened. She would not let me go after Rosmunda. Yesternight she took to her bed in a fever. I should have sent for the healer woman, regardless."

"You are not to blame," Skylar said. "It was good of you to stay with Mam when you have your own place to tend."

He pushed back his chair to rise. "I will go for Rosmunda."

Freda put her hand on his shoulder. "Please, eat first. Perhaps the storm will pass by then."

Anna jumped at a sudden clap of thunder. Skylar sat down again and stabbed a piece of meat from the flat trencher with his knife.

"When you do go," Freda said, "you had best tell Rosmunda that Mariel's illness is of the heart as well as of the body."

Anna knelt beside her mother's bed. There was a tiny window in the chilly room, but the shutter was closed tight against the rain. She could hear that the storm was past. Skylar would soon be returning with the healer. She mopped beads of perspiration from the moist forehead. "Oh, Mam, I need you. Please do not leave me." Her mother was in a deep sleep and unresponsive. "God," Anna pleaded, "where are you?"

Skylar returned with Rosmunda. Anna swept from the sickroom in time to see the tiny healer woman remove a hooded cloak, revealing thin, white hair. The reek of fish permeated the air. *Probably some precautionary measure she uses,* Anna thought.

Rosmunda carried her satchel, bulging with curious-looking pouches of herbs and dark vials, to the hearth and set to work over the fire. "I will need a pot," she said.

Anna rushed to do her bidding.

"I am glad your brother told me your mother was sick of heart, for I have just the thing to heal her heart as well as her body."

"You do?" Anna asked.

Rosmunda leaned close to whisper, and Anna backed up a step. " 'Tis not only called 'fearwort' but 'chestwort' as well. She brings joy into a dark mood."

"*She?*" Anna felt suddenly dizzy from the warmth of the fire mixed with the repugnant smell of the woman.

"The herb. We just need to heat this salve. Works better that way, goes right through the skin. Do not worry, dearie. It is just the thing your mother needs." She stirred. "A little St. John's Wort oil, a little fat, some honeycomb, a touch of mint, and most important, the chestwort."

"Smells good. Like nuts and parsley."

"It has a sweet smell, but a bitter taste. Of course that matters not for the balm. But we will be making a drink, too, after we get her coated with this. And do not sweeten it."

"Sweeten?"

"The drink. Later, later." Rosmunda tested the salve with a single stroke of her long, bony finger. "Take me to her."

Willem and Skylar hovered outside the room. Rosmunda barked at them with the protectiveness of a wolf caring for her pups. "Why you be crowding us?"

Willem jumped backward and crashed into Skylar.

The healer woman's movements were calm and deliberate. With long, even strokes and practiced fingers, she laid back Mariel's gown and rubbed the balm on her wheezing chest. She wrapped the patient with cloth, replaced the gown, and propped Mariel's head upright with a goosefeather pillow. Then she pulled the fur coverlet tight about the sick woman's neck.

"Do this often," she explained, "at least three times a day, and throughout the night." She reached for the cruse by Mariel's bed. "And try to get liquid into her mouth like this." Rosmunda used a small dipper and forced it into the woman's mouth. Her eyes darted nervously from her patient to Anna. "I heard you went to see your papa. How does he fare?"

Anna glanced at Freda, then at Rosmunda. "Papa is dead."

Rosmunda paled, and the dipper began to tremble. It clattered onto the bedside table, where she let it remain. Her voice was creaky as if from disuse. "Let us go and make the drink."

Everyone felt more hopeful about Mariel's recovery after Rosmunda's visit. Even though Anna felt a hollow weariness from the bones out, she told Freda, "It is time you take your family home."

Anna's brothers joined in the urging and thanked the stone-cutter and his family for all their kind deeds.

"Aye, very well," Freda said. She threw her husband and son a knowing look. "I will be back tomorrow or I will send Esther, so you can rest."

"Do you need some help returning the wagon and horses to the village stable?" Horst asked.

"Nay, we will see to it," Skylar said.

As the Cremer family left, Peter paused at the door and spoke privately with Anna, his brown hair disheveled from the storm. Under different circumstances, it might have seemed comical. His expression was solemn, his angular face concerned.

"Brave Anna. I am proud of you."

She arched her brows. "How can you say so? I should have stayed home with Mam, like Willem said."

"Perhaps what you did was not the wisest, but it showed great courage."

"Nay, not wise." Anna's eyes closed at the memories invoked. Peter's hand rested lightly on her shoulder.

"There was nothing else you could do," he murmured.

His words soothed her heart better than any ointment the healer lady kept.

Throughout the night, Anna kept diligent watch over her mother. She applied the balm and did the other things Rosmunda had demonstrated. As she stoked the fire in the big room, she chided herself. *I should have stayed with Mam. I could not help Papa anyway.* The hungry flames she attended leaped upward to torment her with the memory of Valkenburg.

Once, Anna dozed. When she awoke, her mother was thrashing and uttering nonsensical sentences. "No uncle, not the convent. I do not want to be a nun. Kathrina. Dear Kathrina."

Who is Kathrina? Anna wondered. *And what uncle?* Anna's mother was an orphan, and Anna had never heard of any relatives.

Again Mariel murmured, "Prayers . . . Hide, Kathrina, hide!"

Anna stroked her mother's brown hair streaked with gray, and wondered about the strange dream. "Mam, I will pray for you."

"Anna?" Mariel's blue-gray eyes opened but remained unfocused. "Where is your papa? Miles?"

"You must get better for us, Mam," Anna crooned.

"I do not want to be a nun," Mariel moaned again. She tossed her head to the side, her body wracked with chills.

"Of course not, Mam," Anna soothed. "Rest now." She tucked the blanket tight under her mother's chin and began to hum. Mariel grew calm, but her perspiration grew heavier. As the first rays of sun filtered into the room, her fever broke.

"Mam!" Anna's trembling hand dropped the cool cloth she was holding. "Oh, Mam, you are back at last!" She planted a kiss on the flushed cheek.

Mariel's eyes fluttered.

Anna pressed another kiss on her mother's palm. "Try to drink this." She held a dipper to her lips.

Mariel submitted to the bitter nourishment before she slipped back into another deep slumber.

With a backward glance, Anna tiptoed from the room.

The bailiff, Johan van Wijtenhort, patted the two carolus guilders and 12 nickels in his money pouch, his payment for examining and sentencing Miles van Vissers. This, added to the coins the duke had given him earlier, made a tidy sum. He strode through the great Kasteel of Valkenburg to present himself to the Duke of Cleves-Julich.

He bowed before the duke. "Concerning the execution of the heretic from Visserswert, milord, if it agrees with Your Sovereignty, I'll be going about milord's business and confiscate the man's property."

"Remember, I've a special interest in the man's ship."

"Aye, milord."

"I'm greatly disappointed that we did not get a confession from him. A handsome reward awaits you should you bring me the preacher Menno Simons."

"I mean to do it."

"Godspeed to you and your men."

Johan bowed low. When he straightened, his eyes lit on the great coat of arms that hung on the wall behind the duke. The sight of the black lion strengthened Johan. He had lost the duke's favor because of the boatman's silence, and he did not like to look foolish. His eyes darkened. *I will do everything in my power to rout out the heretic that so fascinates the duke and the emperor. I shall look under every rock in the empire if need be.*

Chapter 5

The next day, Anna donned an apron, removed a slab of meat from its overhead rafter hook, and sliced a sizeable portion to satisfy her brothers' hunger. She left the pieces to sizzle on the hearth iron while she walked to the outdoor cellar for milk. The sun's warm rays had scattered diamonds over the wet earth. And Mam was improving.

When Anna returned to the house, her friend Esther was just about to knock on the door. She was a welcome sight, with her blond, coiled braids and glowing complexion. Anna dropped her pail and milk sloshed over the rim. Eagerly she embraced her friend.

"Oh, my dear Anna, how I have worried about you!" Esther sobbed against her ear. "I am heartbroken about your father, about all you've been through. Pray, tell me you are all right."

Anna drew back. "I shall never be the same. But, oh, I have missed you."

"Peter told me of your courage."

"Did he?"

"Aye."

Anna gave her friend one more hug before releasing her. Esther wiped her face with the sleeve of her cloak and reached down for the pail. "Here. Let me help."

"Now that you are here and Mam is recuperating, at least I feel a bit of hope."

"I am glad your mother is better."

There was a rustling noise behind them, and Anna hastened into the house. "I must hurry. Here are the men back from the village, and I have left meat over the fire."

Willem and Skylar lifted their noses to sniff the welcome aroma when they entered the house. Their eyes brightened at Esther's presence, and they were cheered to hear of their mother's recovery. After visiting the sickroom to see for himself, Skylar announced, "I believe I will take my leave tomorrow, if Mam is still on the mend. I have been gone from Hilda and the children too long."

"By all means," Willem said. "Your family needs you now more than we do."

The women joined the men for the meal and listened to their plans. "If Anna can handle things here at home," Willem went on, "I will go into the village tomorrow to see about Papa's business."

Anna jerked up her head at the mention of Papa. "What business is that, Willem?"

"The shipping." He sopped a piece of bread in his warm milk and lifted it to his mouth. His eyes were dull and tired-looking. "Papa would want me to tend his business. It is hard, Anna, but we have patrons to consider."

Anna inclined her head. "I see."

"Make haste and eat," Esther told her. " 'Tis time you got some rest."

After a long nap, Anna found Esther seated on a small bench feeding wool through the spinning wheel. Anna sat on a chair beneath the open-shuttered window to soak in the sunshine. "How is Mam?" she asked.

Esther's hands faltered, and the woolen strand between her fingers slackened. "Better, much better. She recognized me and ate her soup hungrily."

"Then what is wrong?" Their friendship, seasoned by

everything from broken limbs to childish dreams, was close and strong. Anna could tell when something was troubling Esther.

Her friend's blue eyes avoided her, first examining the hearth, then a wall tapestry with ships, trees, and colorful birds before finally settling on Anna's face. "She asked about Miles. I did not know what to tell her, so I said nothing."

"I understand. One of us children needs to explain. But how do you tell your mam that the man she loves has died a gruesome, senseless death? How do you tell her that he was mistreated, thin, and weak?"

"You must also give her a scrap of good."

"Good? Nay, I think not! Only that his last words spoke of his love for her and us. But what is that now?"

" 'Tis everything that is good. Do tell her that."

"I will never understand it. How can life be so unfair? My papa was a good man. Why did this happen to him?"

Esther left her spinning, crossed the room, and knelt before her friend. "He will be rewarded for his kindness in heaven, Anna. Think of it. He is with God the Father now. No one can hurt him anymore."

" 'Tis an unsafe world, and there is nothing to do about it."

"Every person must find his own way," said Esther. "One's beliefs, what one stands for—those are important things."

"More important than life? How can that be?"

"What kind of life would one live, if it were a lie?"

"A safe one," snapped Anna. "You have all changed since I went to live with the Palmkens. I do not understand. I was taught to take mass in the parish church of Eelene. Was my upbringing all for naught?"

"I shan't argue with you, Anna."

"Nay." Anna put her hand on Esther's shoulder. "Nor I with you."

Later that day, after Esther returned home, Anna sat with her mother. "There, now." She wrapped a newly salved cloth about Mariel's chest. "Your breathing is greatly improved."

"Thank you. Daughter, why did you run away?"

So, Mam was going to ask the questions today. Anna tugged Mariel's nightdress and gently positioned her. "Are you sure you want to talk about this?"

"I want to hear all."

"I should have stayed with you. I know that now. But I had to speak to Papa. I thought he would do anything for me. I wanted him to recant."

"I understand. But he would not?"

"Nay." Anna lowered her dark-circled eyes. Her head drooped from sorrow.

"Dear child," Mariel said, "your papa loves you with all his heart."

"I know," Anna nodded. "We went to visit him in the kasteel donjon at Valkenburg."

"Was it awful?"

"Aye. But he did not seem to mind."

"That would be like Miles."

Anna knelt down beside her mother's bed. "Oh, Mam, 'tis so hard to tell."

"I know, but please, if you can, continue."

Anna pressed her mother's hand between her own. "Mam. Papa is dead." She felt her mother's body tense.

"*How?*" Mariel whispered. Her face was contorted with pain.

"Executed. By fire." Anna watched her mother's eyes close and listened to her pitiful sobs and moans. She felt helpless and wished she could remove the pain.

When Mariel finally opened her eyes again, her words were breathy. "Surely you were not there?"

"I was." Anna stroked her mother's face. "Long enough to say good-bye. Then I left." Mariel nodded.

"But the men stayed with Papa to the end," Anna whispered. "At least Skylar did." The event was muddled in her bitter memory. She only recalled begging her papa to recant. Then that heretic had dared to follow her.

Mariel gave a weak smile through her tears. "Good."

The smile brought Anna's attention back. "What?"

"It is good they stayed with Miles." Mariel took a ragged breath. "But I am thankful you did not."

Mam's courage brought to mind Esther's words. "There is more."

"Tell me."

"At the donjon, Papa told us he loved us and he sent his love to you."

Mariel pressed her eyes closed for a time. Then she opened them and said, "Thank the Lord, Miles stood firm for our beliefs."

"But Mam . . . you . . ."

Tears began to stream down Mariel's face. "I know you have questions. We will talk more about the faith. But if you do not mind, I would like to be alone."

Anna squeezed her mother's hand, kissed her cheek, and slipped from the room.

Mariel recuperated in slow but steady steps. She was strong, and determined to heal in body and soul. Anna kept busy caring for her and Willem; the endless tasks of keeping house helped to occupy her otherwise dark thoughts. Willem took several trips to deliver promised cargo along the river, but more often, he kept close to home to keep a special watch over them.

For Anna, each day was an unmarked trail along a craggy cliff where her foot could so easily step off into the darkness below. God had much explaining to do. Many things troubled her—one in particular, her mother's delirious murmuring that first night after their return.

Anna entered Mariel's tiny bedchamber, a piece of cloth in her hand. "If you really think you are able, then here is the sewing you requested, Mam."

"Thank you. I need something to do."

"Mam? I have been meaning to ask you something."

"Pray ask me," Mariel replied, taking the needle and cloth and laying them across her blanketed lap.

Anna drew nearer. "When you were ill, you said some peculiar things."

Mariel's head tilted, her newly brushed hair rippling across her nightdress. "What things?"

"You talked about a convent—about an uncle, and a Kathrina. Did you have a dream?"

A look of alarm flickered in Mariel's eyes, and Anna wished she had not mentioned it. But Mariel patted the side of her bed. "Sit, daughter. I have some confessing to do about my past, things I should have told you a long time ago.

"My parents died when I was twelve." Mariel sighed, the sigh of one thinking of a long-ago time. "I went to live with my father's elder brother. He was a bachelor and did not wish to be shackled with a ward, so he sent me away to live at the Nimbschen Convent."

"You lived at a convent? Why did you not mention it before?"

"I was embarrassed."

"But why?"

"Because I broke my vows and married your papa. A priest by the name of Martinus Luther believed it was wrong for anyone to remain in the convents or monasteries against their will."

"You did not like it there?"

"I detested it! Martinus conspired with a Torgau burgher to help us escape."

Anna's eyes widened.

"It was a clever scheme. The burgher made regular deliveries at the convent. On one of his visits, some of us hid in empty herring barrels."

Anna was amazed. "How many of you?"

"Twelve in all, but the burgher only took nine of us to Martinus Luther's home. We stayed there until Martinus found homes for us. For me, he found your papa."

"Papa?"

"Your papa lived in Wittenberg, and Martinus knew him through the church. Miles' first wife had died and left him with a small child, Skylar."

Anna nodded. She had known Skylar was a stepbrother, though she oftentimes forgot the fact.

"Your papa, like me, had no living relatives. Martinus thought Miles could use a mother for the child and invited him to take a look at his wife candidates."

Anna felt a rush of sentiment. "And he chose you?"

"Nay. He was smitten with another, but too slow in his preparations, and she was not available upon his return to deliver his proposal. So," she shrugged, "he proposed to me instead."

Anna blinked. It had never occurred to her to question Mam about her childhood or courtship with Papa. It was pleasant to envision her mother as a young woman her own age. "But how did he choose you?"

"We collided in Martinus' great hall. My arms were piled high with clothes, and they spilled onto the floor. Miles stooped and helped me retrieve them. I thanked him. He got a twinkle in his eye and asked me if I was adventurous."

Anna scooted closer to Mam. "Were you?"

Mariel smiled in reminiscence. "Aye. After that, Miles often referred to the mischievous spark he saw in my eyes that day."

"Then what happened?" Anna could hardly contain her curiosity and excitement.

"One thing led to another. We talked of his plans to travel

and his dreams to start his own shipping business. He promised to do his best to provide for me and treat me with kindness."

"That sounds like Papa."

Mariel smiled through her tears. "You know the rest. We settled here in Visserswert. In truth, I thought his choice—this isle of fishermen—heaven itself, for Miles was the most handsome man I had ever laid eyes on. I loved him from the start, and it was not long until he loved me too."

"And my stepbrother?"

"Skylar was an adorable little boy, and I loved him at once. That part is as I always told you."

Anna nodded. "But Willem and Skylar look so much alike."

"They both take after your papa. And you look like me."

"Did all the nuns get married?"

"I am not sure, but they all found homes." She patted Anna's hand. "I almost forgot the best part. At the convent, my best friend was Kathrina van Bora. And guess who married her?"

Anna shook her head.

"Martinus Luther, himself."

"I think that is the most wonderful story I have ever heard," Anna murmured. "But what happened to your uncle?"

"He lost all of his landholdings before his death. He died while I was at the convent. That is why I thought I was lost there for good."

"Mam!" Anna clapped her hands. "I have just had the most wonderful idea!"

"What is that, child?" Mariel looked at her with amusement in her eyes.

"You must write Kathrina a letter. Tell her about Papa and renew your friendship."

Anna's suggestion settled over Mariel like the wonder of a season's first snowfall. "Perhaps I shall."

Seeing the sparkle in her mother's eyes, Anna believed she had said the right thing.

Chapter 6

 Anna sensed the approach of a rider before she saw him emerge from the fog and steady drizzle. The thick purr of rain on the thatched rooftop had brought her to the window. She opened the shutters a crack to peer out at the earth's gentle washing. It was planting season, when fourteen out of thirty days were rainy ones, preparing field and valley for growth. A few furlongs from the house, she could make out the river's contour through the fog, but the road was a misty-gray oblivion.

As the rider drew closer, Anna recognized Peter. Quickly, she latched the shutter and snatched her cloak to greet him on the tiny porch. A small gable roof extended overhead. It did little to protect Anna from the gusts of wind that sprayed rain against her face as she waited for him to dismount.

"Welcome, Peter. Did Willem send you to check up on us?" she asked in jest.

"Nay." Peter crowded onto the shelter of the narrow porch, and Anna inhaled the pleasant scents of horse, leather, and wet soil. "I hoped to find Willem at home."

Anna shook her head and looked up into his wet face. "He is sailing." Peter's sodden clothes dripped. "Such a day for a visit," she said. "Come in and dry out by the fire."

Inside, Peter stomped circles in the room as he watched Anna prepare a hot cider drink. When she started toward him, their eyes met. Hers were as blue as her gown, with its square laced-up bodice and gathered skirt.

Peter reached for the warmed goblet. "Thank you," he said, trying to keep his voice calm. If only he knew what Willem would want him to do in this situation.

Anna wiped her hands on her white apron. "Please. Sit down."

They moved to opposite sides of the small trestle table. Peter could scarcely sit still and sip his drink.

"What ails you, Peter?"

He was relieved to hear the question, but his desire to protect her kept him from answering immediately. A moment passed. Peter realized that time was getting short.

"I bring bad tidings, Anna. I wish Willem were here to deal with it, but since you are the only one . . ."

Her eyes darkened, but she urged him to speak with a brave nod.

"The bailiff of Valkenburg . . . he is in the village."

"What? *Here?*" Peter could tell by Anna's stifled gasp that she knew he meant the Duke of Cleves-Julich's man—the one she had seen in Valkenburg, who had arrested her papa.

Peter leaned across the table, yearning to soothe the pain he saw in her eyes. "I saw him and his beadles just an hour past."

Anna's face paled. "And you fear he is coming here?"

"I cannot be certain. But Willem has been expecting him."

Her eyes grew round. "Whatever for?"

Peter gently covered her hands with his. "I pray 'tis not so, but . . ."

"What more can he do to us?" Anna interrupted in a shrill voice.

"Confiscate property."

"Can he do that?"

"Indeed, he can."

Anna pulled her hands from his and rose from the table. Pacing across the floor, she grew more hysterical with each passing moment. "But Papa said they would not. What shall we do, Peter? God help us!"

Peter hurried to her and put steadying hands on her shoulders. "You must stay calm. You can stay with my family."

"But what about Mam? She is unable to travel." Anna pulled away from him and motioned toward the window. "Especially in this downpour."

Suddenly, they heard a clomping of hooves and the creaking of leather. The peal of a human voice rose above the sound of the rain. Anna gasped and turned back toward Peter with a frightened look.

He moved toward the door. "Stay back by the fire. I will answer the door. Please, Anna. Let me handle this."

The heavy knock pounded through Anna's heart, and a rough voice pierced the air. "Open! We are here upon milord's, Duke of Cleves-Julich's, business."

Anna's whole being focused on the door as Peter thrust it open. Four large men burst in, dressed in plated armor and red surcoats with the duke's coat of arms embroidered on the escutcheon across their chests. Anna clenched her fists in the folds of her skirt.

The leader stepped forward. "I am Bailiff Johan van Wijtenhort." He reached inside his dripping surcoat and took out a small scrolled parchment. "I have a writ from the Duke of Cleves-Julich to confiscate the property of Miles van Vissers, including his boat."

Peter reached for the writ, but the bailiff jerked it back. "And who might you be?" he sneered through yellowed teeth.

Peter withdrew his hand, and instinctively put it on the hilt of his dagger. The bailiff's eyes narrowed and his beard jutted out.

"I am Peter Cremer, village stonecutter. Willem Mileson

van Vissers heads this home, but upon his leave I have watch over his sister and mother."

"And where is this Willem?"

"Visiting his brother."

The bailiff looked Anna up and down with a lecherous eye. She shrank back a step, but Peter remained planted, his expression fiercer than Anna had ever seen it.

The bailiff strutted about the room. The beadles, whose swords had been drawn since they entered the dwelling, stepped forward to obstruct Peter while their leader surveyed the premises. Wijtenhort's heavy boots made a crushing sound on the reed- and mat-covered floor. He slashed his sword across a long, narrow shelf, knocking its precious contents on the floor. Metal dishes, decorative tankards, and a bundle of beeswax candles rolled and clanked noisily.

Anna flinched.

Wijtenhort motioned to one of his beadles. "Go get a sack and pick up these things." The beadle immediately left the house. Only one piece remained on the shelf, a carved wooden ship with tiny masts and sails. The bailiff removed it with his gloved hand and examined it, then tucked it beneath his arm. The beadle returned dripping wet, with a canvas sack in his hands, and scooped up the wooden tankards and metal dishes.

Anna moved forward, but Peter held up his hand to stay her.

Wijtenhort tapped his sword on a tapestry, acquired by Anna's papa in his travels. "See that this remains," he ordered. He continued to inspect the house, remarking that various items would "best be left behind."

When he moved toward Mariel's tiny bedchamber, Anna cried out in fear, "Mam!"

The bailiff looked at Anna, then jerked his head toward the open doorway. Mariel was leaning against it in her nightdress, pale but angry.

Wijtenhort strode toward her.

"Please! Let her be. She is very ill," Peter said.

The bailiff stopped and frowned. "What ails her?"

"Lung fever," Anna blurted.

The man stumbled back. His dark, sinister brows arched. "Get back from me!"

Mariel winced, then collapsed onto the floor.

"Mam!" Anna rushed passed the bailiff to her mother's side and knelt to care for her.

Wijtenhort glared, then moved close to Peter. "I will be back tomorrow. See that they," his head nodded at the women, "are gone. Leave everything behind. 'Tis milord's now."

He headed for the door, with the beadles before him. As he stepped outside, he turned his head to say, "That includes the boat. Milord is especially interested in that." Then, raising his voice, he added, "If the women are not gone, we will remove them."

When Peter did not reply, the man baited him. "Is that understood, stonecutter?"

"Yes, milord," Peter said, his jaw clenched and eyes steely.

"Good. Go back to protecting Willem's women, then." Johan Wijtenhort threw back his dark, roguish head and laughed.

Peter watched from the doorway until the bailiff and his men rode away, then turned and hurried to Anna's side. "How is your mother?"

"She is all right. Please help me get her back to bed."

Peter knelt to lift Mariel and return her to bed. "Thank you, Peter," Mariel said. "God bless you for being here."

"Sleep now, Mam," Anna murmured. "You need your strength for what lies ahead."

Mariel nodded. "Please fetch Freda, will you, Peter?"

"Of course. I will fetch both my parents. Do not worry. We will take care of you." Mariel gave a weak nod and closed her troubled eyes.

Once they had left the bedchamber, Anna ran toward the outer door and thrust it open. She ran onto the porch and screamed into the misty distance. "I hate you! You killed Papa. I hate you!"

Peter drew her inside quickly, and she clutched at his sleeves desperately. "Oh, Peter! Whatever shall we do?"

Peter's chest rose in anger. "In truth, I should like to slit that man's throat. But my duty lies in protecting you. I am outnumbered. It is a battle I cannot win. They would just turn their revenge on you." His face twisted. "But still, I can taste that bailiff's blood."

Peter's words matched Anna's emotions.

Gradually his distant look focused on Anna, and he remembered her needs. His voice softened. "My family will help you get through this."

"Nay." She shook her head. "This cannot be happening. Soon I will wake and find 'tis all but a bad dream. Tell me, Peter. Tell me 'tis only a dream." She clutched his sleeves again.

"I wish I could," he said. "Someday it will seem like that, but for now you must be strong."

Anna dropped her arms and turned away from him. "I cannot. I have not the will."

Moving closer, Peter laid his hands on her drooping shoulders. His words were kind but firm. "Then get the will, Anna. You have your mother to think of. She is depending on you."

"I cannot." Anna began to sob. Peter drew her against his warmth, and she felt less frightened.

"Anna?"

"Aye." She lifted her head.

"Willem is not here. You must be brave for me."

Finally she sighed and gave a slow nod. "Very well. Tell me what to do."

Peter scanned the interior of the house where he had spent so many happy times with his friend Willem. "You need to pack up all your clothes while I go to fetch help. That should keep you busy until I return. Can you do that?"

At once the fear returned. "Do not leave, Peter! What if they return? The way they looked at us . . ."

"Nay. They shan't be back so soon. The bailiff is too frightened of the lung fever."

His answer and light touch on her cheek soothed her.

"Someday your world will right itself."

But Anna felt only despair and hopelessness.

Chapter 7

Anna threw clothes into a trunk. She came across the serving girl's dress from Valkenburg and stuffed it in with the rest. Then she carried an armful of boots, shoes, and cloaks to the door and dropped them. She remembered Mam's ointment and healing herbs and hurried to the hearth to place the remedies into empty pails with some foodstuffs.

Then she ran to check on her mother.

"Anna?"

"Aye, Mam."

"Are they really gone?"

"Aye. They are gone."

"They have come for the house then? I have dreaded this day. We will go to Skylar's—he will take us in. I must talk to Willem."

"Willem is not here now, Mam, but the stonecutter will take us in until he returns."

"He can move the business."

"What, Mam?"

"Willem can run the business from Antwerp, with Skylar's help."

"Aye, Mam. 'Tis a good idea." Anna did not have the heart to tell her there would be no business left once the duke confiscated their boat. There would be plenty of time to discuss such things later. "But for today, we will go to the stonecutter's."

"Where is Peter? I thought I saw him here."

"He was here. He went to fetch his parents, remember? In fact, I believe I hear him now." Anna patted her mother's arm and rushed back into the big room. She opened the shutter. The rain had ceased, and her heart quickened with relief to see that Peter had returned with Horst and Freda.

"Aye, 'tis them, Mam. Be patient now," she called, before opening the door to their friends.

Freda embraced Anna. "We came as soon as we could."

"Thank you."

Horst asked, "Do you need help packing?"

"Nay. 'Tis done." She swept her gaze over the room.

Peter looked at the trunks and other collected items and gave her a reassuring smile. "You did well."

"I know of some things your mother will want," Freda said.

Anna was instantly curious. "What might they be?"

"Mariel had me hide some things while you were in Valkenburg. Before she took ill, she worried about this happening. Come, Horst," Freda told her husband. "I will show you."

Good for Mam. Even as Anna admired her mother's pluckiness, new fear seized her. She picked up her skirts and hurried after the couple as they headed toward the shed. Peter joined them.

"I am worried about Willem," Anna said, falling into step with Horst.

"Why is that?" he asked.

"The men mentioned Willem's boat. What if they take Willem captive?"

Peter replied, "Nay, Anna. 'Tis *this* boat they referred to." He pointed toward the skiff that was docked by the shore.

"But that is not Papa's ship. 'Tis just a skiff."

"*We* know that. But they do not."

Hope swelled in Anna's breast like waves on the sea. "They do not know about the other?"

Peter and Horst exchanged a conspiratorial smile. "By the time they realize their mistake, Willem will have hidden it. But we must pray that he doesn't return until they are gone."

"He only planned to be gone a few days," Anna said.

"We will get word to him somehow."

Anna clung to this new scrap of hope. Her papa's merchant vessel was more valuable than their home because it provided their means of support.

Freda showed the men the barrels that contained Mariel's hidden cache, then said to Anna, "We must go inside and prepare your mother for travel."

They bundled up Mariel for the weather while the men finished up in the shed. Then Peter returned to the house and carried Mariel to the wagon, where they settled her into a bed in the back.

Anna lingered alone inside the house. She took a slow turn around the room and caressed her papa's tapestry that they must leave behind. Many of their furnishings had come from her papa's shipping connections. She caught sight of the shells her papa had given to her and her mother and scooped them into her apron.

"Anna, are you looking for something?" Freda asked from the door. "Come along now, love. 'Tis time to go."

The shells settled into the bottom of Anna's pocket. Reluctantly she followed Freda toward the wagon.

"Did you get the coins?" Mariel asked, her voice weak.

"Were they with the rest?" Anna asked.

"Nay, child. They're buried."

Everyone exchanged puzzled looks.

Anna placed her ear close to her mother's lips. "Buried where?" she asked.

"In the shed. Northeast corner. 'Tis all our savings."

Anna wished she had spent time searching through the things in the shed herself. "We will find it."

"Do you know where she means?" Horst asked.

Anna nodded.

He said, "This weather will never hold. Let us take Mariel home, and I will return to search the shed."

Anna glanced at her mother's tired face. "Nay! Those dreadful men may soon return. I must check Papa's shed myself. With Willem gone, 'tis my responsibility. Take Mam, and I will find the coins."

"I will stay with Anna," Peter said at once. "You can come back for us."

"Peter, you can look for the coins yourself. That would be best. Come along, Anna," Horst urged.

"Nay! I must stay," Anna persisted, glancing at the sky. "Please. Take Mam and come back for us."

"I will be back as soon as possible." Horst said reluctantly.

Anna knew she had angered him, but it seemed the least of her worries. As soon as the wagon pulled away, she started toward the shed. Her soggy skirt clung to her weary body. "Hurry, Peter!"

"Where shall I dig?"

Anna pointed. "Try here." She leaned forward in expectation.

The muscles in Peter's broad shoulders rippled beneath his white linen shirt, and the tip of the shovel cut into the crust of earth. When they unearthed no coins in that area then tried another with no success, Peter leaned on the handle of his shovel.

"If we dig up this whole shed, the beadles are sure to be suspicious. You had better stomp down the area where I was digging and try to remove evidence of our search."

Anna started to do so, and let out a shriek followed by a giggle. A frightened mouse shot across the ground and disappeared beneath the shed door.

Peter chuckled, too. " 'Tis good to hear you laugh again."

There was a moment of tense silence, and Anna straightened. "This is not a time for laughter."

Peter returned to his digging and Anna to her stomping. Time passed. Anna examined the two barrels close to where Peter was digging. One contained grain, the other implements.

"Look! This barrel seems deeper on the outside than on the inside."

Peter threw down his shovel and leaned forward. "Let me see." Hurriedly, he removed the contents of the barrel. "You are right." The empty barrel still felt heavy. Peter grinned. He prodded and pried until a portion of the false bottom gave way.

Anna hovered over him and held her breath as he stuck his hand inside the hole.

"I believe we have found it. You are a genius!"

"Nay. I just know how Papa thought."

Peter nodded. " 'Tis time to finish this job."

Soon they had recovered a small leather bag bulging with coins.

Peter set it near the door, replaced the false bottom in the barrel, and put back the implements. Anna firmed up the ground around the disturbed area so no one would detect their activity.

When they were finished, Peter peered out the door. "It should not be long until Father returns." He glanced back at Anna. "Are you warm enough?"

Anna stood beside him and looked out. " 'Tis cold. Looks as if it could rain again at any moment. But I am fine." Suddenly, she clutched Peter's arm. "Look!"

She pointed toward the road at the edge of the woods. " 'Tis Rosmunda. She seems to be headed this way."

Peter followed Anna outside the shed, and Rosmunda saw them at once.

"I was hoping to find you home," the healer woman puffed, as she drew close.

A strong fish scent accosted Anna, and she took a step back as she said, "Mam is much improved."

"I fear you are going to get caught in the weather," Peter said, with a skyward glance.

"I thought I might find lodging here to wait out the storm." Before she even finished her statement, thunder cracked. Large drops stung their cheeks. "I would be obliged if I could sleep in your shed tonight."

"Nay, you cannot." Anna said. *What a strange request*, she thought. Nevertheless, she explained, "Neither can I stay. The bailiff has confiscated our property, and we must leave. He could return at any time. He is evil."

"Nay, not you, too," Rosmunda's face grew alarmed. "To tell the truth, I seek refuge from the same evil."

"I do not understand," Anna replied.

"They have a writ for my arrest."

"Why? What have you done to merit their disfavor?"

"Can we not enter your shelter?" Rosmunda asked, for the rain was now pouring down. The old woman reached out her bony arm and gave the shed door a hard shove.

Before Peter could stop her, she had disappeared inside the shed. Anna gave Peter a frantic look, and they hastened in after the woman.

"Ah!" Rosmunda exclaimed, her eyes lighting up at the sight of the bag of coins. "Trying to keep a secret from the bailiff, are you?"

"I . . . we . . ." Anna said.

Peter frowned.

"As I was saying," Rosmunda said, "I am fleeing Visserswert. My sister lives in Emden. A few of these coins would help."

Anna felt her cheeks get hot. Peter's frown deepened.

"As you said yourself, I did help your poor mother. Got her right off her deathbed, I did. And you," Rosmunda pointed a finger toward Peter, "how many times have I nursed your family? Now you have the means to help this old woman, and I can help you both by keeping my mouth closed and going on my way. Can I not?"

A noise outside drew their attention.

" 'Tis them!" Rosmunda squealed. The sound of men and horses could not be denied.

"They have returned!" Anna cried.

Peter yanked the shed door closed and pulled Anna behind him.

"I shall disappear in those woods and you'll not hear another word from me," Rosmunda said. She thrust her open palm at Peter.

Peter hesitated.

Anna brushed past him to grab the bag of coins.

"Nay, Anna," Peter said.

"Hush," she replied. "The woman did help us. Here." Anna thrust two guilders into Rosmunda's outstretched hand.

Rosmunda remained planted.

"Here." Anna scooped out a small handful of coins and thrust them at the woman.

"I am on my way." Rosmunda gave them a grand smile, then furrowed her brows. "Watch out for those men. They are evil as the devil himself."

"Be careful," Anna whispered after her. The door opened, and Rosmunda disappeared. Peter rolled his eyes at Anna, but she merely arched an eyebrow at him.

"Aha!" the one called Wijtenhort bellowed from outside.

Peter drew his dagger. He and Anna crept toward the door to listen. She felt his arm slip around her to shield her.

"Their protector's horse is gone. What a pity the women have been left alone. I believe we have discovered our night's lodging." The bailiff laughed a cruel laugh. Then there were sounds of squishing earth, squeaking leather, and grunting horseflesh.

"Thank God. I thought they spotted her," Anna said, her hand at her breast.

"No. They are dismounting," Peter whispered.

"Think they will give us a better welcome than the village folks?" one of the beadles asked.

"Unfriendly burgher!" the bailiff said. "He shall pay for it, indeed he shall. I will make plans for him this very eve. But first let's go inside and pay the women a visit." He laughed.

"What about the lung fever?" The voice trailed off.

Anna pressed her hand against Peter's back as they leaned toward the door and listened with disgust to the men's voices and raucous laughter. They seemed to be moving toward the house.

When the bailiff and his men had gone inside, Peter grabbed the bag of coins and tucked it in the crook of his left arm. His dagger in one hand, he reached for Anna with the other. "Quickly. We must go."

They ran to a copse of trees behind the house. Within its cover, they paused long enough for Peter to replace his dagger in its sheath.

They heard an angry shout. "They have gone!"

"No matter," another voice said. "Go and take care of the horses and . . ." the voice faded away.

"This way." Peter motioned with his head, and Anna followed him from cover to cover.

She searched through the rain for a glimpse of Rosmunda, but could not see her. Eventually, Peter and Anna made their way to the river road and started in the direction of the stonecutter's house.

When they had caught their breath, Anna said, "Those men are wicked. They plot evil against all men. And they do it all in the name of religion." Her chest heaved indignantly.

"I would love to cut them into tiny pieces," Peter replied. "Unfortunately, they have the duke's power on their side.

One has to be careful. If only there were not so many of them."

"Aye."

As they trudged along the muddy road, Anna's dress became drenched and soiled and her boots caked with mud. The walking taxed her strength, and her body grew warm under the layers of drenched clothing. A fire coursed through her, a deep seething anger. Nay, it was hatred.

Once, they heard horses approaching, and hid in some nearby brush. It was only villagers. After that, it was not long until Horst appeared. He pulled Anna up into the safe confines of the wagon.

"Get us out of here," Peter ordered.

Chapter 8

Spring rains drenched the countryside, and gloom fell with the drizzle over the stonecutter's house. A runny nose and stuffy head kept Anna in bed for two days. Peter was sick as well, though he recovered quickly and never kept to his bed. Even Mariel experienced a mild relapse.

Half of Anna's sickness was of spirit. When she was not thinking of revenge, she entombed herself in sleep. But even in her dreams, she envisioned herself slipping Peter's dagger from his belt and lying in wait to lop off the bailiff's evil head. She would avenge her papa's death if only she could, but she did not know where to direct her hostilities. In the donjon that day, Papa had said the orders came from the emperor himself. And was not the emperor God's anointed? Nay, that would make her papa the offender, and even a child could tell Miles had been no man's enemy, but a decent, kindhearted man.

On the third day, with gentle coaxing from Freda and Esther, Anna rose from her bed and walked absently about the stone-cutter's house. Then she sat for several hours quietly watching the low fire that burned in the hearth.

Esther eased down beside her on a bench-trunk near a window cut into the stone wall. "The rain has ceased," she said.

"Has it?"

"Weather changes. Seasons change."

"If you are trying to give me hope, I have none."

71

"There is always hope."

Anna jerked her blue eyes away from the flames and stared at Esther. "First my papa's life was snuffed out, without even a decent burial. Now our home is taken from us. Do you not understand? Without it, all traces of my past are gone. I am left naked, cast out into a cold world."

"You are not naked. You have your friends and your faith. Consider my home your home—you have memories here. And no one can take away the ones stored in your heart. Life comes from within, Anna."

Anna lifted her head and gazed into the flickering orange flames.

The day after that, Anna became aware of her mother's needs and helped to care for her. With each passing day, Anna improved. Gradually she entered into the routine of the stonecutter's household, helping Freda and Esther with mundane chores.

One day the sun peeked through the clouds, so after the women heated water in the bricked-in kettle, they washed clothes and hung them outdoors to dry. Anna worked alongside Esther as if in a dream. Esther tried several times to cheer her, but to no avail.

Only when Esther asked if she would like to see what the men were doing in the work shed did Anna respond with any interest. The old stone shed brought back fond memories of her carefree childhood days.

Anna had always loved Esther's home. Horst had built it, not from timber like her own, but from stone he hauled from the river Maas and its nearby hills. The stone shed was situated about four or five furlongs from the stonecutter's house. A copse of pine and a screen of vines sheltered the area.

"I have missed this place," Anna said, inhaling the chalky, mossy smell. "Such a peaceful spot."

Because of the fair weather, the men were working in the shed's courtyard. The courtyard was small, but it provided a blend of beauty and work area. Block walkways, benches, and sculptures showed the stonecutter's craft. Pine, willow, and hawthorn trees added to its charm.

"Why, they are beautiful," Anna said, looking at the sculptures the men were creating.

Horst and Peter looked up from their work, pleasure lighting their faces.

"May I look at them?" Anna moved closer.

While Anna browsed, Esther joined her grandfather on a stone bench. Jarvis Cremer raised one of his white, bushy eyebrows.

"Indeed. Feel free to inspect our work," said Horst. He laid aside his chisel and limped back a step. Peter, however, continued to shape the wings on a small angel sculpture. Occasionally, he rubbed the piece with his thumb.

Anna stroked Horst's stone piece with her palm. The cold marlstone felt smooth and pleasant. "Who is this for?"

"Lord Nicolaas Hoen commissioned the work."

"The Lord of Visserswert," Anna breathed in awe. "How lovely."

"The statues are for his courtyard," Peter added. He set aside his tools.

"Your work is exquisite," Anna murmured. Then she whirled and made a sweeping gesture. "You could be commissioned to work in a grand cathedral, yet you remain in our obscure hamlet."

"Aye. They could be soldiering for the emperor!" The rusty voice of Peter's grandfather brought Anna's head around. She had almost forgotten his presence. His leather-brown eyes, the color of Peter's, sparkled with intensity. "In my time, stones were used for hurling at the Turks." Ever since Anna's arrival at the stonecutter's house, the weak old man had been on the same track, managing to steer the conversation to his soldiering days.

Esther patted his hand. It was large and withered with age, but his ideas were as rigid as the armor he had once worn.

Peter ignored his grandfather's outburst, his eyes lit with passion. "The stonecutting work at the Thorn abbey keeps us busy," he said, "but someday I should like to travel. Father prefers to stay near the family."

The mention of family brought back Anna's hollow longing. Her papa was gone, her brother absent now for many days. She understood the love of family. She knew that many times the stonecutters had to content themselves with mundane hard labor—cutting blocks for the abbey or working at repairs on the village wall. Sometimes Horst even worked in the quarry if work grew scarce.

Occasionally, he did travel. Oftentimes Anna's papa had transported Horst upriver or brought word of a job to him. She was grateful now for this grand commission from their own village that gave father and son a chance to display their talents.

"You are both gifted," she said with reverence. Then, joining Esther and her grandfather on the bench, she pondered this stonecutter and his son. Horst had always seemed so steady and patient. She could understand his contentment to work in his own village. But Peter was different. He had the rush of adventure in his veins. She could see it in his eyes when he spoke of travel. And he was so talented. "It amazes me to see something so beautiful emerge from a lump of stone," Anna mused aloud.

"Even stone can be chipped away and made into a thing of beauty," Esther said.

Anna cocked her head at Esther and raised a brow. "Aye?"

"You are so beautiful." Esther's voice softened. "Do not let what has happened to your papa turn your heart to stone."

"My heart is not stone." Anna's words tumbled out. "It is a burning, seething fire—an uncontrollable storm."

"Aye, girl!" Grandfather Jarvis said. "As it should be. A seething fire."

Esther ignored him. "Fire burns out impurity, and even storms are in God's hands."

Anna was not in a mood to argue or even to think. "I am ready to return to the house. I should check on Mam," she replied, as she rose from the stone bench.

Esther rose, too, and followed with a sigh.

⊱❦⊰

Johan van Wijtenhort, bailiff of Montfoort and subject of the Duke of Cleve-Julich, galloped on his black horse trimmed in fineries of red, yellow, and black. The dark was too deep for the village folk to see his fine clothes—high collar, soft dark vest, and gold sleeves with embroidered cuffs. A long sash draped over his shoulder and wrapped around his waist. It bore the duke's colors: red, yellow, and black.

Johan's deeds were linked to the duke's name, but he performed them not just for duty alone, but also for the pleasure of murder, rape, and plundering. Some inner beast drove him to perform these acts again and again. He imagined that it was the lion on the duke's coat of arms, an animal demon within his soul spurring him on to devour, strengthening and empowering him—a noble, black beast. Johan did not need to justify his acts to himself; he just needed to stay within the bounds of the law of the empire. Tonight he and his fellow riders would satisfy their lust.

They galloped hard into the small river village, their insides aflame with ale, their hands held high with flaming torches. The village folk scurried to their windows to see what caused the flickering lights. They did not often hear the thunder of hoofbeats on the cobblestones this late at night. Only thieves or evildoers wandered the dark streets.

"Whoa!" Johan shouted. His band of armed beadles stopped in front of the shop and dwelling owned by Burgher van Sipkes. Now Johan would have his retaliation, his revenge. Only then could the lion's roar turn to a purr and let him rest for a time.

❧

"Did you hear word of Willem?" Anna asked, the next evening at supper. Peter had just returned from the village, where he had taken some tools to be sharpened.

"Nay. But I believe that is good. Willem must have received our warning, since he is several days overdue."

"I hope so," Anna said.

Horst entered the conversation. "What other news do you bring from the village?"

"Not good." Anna met Peter's hesitant gaze. "Bailiff Wijtenhort and his beadles took a disliking to Burgher van Sipkes and burned down his place of business and his lodging."

"When was this?" Horst asked.

"Last eve."

Anna remembered Johan's remark to his men that she and Peter had overheard in the shed. "So that is what his evil plans turned out to be."

"They are lodging at your house," Peter said, his eyes narrowed and his face grim.

Anna tightened her voice. "Do you think they are waiting for Willem?"

"Perhaps, but they will not stay around this hamlet for long. They will be itching to get back to the city with their spoils." Peter jabbed a piece of meat with his knife.

"Unless they have a mind to burn down a few more places," Anna said. The faces encircling the table grew sober and silent.

"How is this, Mam?" Anna asked, exactly one week from the day the bailiff had confiscated their home. It was the first time Mariel had risen from her bed.

"Ah, 'tis just right, daughter," Mariel said.

Anna helped her mother walk to a chair by her open-shuttered window.

"Any word from Willem?" Mariel had asked the same question each day since their arrival.

"Nay, Mam."

A tap by the open chamber door interrupted their conversation. "May we come in?" It was Horst and Freda.

"Aye," Mariel replied. "It feels so good to be up, and it appears to be a fine day." She cast a glance toward the window.

Horst eased onto the edge of Esther's bed. Freda joined him. Anna's hand rested on her mother's shoulder.

"I've news of the Bailiff Wijtenhort," Horst said.

"Pray tell us." Anna did not like the expression on his face.

"He has left Visserswert."

"Praise God," Mariel said.

Anna had not been able to thank God for anything of late. And, in truth, she felt Horst was not finished with his news. "And?" she asked.

"He left after burning down several properties. He scattered people's possessions about the countryside and seized valuables for the Lord of Visserswert and the Duke of Cleve-Julich."

Mariel's shoulders sagged. "*Our* home?"

Freda crossed the room to Mariel. "We are so sorry."

Mariel's head drooped. "I expected it—'twas only a matter of time. So many memories in that house. To lose it only takes more of Miles away, makes the grief harder."

Anna's hand slipped off her mother's shoulder, down to her side where she formed it into a tight fist. She felt a rush of anger so powerful that she could hardly contain herself. *That bounder. That evil, horrid man.* But as soon as the anger had filled her, there came another concern—worry for the stone-cutter's welfare. She asked Horst, "Did you say the Lord of Visserswert? But surely he knows by now that we are lodging at your home. Will he make trouble for you?"

"Have we put you in danger?" Mariel asked, echoing Anna's concern.

"Nay," Horst said.

"But your work. The statues," Anna insisted.

"Milord is a fair kind and wants the work done. I do not think there will be any more trouble."

"Well, I hate that evil van Wijtenhort and his beadles!" Anna said.

"I understand. Try to remember they are just men doing their job," Horst said. "I was once a soldier."

"Surely you cannot justify killing innocent men and burning the homes of law-abiding citizens."

"In the authorities' eyes we are not law-abiding citizens. They still hold to the old ways. Laws will need to change," Horst said.

"Miles said religion must be separate from the law. We are caught in changing times," Mariel murmured.

"Then I hate these times!" Anna felt as if no one understood her feelings. "Pray forgive me," she said, as she fled from the room.

She sought refuge in the thick woods that bordered the stonecutter's house. Inside the protective covering of pine and thicket, she meant to settle something she had put off long enough. Her chest heaving with anger and exertion, she braced her back against the rough bark of a tree and looked defiantly up to the sky. *If you are up there, God, do something!*

The atmosphere at supper was unusually subdued. Anna guiltily wondered if it had to do with her earlier outburst. But later she sensed it had more to do with the sudden departure of Peter, Horst, and Freda. They had left the house about twilight without telling their plans.

"Where is your family going at this time of night?" Anna asked Esther.

Esther calmly replied, "Menno Simons is holding a meeting. They have gone to hear him preach."

"Nay!" Anna grabbed Esther's arm. "Tell me 'tis not true." Was there no end to this madness? Did her friends not understand the risk?

"It is true, but I shan't tell you anything else if you are going to rail at me." Esther disengaged her arm from Anna's tight grip and gave her a stern look.

Anna could not believe her friend's naïve attitude. "But the bailiff is barely gone, and 'tis so risky." Anna paced across the rush-covered floor. "How strange that Menno Simons would just miss the bailiff like this." At Esther's odd expression, she stopped pacing. "What? Surely he was not here all along?"

Esther gave a smug nod. "Hiding this whole week past."

"Mercy!" Anna plopped down onto a nearby chair. "I cannot believe this is true. And you have said naught to me."

"You could believe, too, if you would not bury your head in the ground."

Anna's expression grew blank at Esther's harsh words.

Instantly, Esther's voice became gentle and apologetic, "Blinded by all your grief." Her eyes pleaded for Anna to understand. " 'Tis not some passing practice. This Christian way is a new and better way, the true way, and people will continue to meet and worship God."

"The Christian way is not new," Anna said.

"Perhaps 'tis not new, only hidden from the people until now. The priests alone had access to the Bible. Can you not see? It gave them too much power, so they fell to temptation."

"And, pray, what temptation is that?"

"The temptation to interpret the word in ways that suit themselves and their pockets."

"To rebel against the pope is to commit sacrilege!" Even before the words spewed out of her mouth, Anna saw their irony. If what she was saying was true, then her papa's death was just. "The wealth of the church is devoted not to humans but to the greater glory of God."

"Men who acquire power, be they priests or kings, work closely together to control people's souls, as well as their bodies and possessions. "

Anna covered her mouth and gasped, shocked at Esther's boldness. The truth in the words pierced her chest like fiery arrows. Still, it was heresy to speak and believe such things. She jumped up, her skirt swirling around her ankles. Rushing to the window, she glanced out into the dark. "If someone hears you speak such things!"

She hurried back to Esther and grasped her arms. "Have mercy! I do not want to lose my good friend too."

Esther removed Anna's hands again, with a gentle rebuke. "I must not be explaining myself properly. But when the Holy Spirit is in you, faith rises up, and you just know the truth." Esther smiled. "You must attend a meeting and see for yourself. 'Tis something you have to experience to believe."

Anna pulled herself upright. "I shall never."

"Anna?" Mariel called from her room. "Is something wrong?"

"Nay, nothing, Mam." Giving Esther a departing glare, Anna snatched a candle to take to her mother's dark room.

She flinched at Esther's quiet retort to her back. "We shall see."

The following midmorning, Anna and her mother entered the kitchen. Horst was savoring a hot hemp drink he used when his leg bothered him. Peter was sitting beside him. "We've news from Willem!" he said.

"Tell us, quickly," said Mariel.

"A ship from Antwerp is harbored upriver. A weaver and his wife on board bring news that Willem is safe in their city. When he received our warning about the bailiff, he went on to Antwerp to stay awhile with Skylar. He sends word that he will come for you when things settle."

Anna and her mother were greatly relieved that Willem was safe. Yet so many matters troubled Anna. *How long will it be until Willem returns?* she wondered. *Will he be safe when he does? Will we sail back on Papa's ship? Will we live with Skylar or have our own place? Will I ever see Esther and Peter again?* Suddenly, she realized how lonely she would feel if she did not.

As if reading her mind, Peter drew near. "See, Anna. I told you your world would right itself. I know you have much to put behind you, but God is watching out for you. Trust him."

The emotions in Anna's heart—joy that Willem fared well and was making a home for them, uncertainty of future plans, sadness that they would leave old friends—made her chest feel tight.

"I will try, Peter," she said. Indeed, she wondered if her world would be better in Antwerp.

Chapter 9

 It was the first sunny afternoon in a week. Mariel sat outside, basking in the shaft of sunlight that came through the twining ivy into the mossy stone house. Anna watched her mother as she inhaled the fresh air and said, " 'Tis like taking a breath of God's beauty." Mam was determined to forge ahead, to experience the fullness of life. She often spoke as if Miles were away on some wonderful journey.

In the next minute, when Mariel's face lit up with pleasure, Anna assumed her mother was imagining some heavenly scene. But the familiar tug on her hair brought her around with a squeal. It could only be one person.

"Willem!"

Her brother planted a kiss on her cheek and hugged her tightly to his sturdy frame.

"Oh, Willem, you are safe!"

"Thank God you are both safe! I have been so worried." His face grew serious. "I am sorry about the house."

Willem released Anna and walked into Mariel's outreached arms. Mother and son held each other for a long while. When Willem drew away, his eyes were moist. "But we have each other and, Mam, you look good."

"And you, son. I knew you would return for us. You are a wonderful sight for these old eyes."

"Old eyes? You are not old, Mam!"

"Help me up, and we will take you inside for some food."

Mariel leaned on Willem's arm, and Anna danced around to slip her hand through his other arm as they made their way into the house.

Word of Willem's return spread through the household. Freda scurried to prepare a light meal for the traveler while he listened to details of the bailiff's evil doings.

"But we have tricked them, have we not? We still have our ship, and I've good news besides," Willem said, between hungry bites. "The business in Antwerp is good. Why, the city explodes with commerce and trade. I cannot begin to express the opportunities for us there."

"Tell us," Anna urged.

Willem motioned wide with his arms. "There is no comparison, love. 'Tis the loveliest city in the world. It is close to the sea—water that goes on forever, with houses and kasteels and more ships than I can count."

"More than ten?" Peter spread ten fingers in the air as he entered the room and greeted his friend. Horst and Esther were with him.

"Go ahead, have your laugh," Willem said, with a smile.

"What is this talk of ships?"

"I was telling Mam that Antwerp will be good to us."

"You intend to live there?"

"Aye."

"I am glad you like it there, but I will miss you," Peter said.

"Then come and visit," Willem said. "Our door is always open."

"What door is that?" Mariel asked.

"Give me time to tell, Mam. I am getting ahead of my story now."

"Just start at the beginning," she urged.

"While traipsing after Skylar, I became acquainted with a group of merchants who took interest in the business. They want to market their wool and local wares along the coastal ports in exchange for currency. They need it to buy the spices and other foreign goods that pour into Antwerp. I already have got shipments lined up." He thrust his arm in the air. "Well into harvest time."

The ruddy glow in his cheeks and light in his eyes encouraged Anna. She kept her hands folded in her lap, but in her mind they clapped with delight. Willem's joy was contagious.

"Good news at last." Horst gripped Willem tightly on the shoulder. "Miles would be well pleased with his sons."

"Indeed he is," Mariel said, forever bringing Miles into the realm of the living rather than the deceased. She pointed heavenward, and repeated, "Aye, he is. How is Skylar doing? I scarce remember his visit on your return from Valkenburg."

Willem's voice filled with pride. "Skylar is going to be a papa again, probably before the harvest season. Hilda and the other children are fine. They are anxious to see you, Mam. You, too, Anna."

While Mariel digested the news of a new grandchild, Anna asked, "When will we go, Willem?"

"The river air is still quite cold, and I fear for Mam's health. But when the weather stays warm and she can travel, I will return. By then, the house will be ready." Willem turned toward Horst. "If it does not inconvenience you too much."

"Nay. You are all welcome to stay as long as it takes, until it is safe to travel."

"What is this about a house?" Mariel asked.

"There is a house available just a stone's throw from Skylar's place. It needs repairs. After a few shipments, if all goes well . . ."

"Willem, your papa had some savings. I shall send money back with you."

Willem's blue eyes gleamed. "This is more than I expected. It is settled then. I shall prepare the house on my return and come for you as soon as the weather permits."

Anna's thoughts went back to the day the bailiff had confiscated their property. Peter exchanged looks with her. He was also remembering the coins in the barrel.

Willem changed the subject. "Skylar was baptized. Just before I left there."

"Was he?" Horst inched closer, and Peter leaned toward Willem, eagerly listening.

"The believers are multiplying here as well. There is a meeting tonight," said Peter. Willem glanced at his family. "Mother and Esther have gone to the believers' meetings," Peter went on. "Is that not so, Father?"

"Aye. What better way to celebrate your good fortune, Willem, than for all of us to attend the meeting. We can thank the heavenly Father for his provision."

"I shall stay with Mam," Anna said.

"Nay, I shall be fine," protested her mother. "I believe you should go with your brother, Anna. 'Tis exactly what you need."

The matter was dropped, but later, when the others prepared for the meeting, Anna sought out her mother. "I'll not go to the meeting tonight, Mam. I would really rather not. Do you not understand how I feel about this?"

"Come here, daughter."

Anna crossed the room to Mariel's chair. "Trust me. I truly believe God wants you to go," her mother said.

"What about Papa? Who did he trust? God?"

"That is why you must go. You need to learn about your papa's faith. I wish we had talked to you about it while Miles was alive. We had just become believers ourselves, while you were away. We did not realize how short Miles' time would be. Perhaps if you could understand more about the faith, it would help you to work through the grief you carry."

"Am I the only one with grief?"

"I am ashamed that you said that."

Anna hung her head. It was a foolish thing to say. She knew

Mam and Willem loved Papa as deeply as she did. But how could a person live in such peace—nay, joy?

"I am sorry, Mam."

"Go tonight, Anna. Then report to me all that went on. I need to know as well. Then we will discuss it. You have done many things to help me during my sickness and my grief. But this would mean the most of all."

Anna swallowed hard. Mam had always been so good to her. How could she refuse her now? "Then I shall go."

❧

Johan van Wijtenhort stood so quickly that his chair toppled over backward. He threw the scrolled paper onto the table. "The duke is not satisfied with our work in Visserswert."

Two of his beadles sat across the dicing table. Since the message had been delivered, they had been watching Johan, waiting to see if he would share its contents.

The boldest one sneered, "Is he still whining about that preacher?"

Johan picked the paper up again and unrolled it. He thumped it with his finger. "Says we got the wrong boat."

"I was hoping we were done with that village. 'Tis a dull place."

Johan's eyes were suddenly aglow. "Maybe the village folk think the same."

"What?"

"That we are done in their village. A surprise visit might get us some information. If we could just catch them in one of their meetings! The duke would quit complaining if he got his preacher."

"What about the boat?"

"Forget about the boat. The preacher is a bigger prize," said Johan, grinning wickedly. "And he comes with a bounty."

"I do not take much to the sea, and I do not relish sailing all over after some lost ship."

"Aye." Johan picked his chair off the floor and reseated himself. Now that he had a plan, his mind was at ease. He smacked the table. "Let's see what the dice say."

The beadle who had been quiet through the entire exchange picked up the dice and tossed them onto the table. He smiled. "My luck has turned. A sign for us?"

Johan threw back his head and laughed. "You are matchless. Did I ever tell you how much you remind me of my cousin? Ah. There are times I miss that lad. He is a printer in Wittenberg. A rising star, that one."

The path that wound along the river and led to the craftsman Jacob Vrenken's house was dimly visible in the light of the crescent moon. Before they even arrived, Anna was spooked. Could the others not see how wrong this was?

At the Vrenken's, Anna's spine prickled with more fear, for the worshipers became even more secretive. They hid their horses and wagons at a secluded meadow close to the river, then followed a stony footpath to a place where eerie circles of light dotted the night and a harmonious tune murmured in the air. Esther squeezed Anna's hand.

As they neared the place of worship, they could recognize the singing. Shadows turned into village friends. Logs and blankets were used as seats. Anna and the others moved among them until they found places. Both amazed and repulsed, Anna discovered who among her friends held this new faith.

Even in the darkness, lit only by the moon and oil lamps, Anna could see that they were singing earnestly. She had to admit the words were moving.

Soon a man stepped forward and began to preach. "That is Menno Simons," Esther whispered.

Anna stiffened and snapped under her breath, "Papa died because of him!"

"Nay. Miles died for his Lord," Esther said.

Anna glared. Her friend could be infuriating at times. But Esther had turned her attention back to Menno Simons.

"He is rather old," Anna snarled through the side of her lip.

"Shh! Give him a chance. Just listen."

Menno Simons began to tell the story of a man named Martinus Luther. *Where have I heard that name before?* Almost at once, Anna remembered. *'Twas the priest who helped Mam escape from the convent!*

"Luther writes that children should be baptized in their own faith, which lies dormant and hidden until they come to the years of understanding, as if they were asleep. We do not read in Scripture that the apostles baptized a single person while they were asleep!"

How confusing, Anna thought. *But 'tis true. Babies do not comprehend what is taking place. But the parents know . . .*

"Why then baptize children before their sleeping faith awakes and is confessed by them? Infant baptism is nothing but human invention."

Human invention? But, of course, the priest is human, is he not?

"The church is a free church—not made up of every person born into an earthly empire—but made up of persons who believe in their hearts in Christ, those who have faith."

But does not everyone believe? How frightening it would be if we were judged by our faith. "Do you have this faith tonight?"

I do not know. Do I? "If not, you must repent and believe the gospel."

I wonder if that is the same as confession? "Anyone wanting to take that step can come forward right this minute. We will wash you in the river."

Menno Simons motioned to another man, one of the elders. Anna recognized the man who trod right through the river reeds and waded in his socks and breeches. He stopped where a halo of light shone over the murky water, not even flinching at the cold river water. Then he held open his arms to the group of believers.

"Who will come?" he asked.

Anna was stricken then as she saw her own brother, Willem, rise and stride toward the river. Her heart beat rapidly against her gown. Three others stood and waded right into the river.

The elder pushed Willem's head beneath the water. "I baptize you in the name of the Father, the Son, and the Holy Spirit." Willem came up gasping, then smiled.

"Blasphemy," Anna moaned.

"But my entire family is baptized," Esther said.

The news confirmed Anna's worst fears. When the service ended, the group gathered around the new believers to welcome them into the fold. As soon as possible, Anna picked up Willem's discarded cloak and hat and started toward the wagon, intending to wait there for the others. But she had gone just a few steps when she heard her name.

"Anna."

It was a woman who knew her mother, one of many who had brought food and condolences to the stonecutter's house.

"How is your mother doing?" she asked.

"Almost recovered."

"I've never had a chance to tell you how sorry I am about your father. Miles was a wonderful man."

"Thank you for your concern."

"I see your brother follows in your father's footsteps," the woman's husband said.

"I had better take Willem his cloak."

Esther gave her a sympathetic look, and Anna made her escape. The circle around Willem had thinned. He was shivering. Instead of going to the wagon, she made her way to his side.

Willem welcomed the cloak, with joy shining on his face. Anna felt discouraged. She had to remove herself from this scene, from the preacher who endangered all their lives.

Willem touched her arm. "I will be a moment."

"You are Miles' daughter, are you not?" Anna turned toward the man's voice. It was Menno Simons. She could only nod, for there was a catch in her throat.

"I thought so. I wish to tell you how I've grieved over your father's arrest and death."

Anna stared at the man. He had not been the one to love Papa. Her emotions overwhelmed her. He had not been the one to see Papa die. Her head felt as if it would explode from the rush of anger that swept through her. This man was the cause of Papa's death.

"I would gladly die in the place of all those suffering for their beliefs, if it would stop the bloodshed," said Menno Simons.

"If you want to stop the bloodshed, then turn yourself in to the authorities and quit preaching lies."

His eyes flickered with pain. "You are not a believer, then."

"Nay. And I believe you are responsible for the death of many innocent people. Now you have deceived my brother and my friends. I despise you!"

Anna turned and hurried toward the footpath that led into the darkness. She would wait in the wagon. Once, she stopped to look back. She could not discern which black figure among the clusters of shadows was Menno Simons. Anger burned in her breast. She did not know if anyone had overheard her conversation with the preacher. Neither did she care.

Anna followed the neighing and rustling of the horses to find her way to the wagon. Halfway there, a voice stopped her.

"Anna?" It was Willem.

She halted and said, "Aye." Her voice was curt.

"I saw you go. You should not be alone."

"Why? Our friends and neighbors might ambush me in the dark?"

"I know you are angry with me."

Anna felt her shoulders sag. She did not want to be angry with Willem. "I think I am afraid for you."

She felt his arm slip around her. "Let's go to the wagon and talk about this."

It was comforting to let Willem guide her along in silence. When they reached the wagon, he helped her up, then sat close. Anna handed him a blanket to wrap around his wet legs.

"I think I know how you must feel," he said. "I did not want to lose Papa either. And I do not want to lose any of my family or friends. But I know now that Jesus is real. He lives in me. I have to follow him."

"But why can you not follow him at the church? The church is where God is."

"The way we were taught is a following of tradition, of rules and regulations. The church is a beautiful building where the priests offer the sacraments. The Christ I know is a living person. He is alive today." Willem blew out a long breath. "I am not doing this well," he said. "Anna, 'tis everyone's free choice to follow Jesus or not. A baby cannot choose, so how can infant baptism save a person?"

"But 'tis not a choice," argued Anna. " 'Tis the religion of the kingdom. We do all that is required, and then we are saved."

"Nay, Anna. No one could ever live a life good enough.

That is why Christ died. He is our ransom. We must believe in him to be saved."

" 'Tis the same thing, Willem."

"Nay . . ." Willem gestured wide with his arm and accidentally knocked Anna on the nose.

"Ouch!"

"What a clumsy oaf I am. Are you hurt?"

Anna wiggled her nose from side to side and gave it a few gentle pokes. "Nay."

Willem gave her a hug. "Brave girl. Always the brave girl."

Anna was about to protest when she heard voices. "The others come."

"Aye," he whispered. " 'Tis real, Anna!"

"What?"

"Ah, Anna. The Spirit of God is sweet."

"Hush, Willem."

Chapter 10

The following day, Anna and Esther took a jaunt to the village fish market.

"I saw you were talking with Menno Simons," Esther said.

" 'Tis good to put a face to the one that I hate."

"Do you think it is right to hate? Is that not a sin?" Esther tipped her head and caught the sunshine in her golden braids.

Anna gave her a look of contempt. "I could not stop even if I wanted to."

"You can pray about it. Only God can help you forgive what was done to your papa."

The girls climbed the long incline that led to the village bridge. Anna considered Esther's reference to prayer. She had not done much praying lately, except that day in the woods when she had dared God to do something.

She stopped and leaned over the stone ledge at the middle of the bridge. Esther joined her.

The river that edged the village sliced into Visserswert at this point, creating a deep gorge. Anna stooped and picked up a small smooth stone, then bent over the ledge and dropped it. As they had done so many times before, the girls rested their elbows on the ledge and watched the stone drop. Anna counted aloud, just as her papa had taught her. Esther joined in. The stone hit the water at the count of ten. Anna knew what number it would be.

Papa had taught her how to measure the distance from the

bridge to the bottom of the gorge by counting the drop of a stone. She thought of him now and said, "See how the water rushes below?"

Esther nodded.

"In this very spot, my papa told me this river was like life, rough in spots, flowing calm in places, ever changing."

They remained quiet for a period of time, thinking about Miles' observation. Suddenly Anna straightened and said, "I do not like change. I still cannot understand why people want to take sacred rites and sacraments away from the priesthood. Christendom has existed for centuries. Why change it now?"

Esther stepped back from the ledge. "Do you want to go to heaven when you die?"

"I do all that is required. You know I attend mass. I suppose you believe that no one went to heaven until this new way of faith!"

"Nay. I do not believe that. I think some sincerely worshiped God, but many thought their infant baptism assured them of eternal life. The Bible says that only by faith in Christ are we saved. Baptism is a public admission to this kind of faith. The faith is what we need."

"Surely one can have faith and still hold to the traditional ways of showing it."

"I cannot answer that. But God knows what is in everyone's heart."

"That is a frightening thought."

" 'Tis true we all sin and make mistakes. But since I believe and his spirit lives in me, I want to please him. Knowing Jesus has changed my desires."

My desires are not very pure at this moment, thought Anna. *If God were looking in my heart right now, I would be ashamed.* They moved off the bridge, each steeped in her own thoughts.

Soon the village activities drew their attention. Children

played and people sold their wares in the market. Anna wrinkled her nose at the smells coming from the deep wooden barrels laden with sea fare. She poked at the iridescent scales of a fish and remembered how her mama had hidden in empty barrels to escape the convent. The fish slid from the top of the heap, and Anna caught it by the tail, careful to avoid the sharp ridge along the center of its belly.

At the same time, the seller's hands lunged forward, then relaxed.

With a smug smile, Anna dangled the herring. "Fresh?"

"My fish are always fresh." Ansel, the dark-haired, tiny fish seller, gestured with his hands as he spoke in his thick French accent.

"We will take four," Esther said.

Anna watched her search in her pouch for the necessary coins. After the trade, Esther placed the fish in her basket, and began to thank the seller. But his attention was across the street.

Both girls followed his gaze to a pair of beadles in armor. Anna recognized the men as ones who accompanied Wijtenhort. She froze with fear. *I thought they had left Visserswert!*

The beadles were apprehending a man. It was the mason hired by the village to work on the well, a man who had participated in the secret meeting at Vrenkens'. Anna gasped as Esther lunged forward.

The seller reached out and grabbed her arm. "Nay," he said. "There is nothing you can do."

Anna stole a glance toward the harbor across from the marketplace, where her papa used to dock his ship. Of course it was not there. Willem had left early that morning. Her head pounded to think of his narrow escape. She wondered if Willem was the reason that the beadles had returned.

One beadle slapped the bricklayer across the mouth and blood trickled down. Another twisted his arm. "Dirty heretic!"

"Do something!" Esther cried out, but at that moment, Anna's feet felt too heavy to move, her body paralyzed with terror.

At Esther's outburst, the beadles looked their way. The fish seller's face paled. His eyes darted from Esther to the beadles. The first beadle, seeing the women's fair complexions and pleasant figures, leered openly. From the foul glint in his eye, Anna thought he might even recognize her. He made a move in her direction.

Anna shrank back, but the other beadle intervened and shook his head. With a departing smirk at the women, the first man gave their prisoner a severe jab.

The fish seller let out a deep sigh. "Go home at once!" His hands brushed them away.

The beadles dragged the man down the street.

Heads poked out of businesses and homes. Two young lads yelled obscenities from a turreted tower. Soon a small crowd assembled and blocked Anna's view.

"Someone is a spy," Esther whispered.

"Let's go." Anna drew Esther away from the market and toward the bridge.

Before they crossed, Esther cast a final backward look. Then she lifted her skirt and the girls broke into a run.

When they reached Esther's home, they ran behind the house to her father's work shed and dropped the fish basket on the cobblestones in the courtyard.

Esther gasped, "Papa! Peter! The beadles took the bricklayer. They said he was a heretic, and they beat him and dragged him away."

The men's faces paled in alarm. Horst's jaw tightened.

Peter jumped up. "We cannot let this happen again!"

His father grabbed his arm. "Stop. Have you not listened at the meetings? The way of peace is the better way."

Grandfather Jarvis rose and reached out to steady himself

against the stone bench. "You have turned into a coward, Horst. Now you mean to shame your son. Have you no regard for the honor that goes with that dagger?"

Peter clutched the dagger. "What Grandfather says has merit. You were a soldier. I cannot understand this new way. I believe in the faith. But this . . ."

"I cannot change the past. I put a knife into your hand at an early age and taught you all I know. I regret those years wrought with steel and force. I wish now I had used a blade only for good." Horst gestured toward the sculptures.

"Menno Simon's preaching on peacemaking has swayed you?" asked Peter.

"Aye, son."

"What about protecting one's rights?" Grandfather asked.

Horst picked up the fish basket. "Let's go inside."

The girls trailed after the men, following them into the house and listening to the ongoing debate. Horst explained, "In following Christ we give up all our 'rights.' We love one another. This does not allow for revenge."

A knock at the door startled them all. Anna jumped and Esther shrieked. Horst motioned for them to be quiet, and they backed away from the door. He opened it a crack.

It was the fish seller. "Come in." Horst reached out to draw the man inside.

"I need to talk to you." Ansel's desperate voice was more thickly accented than usual.

"Can we get you something to drink?" asked Horst.

The man nodded. "Aye."

Mariel and Freda had joined the others, and Freda rushed off to fetch some water.

Ansel gestured to help his words along. "I know the boatman's family stays with you. I hear they will soon depart. I wish to go with them."

Horst glanced at Mariel. "I do not understand."

"I have eyes and ears. I know what happens in this village. I want to leave before I am forced to betray my friends."

"You are not a believer?"

"Nay."

"Why not go back to France?"

"I have no family there." He turned to Mariel. "I believe that wherever your son docks his boat would be a good place to sell my wares. I have been in this village too long to turn on my fellowman. But the bailiff's men, they work their way through the village, asking questions, routing out the believers. 'Tis only a matter of time until . . ."

"If you are not a believer, why should we trust you?" Horst asked.

The fish seller tapped his heart with a closed fist. "I speak only the truth."

Horst studied him closely, then decided, " 'Tis enough. Willem will come for his family when the weather warms. We will let you know when he arrives."

"And where will he be heading?"

Horst looked at Mariel, and she nodded. "Antwerp."

"Good," Ansel said, a light in his eyes. "I have heard 'tis a big trading center."

Freda returned with Ansel's drink. When his thirst was quenched, he rose to leave. "If something better comes along, I shall take it. If not, I shall wait for Miles' son to return and pray 'tis not too late. Good-day to you."

"Good-day. Take care."

When the man left, Anna asked the question on everyone's mind. "Do you think we can trust him? It could be a trick to find Willem."

"I pray not," said Mariel. "I only know 'tis like the man says. He has lived in the village for a long time and has a good reputation. He was Miles' friend. We cannot turn him away."

"He seems to know all about the believers. He could have betrayed us already if he had wanted to. But he has not. Anyway, we will have time to think about it until Willem returns," Horst said.

"But we already told him that Willem is in Antwerp."

"Antwerp is a big place. We shall pray for him."

"I would like to go to the church," Anna said. "Would anyone care to go along?"

"But you have just returned from the village," Esther said.

"I want to go to the church. I need to pray."

"I will go with you," Mariel said.

Chapter 11

 Several days passed. Freda said she wanted to bring the spring into the house. Anna helped to replace the rushes on the floor with fresh reeds from the banks of the river Maas. She enjoyed her treks into the woods with Esther to search for sweet-smelling herbs, catnip, thyme, lavender, and grasses to mix in with the reeds. Even Mariel joined in the spirit of spring.

The next chore they tackled was baking, and Anna dreamed of Willem's return as they worked. When Peter spoke from behind her as she carried pies outside to cool, she gave a start.

"Let me help. I did not mean to startle you."

Peter took one of the pies and fell into step with her.

Anna glanced up at him, suddenly acutely aware of his presence. The fringes of his brown curls brushed his broad shoulders. He combed his hair straight back, but it had a tendency to fall across his forehead on one side. His eyes were deep set and dark beneath heavy brows.

When Peter was serious, his eyes could probe deeply and quite unsettle her. Even when he teased, like now, he looked at Anna with a deep, searching expression that made her feel as if her heart and soul were exposed.

He leaned against the stone wall of the house as he watched her rearrange the pies. "I have noticed you seem more relaxed these past few days, Anna," he said. "Even happy, in a quiet sort of way."

Anna nibbled her bottom lip in thought for a moment. "I

have attended mass regularly. Sometimes Mam goes with me. I think it has helped."

"I am glad you are seeking God."

"I still feel so . . . restless."

"What you need," he said, tapping her chin with his finger, "is a diversion."

With a wide grin, he grabbed a pie and ran toward the woods.

Anna planted her hands on her hips. "Peter Cremer! What will your mother say?" When he did not stop or slow his pace, her mouth curved into a smile, and she joined in the game. "Stop, thief!"

By the time they reached the woods that edged the riverbank, Anna had gained some ground. Inside the woods, however, she trailed further and further behind. Her gown seemed to get caught on every stray twig and bramble.

She followed Peter around trees and over logs. How often in the past had she pursued him and her brother through these woods? A bush snagged her skirt, and she was forced to stop and work it free. She could hear laughter nearby. Peter had straddled a stump, pulled out a knife, and dug into the pie. His shirt was untucked, and he looked as disheveled as she felt.

Her laughter trilled through the trees like a bird's song. "Peter, you have not changed a bit over the years."

"Mmm, delicious. Have some?" He offered her a piece of pie that clung to his knife, and she came close and licked it clean. He scooted over and patted the large stump beside him. She sat, and together they shared the forbidden snack.

After a while, Peter cleaned his knife and moaned. "I am full."

Anna giggled. "What will your mother say?"

"She is accustomed to this sort of thing."

"I suppose she is."

Presently, Peter leaned close and fixed her with one of his intimate gazes. "I have known you a long time, Anna. Lately

you've become a lovely young woman. I shall have to tell
Willem to watch out for you in Antwerp."

"Such foolishness." Anna smoothed her skirt and said
wistfully, "I pray that Willem is not in danger."

"Menno Simons is gone again."

"Good riddance. If only his beliefs would vanish as well!
But they linger behind to spoil people's lives."

"I am sorry you feel that way."

"I hate Menno Simons and his beliefs. They will burn
people in hell!"

Peter's face turned red with anger. "That is a spiteful thing
to say! You are a . . . a foolish, stubborn girl." He got up, set
the pie in her lap, and turned his back. Then, to Anna's surprise, he strode away.

She felt ashamed to the soles of her feet. What horrible things
to say to the person who had saved her from the beadles. She
had just inferred that he was destined for hell. What must he
think? She took a few steps forward and called his name.
"Peter!"

He flinched at the sound of his name, but he did not look
back. Anna did not see him again until supper, and then he
did not meet her gaze. She felt miserable, and she did not
know how to make things right.

That night, Anna's side of the bed looked like wild animals
had been in it, so many times had she tossed and turned.
Finally she rose, careful not to awaken Esther or her mother.
She pulled on a wrap and shuffled to the kitchen. Perhaps
food would soothe her upset stomach.

A candle was lighted in the kitchen, and she gave a start
when she saw who was sitting at the table.

"I did not know anyone was up."

Peter did not smile. "You could not sleep either?"

"I was hungry."

"Now that you mention it, so am I. How about some milk?"

"Aye," Anna replied. She brushed by him. "That sounds delicious. Ah, some cheese and some bread." Her tone sounded stilted, even to her own ears. She prepared the food while Peter poured tankards of milk. He placed them on opposite sides of the table.

When she joined him, she noticed his book for the first time. "What are you reading?"

"I am reading about peacemaking."

Anna took a drink, thankful for the shadows. "What do you mean?"

"I was thinking about my conversation with Papa. You are now looking at a peacemaker, Anna."

With a few little chokes, she finished her swallow.

"I apologize for the things that I said earlier," Peter went on. "Will you forgive me?"

Anna's eyes widened. She wished she had apologized first. But quickly she answered him. "Aye, if you will forgive me for the things I said."

He smiled. " 'Tis forgotten."

She studied him and edged closer. "May I ask what brought on this new way of thinking?"

His steady gaze grew tender as he thumped the book that lay on the table. "This. Our Lord's words."

"Who? Is it an edict from the Lord of Visserswert? Has he found error in your ways?"

Peter watched the sparks light Anna's face as she argued on his behalf. " 'Tis unfair to be ordered about in such a way. And after you made him such lovely sculptures. 'Tis . . ."

"Anna," Peter whispered. "Whoa." He captured her flailing hand midair and held it in his own, bringing it to rest on the table. Her concern touched him. "Rest easy. 'Tis not an edict from the Lord of Visserswert."

"No? Then who?"

"Do you promise not to get angry if I tell you? I do not want to argue again."

She removed her hand. "Aye, I promise."

Peter leaned forward to explain, "This is a Bible, and I have been searching its pages to determine what God says about fighting, killing, and reconciliation. Menno Simons preaches about peacemakers, and I wanted to see for myself what God really says."

Anna gasped.

Peter hastened to say, "Now remember your promise."

She nodded and swallowed. "You can actually find something like that in there? I mean, find out for yourself?"

"Aye. Is it not wonderful?"

"Nay, Peter." She shook her head, and her hair glinted in the candlelight.

Peter watched her, intrigued. Anna was getting worked up again. Her cheeks were red and her eyes sparked like a lioness ready to pounce. Would she pounce on him? No, she was fighting for control. She remembered her promise.

" 'Tis wrong." Her voice squeaked.

"Are you sure I did not see a spark of interest light your face?"

"Well, I am glad you are checking up on what that despicable . . ." She bit her tongue and started again. "On what Menno Simons says. That is all. I shudder to think of all of the people that follow him blindly to their . . ." she cut off her sentence. "Where did you get it anyway?"

"It is Father's."

Her brows rose, and she frowned.

"I am allowed to use it whenever I want. Come closer. I will show you what it looks like."

Anna leaned forward.

Peter caught a whiff of her delicate scent before she jerked back.

"Nay. Never. 'Tis forbidden. Do not tempt me so, Peter."

With that, she rose from her chair. "I must go back to bed."

"Wait. Do you not want to hear what I've discovered?"

She folded her arms. "Make haste, if you must."

Peter thumped the page Anna had refused to examine. "It says here: 'You have heard that it was said, an eye for an eye, and a tooth for a tooth: but I tell you, do not resist an evil person. If someone strikes you on the right cheek, turn to him the other also.' "

He paused. "It is a hard lesson for me. Something inside me compels me to react, protect. This seems a cowardly way, yet the more I read, the more I am persuaded that Christ wants us to show love to all, deserving or not."

"What a perfect dilemma. Now do you see why 'tis forbidden to study the Holy Script? These things have been all worked out for generations."

"I must serve God the best I can. I hunger for truth."

"Are you sure you are not just hungry for trouble?"

"You have known me a long time. Is that what you think?"

"Nay," she admitted. "I think you are an honorable man with some mixed-up ideas, but I do not want you to get hurt."

"Is that a compliment?"

"Aye, and with it, I shall return to my bed."

"Sleep well, Anna."

Anna gave Peter an indignant look. "You know that I shall not," she said, and swept from the room.

He chuckled, but soon grew somber. Willem's little sister was not a child anymore. She was a woman, appealing in every way. Nay, irresistible. And that would turn out to be enough to keep slumber away from him for more than one night.

He had always wanted to protect her, and she had been through so much lately. Maybe it was just sympathy. Would not any friend feel protective when another friend went through such troubles? Still, he could not ignore these new feelings or deny the attraction.

Chapter 12

 Esther prattled on gaily, her hands darting in and out to weave a basket on her lap. Anna nodded and smiled. Her hands, too, were occupied with weaving, but her thoughts were adrift.

Only two years ago, Anna had enjoyed visiting Esther's house above all things. The visits had never seemed often enough. But now, nothing—not even her dear friend Esther's companionship—could satisfy her persistent longing.

Anna had to admit this longing was not new. During her four seasons abroad, she had attributed it to homesickness. But when she returned to Visserswert, she did not find the contentment she expected. Instead, changes occurred so rapidly there was no time to adjust from one to the next—Papa's death, Mam's sickness, being uprooted from their home. The uncontrollable procession of calamities left her feeling restless. But restless for what?

She looked up to see Peter coming into the house. He was waving a letter. "For Mariel."

Anna cast aside her handwork and jumped to her feet. "I will take it to her." She snatched the letter from his grip. "Thank you."

Peter gazed at her with amusement. "At your service." His behavior seemed almost flirtatious, but Anna ignored it as a tease and chose not to respond. With an acknowledging smile, she went to search for Mam.

Anna fought back her feeling of dread. "Mam, you have a letter. Perhaps 'tis from Willem."

Mariel smiled in anticipation. "Let's see, shall we?" She tore open the seal. Anna watched her as her eyes anxiously scanned the parchment, then widened in wonder.

"What is it? What does he say?"

"Nay. 'Tis not from Willem, but Kathrina Luther."

Anna rushed to her side with a squeal. "Truly?"

"Aye. She is sad to hear about Miles, but she . . ." Mariel laid the letter on her lap. A dreamy look came over her face.

"What, Mam? Pray tell me."

"She wants us to come for a visit."

Anna considered the idea. "Why, that is wonderful news. And just the thing for us."

"You think so?"

"Aye. The house in Antwerp is not ready, but you are able to travel. 'Tis just the diversion we need."

"We have imposed many days upon Horst and Freda," Mariel agreed.

Anna knelt, placed her head on her mother's lap, and felt her tender strokes on her hair. "Oh, Mam, that is exactly how I feel."

" 'Tis hard to be uprooted from one's home," Mariel said.

"Aye."

"I cherish the idea of seeing Kathrina again. I feel young just considering it. But it might be troublesome or costly to make such arrangements."

Within the week, plans were underway. Mariel sent word to Willem by a sea merchant who stopped in Antwerp on his regular route. It so happened that Willem was not at sea, and he sent an immediate response. He was delighted with their idea. His only concern was Mam's health.

He would come at once and judge for himself. If Mariel was able, they would sail first to Antwerp to visit Skylar. Then Willem would take them by ship to Wittenberg. The trip would be good for his business, and they could rest assured the idea was not outrageous or costly.

With each passing day, Anna watched her mother warm to the idea and anticipate visiting Kathrina. The trip would do them both good. Since Papa's death, Mam had tried so hard to press on. She needed a change.

They sent a letter about their plans to Kathrina. The prospect of the journey was exciting, but it would still be hard for Anna and Mariel to leave the village that contained so many memories.

Anna hoped Martinus Luther's home would be a place where she and Mam could rest and recover. Even the preacher Menno Simons had accused Martinus Luther of upholding infant baptism, so his home must be a safe place where people adhered to tradition. And surely he was a kind man. Had he not helped her mother those many years ago?

The next day, Peter coaxed Anna away from her duties.

"Come with me for a walk. There is an explosion of windflowers in the meadow by the woods."

Anna agreed with a warm smile. "That is where you and Willem always differed."

Peter cocked his head to the side. "Willem and I have many differences. To which one do you refer?"

She laughed lightly. "When we were children, I could persuade you to pick flowers with me, but Willem was never interested."

Peter gave her a sideways serious glance. "But you know I have an eye for the lovely."

"Aye. You are the sculptor." Peter seemed to withdraw after that, and they walked in silence until they reached the meadow.

"Oh, they are so lovely," Anna said, gazing at the bobbing heads of purple. "Will you help me pick a bouquet?"

"Aye, on our return. Let's walk a bit."

She shrugged. "You seem troubled."

"Aye."

They left the meadow and walked toward the riverbank. Anna cast him a glance. "Are you worried that you will not see Willem after we leave?"

"Nay . . . I mean, aye. But 'tis not what I wished to talk to you about."

"Oh?"

They reached the river's edge and came to a large flat rock where Peter often fished. He motioned to her to sit down. Anna allowed him to take her hand and help her. "Comfortable?"

"Aye."

The balmy day offered a gentle breeze, which teased Anna's skirt. She brushed away some stray hair and tilted her face to study him.

Peter plucked a blade of grass and stared at it. "I shall miss you."

His face looked so serious that he appeared older than his twenty summers. There was even a trace of pain in his eyes. Anna tried to lighten his mood. "The village is not so far that you cannot find some girl to tease when you feel the urge."

His mouth curved and she relaxed. "Nay," he answered, "there'll not be one that can take your place." Then his brown eyes turned sincere again and probed into her own. "You have made a difference here," he said, placing a hand on his chest, "and it will be lonely without you."

The gesture moved her. "Why, Peter. That is the sweetest thing you ever said to me."

His eyes dropped to the blade of grass in his hand. "It is the truth. My heart has just revealed to me how much I care. Now I fear I am losing you."

Anna was shocked. "Are you telling me . . ?"

Peter nodded. "Aye. I know not when it happened, but

next to family and God, you are the dearest person to me. The thought of you leaving and my not being near you or able to protect you . . ." He shook his head.

Anna felt strange stirrings in her own heart. Part of her wanted to sing for joy, but she could not. Her heart was still too broken. Certainly, she admired Peter—she always had. He was handsome and brave. And she had felt drawn to him since he had returned to Visserswert. Peter had been there for her. She needed him. Was that love? Whatever it was, she did not want to lose him either. But Peter was a believer, and it frightened her beyond reason.

He leaned toward her and reached for her hand uncertainly. "Anna?"

In her confusion, she said the first thing that came to her mind. "I am sorry, Peter. You are a dear friend. I shall miss you, too. But you know I must go." She disengaged her hand and pushed herself to her feet.

"Are you sure? Must you?"

"Aye. We had better go back."

As she turned to leave, she saw Peter's determined expression and wondered if this would be the final word on the matter. She called back over her shoulder. "You will not go back on your word, will you?"

"What word is that?"

"We shall still pick the flowers?"

He caught up to her, and she glanced up at him. "Aye," he said, "we shall pick the flowers."

Peter made a gallant attempt to cover his disappointment, but Anna could see the strain in his eyes. She gave him a quivering smile. The quickening of her heart, the urge to flee yet the desire to stay—it was all quite unsettling.

Everyone in the stonecutter's household was gathered around the hearth when Willem arrived that evening.

Anna flung herself into his arms. When he finally released her, she touched the little beard on his chin. "What is this? Something new?"

He nodded. " 'Tis a sign of the believers. Skylar also wears one."

"Oh."

"I think it becomes you," Mariel said with a warm hug.

Peter stood behind the others. "I think you are as ugly as ever."

"I expected no less from you, my friend." Willem gave Peter a sound slap on the back. "But I will not take offense, since we sail in the morning."

"So soon?" Esther objected.

"I fear so. This voyage combines trade with pleasure."

"Aye," Freda said. "I wish you could stay longer. Let's make the most of the time we have left. Come and eat, Willem."

As Willem ate, Horst explained about the fish seller. "Ansel came to us one night with a request."

"Indeed?"

"He wished to know when you would return and where you reside." Willem quit chewing, and his brows arched. "He wants you to take him with you," Horst said.

"We trusted him," Mariel added, "and told him about Antwerp. I hope we did the right thing by you."

"Only God knows," Willem hesitated. "But 'tis done. We shall take him with us."

Anna exchanged glances with Peter across the room. Could she trust God to protect her brother when he had not protected Papa? She had been attending mass and saying prayers on Willem's behalf.

After Willem agreed that Mariel was fit for travel, they sat up far into the night, making plans. Peter took a message to Ansel to be at the ship before daylight, and that evening, the men carried the women's belongings aboard *de Lowlander*.

Anna could not sleep with so many emotions churning in her breast, but the sun rose as usual. It seemed but a dream that they were leaving Visserswert. Freda and Esther wept unashamedly. It was harder than Anna had imagined to say good-bye to them.

Anna, Mariel, and the men made their way to *de Lowlander,* and Ansel met them at the docks. When it came time to say good-bye to Peter, Anna was overcome with deep caring for him—just as he had described, the kind only felt for family. But she must not let him know. Not now, when she was leaving. Not now, when she needed him.

"Take care of that dagger, Peter," she said, feeling the blood rush to her face.

"Be of brave heart, Anna." Peter bent his head and gave her a light kiss on the forehead. "The keeper of hearts."

Anna's gaze followed his finger, which pointed toward the heavens. *He is so gallant.* She blinked furiously to keep back her tears.

After the ship set sail, she wished she had expressed her feelings. But Peter and Horst were now mere dots on the horizon. So instead, she went below deck with an aching head.

PART TWO
Wittenberg

Chapter 13

 After a brief visit with Skylar's family, Anna, Mariel, and Willem set sail on *de Lowlander* down the river Scheldt toward the North Sea.

Willem had been right—Antwerp was the loveliest city in the world. Anna could not take her eyes off the glorious sights from the ship's deck. Hundreds of steeples and gothic towers stretched toward the sky. The docks brimmed with merchants, sailors, wagons, horses, and ships of all shapes and sizes. Mariel waved a handkerchief at Skylar's wife, Hilda. Even Ansel, the fish seller, stood and shouted French farewells.

As their loved ones disappeared from view and they floated further along the harbor, Mariel went below deck. Anna remained at the rail to take in the view. Feeling a nudge at her elbow, she turned.

"Willem! I thought you would be at the helm."

"Nay. The helmsman is doing fine. I like to watch all the other ships."

"What is that large stone kasteel?" Anna pointed at a magnificent fort with round towers.

"The *Steen*, Dutch for stone. Charles V had it renovated." Willem raised an eyebrow disapprovingly. "This is the emperor's territory. Antwerp is a free city, but it falls in the duchy of Brabant. Charles V is by inheritance the Duke of Brabant, so 'tis under his thumb."

"Then will it not be dangerous to live here, Willem?"

"No more than anywhere else. You like the city, do you not?"

Anna nodded. "Aye. And the house is near Skylar's."

"I had a hard time convincing Mam to continue the journey. But the house is not ready."

"Which made it all the more tempting. She told me she wanted to stay and help."

"You will be back soon enough for that. She could not disappoint her friend now that she expects you."

"You are thoughtful, Willem. What would we do without you?" When Willem bent his head and did not reply, Anna wondered if he was thinking about his promise to Papa.

"I had best go check on the helmsman now."

As he turned to go, Anna reached out and squeezed his arm.

The second leg of the trip—from Antwerp harbor to the North Sea, around the coastal lowlands, inland up the river Elbe, and through the land of German princes—was exhausting. Wittenberg was indeed a welcome sight.

From the harbor, they traveled on foot. A merchant in the city gave them directions to Martinus Luther's residence, and they continued past the marketplace to the outskirts of town.

They walked past a board fence through the north gate and entered a shaded courtyard. Anna worried about the way Mam leaned on Willem's arm. The monastery's grand, arched entry was made of sandstone, and it glittered in the sunlight. Willem led Mariel to a low, stone seat carved into the side of the structure. "Rest a bit, Mam, before we announce our arrival."

Mariel eased down and gazed up at the carved apex. An inscription read, *Vivit—He lives*. She glanced up at Willem's anxious face. "I can scarcely contain my excitement."

Willem knocked on one of the dark, wooden doors. Before long, the great door groaned open. The vastness of Martinus Luther's home was most impressive. It was actually part of an Augustinian monastery known as the Black Cloister. But

Anna soon discovered that, though it was not cozy like the stonecutter's house, it did not lack hospitality.

A girl of ten or eleven summers stepped forward to welcome them. She introduced herself as Margaret, daughter of Martinus and Kathrina. She bid them to follow her up a winding tower stairway that ended in a fair-sized hallway. From there, they passed through a door to the right and into an ornate reception room. There, Margaret asked them to wait while she located her mother.

The morning sun shone through a high square window, a warm golden tonic that bolstered their spirits as they waited. Presently, a round, energetic woman appeared and swept Mariel into an embrace.

"Mariel. I cannot believe 'tis you," Kathrina said. Anna immediately liked the pleasant woman with her dancing, wide-set eyes and heart-shaped face.

"Your sweet embrace restores my heart," Mariel said to the smaller woman.

"Welcome, my sister. Are these the children you wrote about?"

"Aye," said Mariel, with maternal pride. "Come forth, Willem. He is twenty, and our daughter Anna is almost eighteen summers."

Kathrina gave each of them a kiss on the cheek. "As I recall, Miles also had a small son when you married."

"Aye. Skylar is married and resides in Antwerp. We just journeyed from there."

"How the years have flown! But come, now, let me show you to your quarters so you can rest up from your journey."

Kathrina led them up another flight of stairs to the third story, where they would stay.

"I was so sorry to hear about Miles' death. Such a good man." After a meaningful pause, she continued, "Stay as long as you like. I will do whatever I can to help."

"Thank you. With such a large household, your duties must be many," said Mariel. "Please, let us serve you."

"All in good time. Did you walk from the ship?"

Mariel nodded.

"As I thought. Then first, you must rest."

Kathrina's hospitable spirit warmed Anna as she and Willem followed along. She felt safer than she had in months, and her heart swelled with gladness. She stole a sideways glance at her brother, and he gave her ear a playful tweak.

Willem left the women to attend to some of his affairs. Anna and her mother settled comfortably into their bedchamber. Mariel was soon reclining on the comfortable straw mattress, which hung suspended from ropes. "The voyage was hard," she admitted.

"But worthwhile."

"Aye, daughter, seeing Kathrina is a blessing from God."

"I feel so, too."

"But it was hard to leave Skylar. I have a foreboding about it."

Anna felt no such foreboding. Skylar's two children had been like sweet flowers, but Anna was eager to experience Wittenberg. "Surely not. 'Tis just your fatigue, Mam."

"Nay. With her mother coming down ill, I fear Hilda will need help with her childbirth."

"Nonsense. Everything will be just fine."

"I pray 'tis so."

"Rest now, Mam. The supper hour will arrive soon enough. Here. I shall just lie down beside you."

Anna climbed onto the straw mattress they would share and patted her mother's hand. Excited though they were, weariness had taken its toll, and in a few moments, both were fast asleep.

A knock sounded on their bedchamber door. Willem had arrived to escort them to supper. Anna discovered that the Luthers' home abounded in activity. Many people passed through the tall, arched doors to clatter about the great stone and wood-paneled rooms of the old monastery.

Martinus Luther was an exuberant man. His body showed signs of age, but his inner person was sharp and full of warmth. Anna observed his wavy hair, deep penetrating eyes, round face, and double chin. He was a large man, and his dark frock took up a great deal of space.

Martinus extended a ringed and gnarled hand to Mariel. "Sister Mariel, I see that my matchmaking skills were not in vain and have born some fruit."

Anna saw her mother blush. Martinus burst into laughter, a pleasant tingling sound. "You and your family are most welcome visitors in my home, sister, and at my table."

Fruit of the womb, indeed! Anna admired her mother's quick composure and gracious response, thanking him and Kathrina for their kind hospitality and personally presenting Anna and Willem.

Children and adults, men and women, encircled the long table. Kathrina explained that at times their home was filled to the brim with people. Some were students.

Across from Anna sat the eldest of Luther's guests, to whom the conversation was most often addressed. Mariel introduced him as an old friend, Elder Lucas Cranach. She had spent many hours in his home in earlier years. During the meal, Lucas cast Anna sympathetic, even grandfatherly looks when she blushed from the students' continual stares.

"Lucas, what shall we debate tonight?" Martinus asked.

Lucas' eyes twinkled as he said, "I suppose the cursed Turks are good for another round."

"The only good thing about the Turks is they keep the emperor busy and needing our military support."

"He means," Lucas explained, "that Charles V, Holy Roman Emperor, needs the support of Wittenberg's good prince and elector, John Frederick, who supports Martinus Luther's religious ideas."

"The electors are the real heads of the German lands," said Martinus.

Anna doubted that. Everywhere she went, the emperor's power was mentioned. His empire included not only her own region under the Duke of Cleves-Julich, but also Skylar's city and now the German princes like John Frederick.

"Most of the emperor's funding, of course, comes from Spain's trips to the New World," said Martinus.

Willem perked up. "What do you know of the New World?"

"Charles V receives one-fifth of those spoils, and most of the explorers are Spanish." Cranach smoothed his long, white beard.

"Do you know anything of Cortez?" Willem asked.

Anna was happy to see her brother's enthusiasm. She was as fascinated as Willem, and the world opened up before her as she listened.

Later, Anna jumped when Luther thumped his fist on the table. "Let us have some music. There is nothing like it to heal the soul and raise the spirits. Without music, man is a stone."

The mention of stone turned Anna's thoughts to Peter and his sculptures, but the music soon drew her attention. A student played a lute, and Martinus taught them a song he had penned himself, "A Mighty Fortress Is Our God."

At last, Anna and Mariel withdrew to their chamber. Anna stretched out upon the inviting straw mattress, her mind a-flurry with talk of Turks and Spanish explorers, the attention of the university students, Kathrina's warm smiles, the children's laughter, and her mother's happiness. There were so many interesting and delightful new things to ponder and dream about. She was glad they had come to this new world.

The next day, Willem bid them good-bye with the promise to return for them at harvesttime. Anna was worried for her brother's safety, and hugged him so tight that he chuckled and placed a gentle kiss on her brow.

"Do not worry about me, love."

His departure put Mariel to bed with such a fit of megrims that Anna administered an herbal application, which she obtained from Kathrina.

"I've such a foreboding," Mariel moaned. "I should have gone with Willem."

"Indeed not! You and Kathrina have much to reminisce about."

"But I feel that Skylar is going to need me."

"Then he can send for you." Anna peered out a tiny window overlooking a garden. Kathrina was working below. For a small woman, she seemed to get many things done and be everywhere at once. "After a rest, you will see things differently," Anna went on. She kissed her mother's brow and let herself out of the room.

The garden was easily accessible. As Anna approached, Kathrina turned to greet her.

"Hello. How does your mother fare?"

"She is resting now. May I help you with your task?" Anna asked.

"If you wish." It was plain that Kathrina's garden was her pride and joy. Anna could see why. It contained an abundant display of growing things—squares upon squares, made up of rows upon rows of vegetables and flowers. And the early roses were in full bloom.

"Your garden is wonderful!" Anna marveled.

Kathrina jumped up to shoo a pig out of the garden area. " 'Tis better yet when you sink your hands into the earth."

Anna accepted the invitation and knelt beside her. Together they pulled weeds, enjoying the feel of warm earth and the smell of herbaceous roots.

A while later, Anna had the prickly sensation that she was being watched. She glanced up at the monastery's distant windows and turreted towers. But the rows of tiny windows looked vacant. She surveyed the rest of the garden and soon spotted the quiet observer. It was Lucas Cranach. He waved to her from where he sat cross-legged on the ground, then returned to his work.

Kathrina gave him a fond smile. "Lucas is doing a wood-cutting of the garden," she said. "You may go and see, if you like."

"Thank you. I shall." Anna rose and dusted off her skirt. A path wound between patches of garden and led her to Elder Cranach.

"Join me?" His twinkling eyes indicated the ground beside him. His hands continued to chisel intricate patterns on the slab of wood propped on his lap.

Anna nodded and eased down beside him on the grassy slope. "I have never seen anyone do this before." She could tell her interest pleased him. The old man's long, thin fingers continued their quick, precise movements.

The monastery portrayed on the block of wood was a nearly perfect replica of the actual edifice that loomed before them. At the present, Lucas Cranach was chiseling the gardens. In fact, Kathrina was in his line of vision.

"That is wondrous," Anna murmured. "Such delicate work."

Lucas smiled at her compliments.

"Do you live here, too?" she asked.

"Nay. The doctor and I are friends and frequent each other's homes. I live but a stone's throw away. I do woodcuts

for his pamphlets. I paint, draw, and etch." He shrugged.
"But this one is just for his pleasure. He is fond of his garden
and often speaks of his wish to retire and spend his time
tending it. I mean to present this as a gift."

"Is it a secret?"

"I am sure Martinus knows. Nothing goes on in this household without his notice, or Kathrina's, for that matter. But it
will still delight him."

"Aye. 'Tis most exquisite."

Anna watched with fascination, and time slid by. Once,
when Lucas paused from his work to stretch his arms and
work the kinks out of his fingers, she asked, "May I touch
it?" She felt the raised ridges. "I have a friend who would
love to see your work. He is a sculptor."

"Is he good?"

"Aye."

"I would like to meet him."

"He lives in Visserswert." Sadness enveloped Anna as she
remembered the vast lands separating her from her old friends.

"And you admire his work?"

"Aye." She might have told him more about Peter if Lucas
had not been distracted by something across the garden. She
followed his gaze and saw a student approaching them.

"Alphonso is an understudy."

When the student joined them, he gave Anna a polite nod
and settled down beside Elder Cranach. He positioned his
woodcut on his lap and sketched black lines on a white-paint-
ed block.

Lucas explained. "After Alphonso has finished his sketch,
he will chip away the white portion, as I have done, see? He
will leave the lines to be dipped in ink."

"I'd best leave you men to your work," Anna said. "I know
that Dr. Martinus Luther will cherish this cutting. Good-day."

Chapter 14

Martinus Luther and Lucas Cranach watched the printing press in action. "Very fine."

Thedric Bettendorf, the German printer who owned the establishment, puffed out his chest. "I am glad you find my press favorable."

"Lucas highly recommends your work. My printer, Hans Lufft, does as well."

"If you would but let me do a printing for you, you could judge my work for yourself."

Martinus did not give the printer a definite answer, but he nodded. "I have nothing at the present, but I will keep you in mind should Hans become too busy."

Once they left the young printer's shop, Lucas said, "That one seems to be a rising star."

"With the abundance of paper from the city mills and the university's constant demands, this new print shop should survive."

It was a marvel to Anna that Dr. Martinus Luther and his wife could find time to get anything done with the throng of people who crossed their threshold. Some came for counsel with personal problems. Many ordinary citizens came, begging Martinus to plead on their behalf before the elector. The intellectuals of the land came to debate. And always a steady stream of university students assembled to sit at Luther's feet.

Nevertheless, even with all the bustle of people coming and

going, Kathrina's companionship seemed just the tonic Mariel needed.

Anna found it restful to tend the cloister garden. One day as she weeded, she heard the shuffle of feet and looked up to see Martinus. His presence surprised her, since Kathrina had mentioned he was in his study preparing a sermon.

"Good-day, Anna."

"Good-day, doctor. How is your leg today?"

"Feels like a river of fire and brimstone instead of flesh and blood."

Martinus Luther always talked in terms of the spiritual. Anna knew his leg had a severe infection, a strictly physical problem, but if Martinus thought it connected to the spiritual, then she was in for a sermon.

Since Anna arrived at the Black Cloister, her perception of Martinus Luther and his world had changed. To her dismay, everything about this big man hinged on reformation of mankind and church, the exact thing from which she had fled. He defamed the pope in nearly every conversation. Daily, new fears crept into her soul.

Hellfire and brimstone, hmm. "I daresay if it were the cold season, you would not need to take coals to your bed." As soon as the words escaped Anna's mouth, she clapped her hand across her lips. "Forgive me, I . . ." Her face felt like fire. Even her tongue burned. If only the ground would open up and swallow her whole.

But Martinus only chuckled. "No need to apologize."

Anna frantically sought to change the subject. "I have a friend in Visserswert with a bad leg. He drinks boiled hemp when it aches."

"I have tried that. It helps sometimes."

Silence hung between them, and Martinus limped off to cut one of the roses. He returned with the flower shortly, rolling the thorny stem between his thick fingers. "You look troubled."

Anna had become accustomed to the comments that came from deep within this man. He was a fount of thoughts and ideas, many of which set her world on edge, but above all, he was perceptive.

"I love it here, but I still miss Papa and my home."

"Ah. The devil does like to heap on worries and depression. He is a sad, sour spirit who does not like the heart to be glad."

Anna sighed deeply. "I miss the joy of carefree days."

"Carefree is a child's word, and you are not a child. But joy, now that is a good word. We find our joy in God." Martinus gestured to the garden. "Just look at his creation. Look at this rose, for instance." He held it close for her to smell.

"True, 'tis beautiful," she said, "but what of our daily troubles, then?"

"Each day has some. We need not worry about them. If we but take them one at a time, God will be faithful to see us through." He smiled. "Would you care to join me on my walk?"

"Nay, thank you. I had better finish up my work here. Enjoy yourself," she said.

"That I will," Martinus said, as he limped away.

Anna plucked a weed from the soil. *I do miss Papa,* she thought. *If only things could return to the way they were before I went abroad, before Papa was executed, before we were uprooted from our home. Is such a wish so childish? I even miss the stonecutter's family, Esther.* She sighed. *Peter.* Her fingers clawed the loose soil. *Will I ever see them again? Dr. Martinus said it is good to hope, so I shall.*

Willem reclined in his tiny compartment below the deck while his capable crew kept *de Lowlander* on course. Gentle waves rocked him, and his blond head nodded. He felt sleepy, but he wanted to pen a letter to Peter before he climbed under the furs on his cot. The next day they would reach a port where he could post his letter.

He smiled as he wrote. If his guess was right, the proposition he offered Peter would suit his friend's needs as much as it would satisfy his own purposes. When he was finished, he placed the letter in his pouch. Then he took off his boots and slipped under the covers. He breathed a prayer, and within moments, the gentle swaying motion of his beloved sea lulled him to sleep.

At the peak of the hot growing season, when the fields outside Wittenberg were green with produce, two important incidents occurred.

First, Anna received a letter from Esther. She missed Anna, she wrote. Peter and Horst had finished with the statues for the Lord of Visserswert and were working at the abbey. Peter was restless.

Memories of Peter filled Anna's mind—the passion that shone in his eyes when he smoothed a lump of stone, his fervent desire to seek God even if it meant reading the Scriptures at the table while the rest of the household slept, his impetuous vow to be a peacemaker. She chuckled. *Passionate, fervent, impetuous—that's Peter. If only he had added a personal greeting to Esther's letter*. She sighed. *But I discouraged him. No wonder he is restless*. She wiped a tear from her eye.

Esther's letter went on to say that the bailiff and his men had been spotted in the village again.

The second incident occurred one evening at Martinus Luther's table. A visitor came to supper. That was not unusual, but the visitor's interest in Anna was out of the ordinary. The gentleman was tall and lean, with dark hair and eyes. He was handsome in a sinister, worldly sort of way. He looked a bit familiar, too, though Anna could not reason why.

Lucas Cranach, the elder, introduced the gentleman as Thedric Bettendorf, a German printer and prominent rising figure of Wittenberg. From their conversation, Anna gleaned that Thedric hoped to publish some of Martinus Luther's pamphlets and books. She was curious, though, about the way he conducted himself.

Thedric seemed determined to include Anna in the conversation. More than once, he caught her eye before he spoke, making it seem an intimate thing between the two of them. And though he was a perfect gentleman, she felt something was afoot between him and Elder Cranach. They kept exchanging knowing looks. Suddenly, she realized that Lucas was matchmaking. He had, after all, accompanied Thedric. Then it struck her that Thedric knew it and did not care!

She was convinced Thedric was aware the instant she guessed the truth, and was delighted that she was in on their little game. The idea brought heat to her cheeks, yet she felt herself succumbing to his charms. *'Tis as if he is putting me under his spell,* she thought.

"How is your sequel to 'Against the Roman Papacy' coming?" Thedric asked Martinus.

" 'Tis progressing, if my health holds out. The pope is Satan's bodily dwelling, you know. Humpf! And he thinks he can appease the population by his councils. Councils that shall never come to pass, for the pope refuses to lend an ear, but only intends to dictate. No one will attend such a thing." Luther grew quiet, then almost reverent. "These days, however, my mind attends to another issue."

"Pray, tell *us* what it is. If you have something new, I can take it with me to the Frankfurt Book Fair." Thedric fastened his gaze upon Anna for an intensely long moment when he stressed the word *us*, then gave his attention back to the doctor.

Anna could only wonder if the heated look between them had been her imagination. She took a large swallow of her drink and waited for Martinus' answer.

"I shall entitle this work 'Against the Thirty-five Articles of the Louvain Theologians,' reiterating that the doctrine of the church must be based on the Word of God or else it is falsehood, godlessness, and heresy. In this work, I shall challenge the sacraments and refute the Anabaptist view of baptism."

Anna choked on her drink. The word *Anabaptist* cut through her like a knife. When she could breathe again, she glanced across the table at her mother. Mariel's face had paled.

"You could make enemies with the emperor," Thedric said.

"Ha! I've already been released from my vow of obedience. The pope has cut me off from his church. The emperor's cut me off from his empire!" His fist hit the table and his tankard of drink bounced and sloshed over the side. "But the Lord took me up. And 'tis far better!"

Anna's temples began to pound. She felt as if she were going to be sick or fall off her chair from a dizzy spell. She pushed her tankard away and placed her hands in her lap. All the while, she prayed the subject would change before she heaved up her meal.

Thedric seemed interested in how Luther's publications would affect his purse, but he was more ardent in his attention to Anna than in his involvement in the conversation. "I pray your health will hold and you will be able to succeed in all your enterprises," Thedric said. "Shall we toast to Martinus Luther's health?"

"May the devil take his leave of me. But I fear 'tis not to be. My time is short."

"Nonsense. You are much needed here." They all raised their goblets and Lucas Cranach repeated Thedric's request, "To Martinus Luther's health and the devil's demise."

The tankards rose and emptied around the room. Most thankfully, it was time to leave the table. Anna's supper might stay down and save her from embarrassment. Her head, however, was aching.

Thedric approached. "Please, allow me." He nodded toward the stairway that led to the assembly room.

Anna nodded, grateful for the arm to steady her, yet wary of her escort. When they joined the others, Thedric took her to a seat in an isolated area of the room and claimed the chair facing her. "May I ask you a personal question?"

"You may ask, but I cannot promise you a reply." Such forward behavior from a stranger! Mariel watched them from across the room.

"I noticed the dinner conversation deeply affected you."

"I wondered which sacraments Martinus intends to challenge," she said in a low voice.

Thedric's brows arched. "I would think that living here, you would be quite familiar with the doctor's opinions."

She smiled and dropped her eyes. "Perhaps you forget, I am a woman." His smile deepened. *Foolish, foolish,* she inwardly admonished. *Why did I encourage him?*

"Nay, I would never forget such a thing. But I do perceive your meaning. And although I would rather expound on the first fact, I will be pleased to numerate the sacraments." His voice lowered to a whisper. "Indulgences, purgatory, the sacrifices of the mass, and celibacy." His smile turned smug.

Anna's hand flew to her lace collar. "Martinus thinks *all* of these are wrong?"

Thedric's fingers drummed against his thigh. "He thinks the church and the pope are consumed with man-made rules that mean nothing to God."

As if lightning had struck her brain, the situation became clear. *Martinus Luther is as much a heretic as the Anabaptists.* "What is this world coming to?" She lowered her voice. "Why must everyone question the authorities and powers that are in place, and for no good reason?"

"I perceive you are devoted to the pope?"

"But, of course!" Her chin tilted upward. "I do not wish to be looked upon as a heretic."

"Ah, the meat of the matter." Thedric scooted to the edge

of his seat and leaned closer to Anna, his expression as glee-
ful as one who had found a long-lost key. "If I may be so
bold—and in no way do I mean you any dishonor—you need
fear no harm. The doctor has full support of Elector Frederick.
The elector brings many issues to Martinus for his counsel.
And the emperor needs the elector's support right now, so
Martinus seems to be safe enough."

"And you?"

"Have no fear on my account." He gestured with a raised
hand. "I am not a reformer, I am a publisher." His smile was
so engaging that Anna could not help but like him. He boasted,
"I will do all that is in my power to conduct myself on your
behalf, Maiden van Vissers."

Anna raised a doubtful brow, and Thedric chuckled.

That evening, when Thedric entered his modest home, he
went to his armoire. The talk about reformation had turned
his thoughts to a letter that he had just received from his
cousin, Johan. It read:

*The duke is obsessed with finding one Menno Simons, an
Anabaptist preacher. He has me trekking across the countryside
in pursuit, but the man is elusive and refuses to be captured . . .
If it pleases you, and if you have any knowledge about the
man, please have a heart and send your poor cousin such information at once. There is a large ransom offered, and I would
share it to put an end to this. How fares the book printing?*

Thedric smiled. His cousin never communicated with him.
He must be in dire need of information on the one called
Menno Simons. He should ask Martinus Luther about the
preacher. His thoughts drifted to lovely Anna van Vissers. She
provided additional incentive for continuing his pursuit of the
doctor. Martinus Luther's influence within the city walls of
Wittenberg, and even beyond, could greatly promote his own
welfare.

Chapter 15

Martinus Luther's daughter, Margaret, entered the room where Anna was doing embroidery and lifted shy eyes. "You have a caller."

"Are you certain 'tis for me?"

The young girl nodded. "In the parlor."

Anna set aside her needlework, ran her hands across the wrinkles of her gown, and hastened to the parlor. Dark-haired Thedric waited on a chair, clad in hose and short breeches. He was balancing a package on his lap and tapping one of his broad-toed shoes. His face brightened when she entered, and he rose.

"Good morning, Maiden van Vissers."

"Good-day. Are you looking for the doctor? I believe he is . . ."

"Nay." He took a step forward. " 'Tis you I wished to see."

"Oh?" She gave him a weak smile, hoping he could not see how his flirtations were affecting her.

"This morning I could not keep my mind at task. I kept remembering the lovely woman I'd met a few nights past. So," he gestured, "I finally gave up trying and decided to see if I was only dreaming or if the lady was real." He paused to give her a meaningful look. "And, indeed, you are."

Anna arched a brow. "I apologize for the annoyance."

Thedric's lips curved slightly. "Not at all. Please do not misunderstand me. It has been a long time since I have enjoyed myself so much. In fact, I wanted to show you my appreciation, so I brought you something." He thrust forward the brown-wrapped parcel.

Anna shook her head. "But I cannot accept a gift from you. We have just met and . . ."

"On the contrary, you must." He leaned forward, his voice low. " 'Tis about the issues." He winked and smiled, revealing a dimple in each scrubbed cheek. "Some of Martinus Luther's pamphlets."

"Oh." Anna cast a guilty glance over her shoulder. "But these are forbidden, are they not?"

"Aye, by the pope and the emperor. But the elector not only condones, but also has built his university around Martinus' theologies. They are merely the words of your most gracious host." He shrugged.

She understood his rationalization and the implications. She had already crossed the bounds of safety by residing in the doctor's household. Could reading his writings be any worse than eating his food? Sleeping in his bed? "Thank you."

" 'Tis my pleasure." Thedric stood, then hesitated. "May I call upon you tonight?"

Anna studied him. He stood at a soldier's attention, his broad-brimmed cap in his hand, obviously not intending to move a muscle until he had her answer. "I should like that very much."

"Tonight then." He gave her a slight bow and departed.

Anna hastened to her chambers with the objectionable package. Inside, she eased off the outer wrappings. The pamphlets were scrolled and tied with a ribbon.

"Oh," she breathed. The ribbon fluttered from her fingers onto the small table by the bed.

When she unrolled the pamphlets and leafed through them, she frowned. In her hands, she held the disputable writings of Martinus Luther, bellwether for the reformation of the church. Though he was not as radical as the brotherhood of believers her papa had joined, she realized that the pope and the emperor frowned upon his writings. And here she was, holding the pamphlets. What should she do?

Hands trembling, she opened the first pamphlet. A picture covered the opening page. Anna's mouth gaped open as her eyes took in its message. The picture depicted the pope and his throne resting in the jaws of hell. Such blasphemy! She snapped the booklet closed. Where could she hide the pamphlets? Quickly, she thrust them beneath her straw mattress and waited for the galloping in her chest to subside.

Once the picture was out of sight, Anna rubbed her hands on her skirt and calmed herself enough to remember the bearer of the gift and his intentions. *I must find Mam.*

Mariel was in the kitchen, busy with meal preparations. As unobtrusively as possible, Anna picked up a knife to help.

But Kathrina turned to speak to her. "It seems you enjoyed Thedric's company the other night."

Anna's hand trembled slightly, amazed that Kathrina had hit on the very object of her concern. But then nothing in the household slipped past Martinus' wife.

"You are a beautiful young woman," Kathrina said, a hint of wistfulness in her voice. "I noticed that he singled you out. I believe Thedric was favorably impressed with you."

"He called this morning."

Mariel, who had been peeling vegetables, paused with her hands in midair. "For you?"

Anna avoided her mother's round eyes. "He wants to call again tonight."

"What did you say?"

"I was unsure if I should answer him without consulting you first, Mam, but he was waiting and I did not know where you were. So I told him aye."

Anna ventured a look. Her mother was busy peeling

vegetables again. "You are of age, and you may answer for yourself. But do not hesitate to say nay, if you've a mind to."

"I will remember that, Mam. I really do not know much about the man. I assume he is reputable, to have been invited here."

"Luther approves of him," Kathrina said, "though we haven't known him long."

Peter rubbed his hands on his apron. "Will you sit?" he asked Esther.

"Who is the letter from?"

With a chuckle, Peter said, "Wait until I open it." His hands worked the paper free. "Ah, 'tis from Willem." Silently, he scanned the letter. "The sea agrees with him." Peter could not disguise his joy.

"What?" Esther probed. "Tell me."

"Willem has connections. He can get me a commission in Wittenberg."

Esther jumped to her feet. "He wants you to check up on Anna and Mariel?"

Peter nodded his amazement. Suddenly he jumped up, too, and grabbed her. He swung his sister round and round, laughing.

That evening, Anna waited for Thedric, hoping his arrival would not cause too great a stir in the parlor, where she and several others were assembled. When he did appear, he maneuvered his way to the corner divan where Anna sat, his face alight with pleasure and charm. He wore a padded doublet beneath a cloak of dark green velvet, embroidered with panels of gold braid.

Thedric opened the conversation. "I hope you know that I am quite taken with you."

Anna's gaze swept the room. Thankfully, her mother's

attention was occupied elsewhere. "As you keep trying to convince me," she answered.

Thedric smiled. "And shall persevere." There was a silence, then he asked, "Did you read the pamphlets?"

Anna's gaze dropped to the floor. "I did not get past the picture on the first one."

Thedric leaned close. "Surely you have heard Martinus call the pope the antichrist?"

"Aye. But I do not understand its meaning."

"In the Scriptures it speaks of earth's final days when a false prophet shall rule the world. He is called the antichrist."

"And the doctor thinks that . . ."

"He is sure of it. He also thinks the end of the world is upon us. Perhaps tomorrow."

"How frightening," Anna said.

"And what think you?"

"Nay, I do not believe it. And you?"

"Nay," Thedric said. "If you read the doctor's pamphlets, you will better understand his theology."

"You have read them, yet you do not agree with his theology?"

Thedric shrugged. "You read them. Then we will discuss it." He dismissed the topic and gazed about the room.

Anna, too, took in the frescoed walls, the decorated panels, and the groups of people in the room. She did not hear their conversations, being absorbed in her own thoughts. She scrutinized the flowers on one panel, then her eyes swept over the bench built into the wall and up to the beamed ceiling, which was divided into squares and profusely decorated.

Finally, after she had finished inspecting the room, she relieved the silence. "Tell me about yourself."

"There is not much to say. I live alone. My greatest joy is my printing press."

"And what joy do you find in this press?"

"It is not the press itself so much as what it allows me to do."

"Indeed?"

"To be present in the central hub of literary works—the university, and distinguished personalities—is quite stimulating."

"So you are an intellectual?" Because their voices were low and the room full of people, they could carry on a private conversation without the worry of being overheard.

"Nay, I just reap the benefits of such circles. Let me explain. No doubt, you take the view that the established church brings unity to the empire. Am I correct?"

"Yes, I agree with that statement."

"I believe it is disunity, diversity, that strengthens my empire."

"How can that be?"

"Disunity weakens the empire and empowers the cities. As cities increase in power, merchants become richer. And I, my dear, am a merchant." He arched a dark brow. "Do you not enjoy the things money can buy?"

"It is good we had this little talk," said Anna, fingering the high, embroidered collar of her blue gown. "I do not wish to be disrespectful, but I fear we have little in common."

"Don't look so distressed. Please explain."

"You are open to new ideas, and I am traditional." She gestured with her hand. "You are worldly. I am but a village girl, with no aspirations toward wealth."

"Wittenberg was once a village, and," he leaned close, "were it not for good fortune, good business, and prosperous friends, I would be in a village, too." He shrugged. "So, you see? We are not so different. And things of the world are fun and easy to learn. Trust me on this."

He had missed the point. The conversation ended when refreshments were served, and afterward Thedric introduced the subjects of literature and art.

Anna soon discovered he was a connoisseur of all fine

things. The way he wooed her with his eyes was flattering. He was attractive, and she could not deny his worldliness set him apart from any man she'd known. She rather liked him, when he did not talk about seeking wealth.

At last, he remarked on the lateness of the hour, and Anna accompanied him to the door. He picked up his lantern with one hand and took her hand with the other. "The city fair is a few weeks away, and there will be a theatrical production. Will you come with me?"

It was an irresistible invitation, for Anna loved fairs and had not ventured into the city often. She was eager for lively amusement.

" 'Twould be a pleasure," she answered.

Chapter 16

 A week passed. Anna's curiosity over Luther's pamphlets had returned. One midmorning she was inspecting them in her bedchamber when the door creaked open.

"What are you reading, my dear?" Mariel asked.

"Oh, some of the doctor's writings." Anna felt almost relieved that her mother had found her out.

"He is quite the reformer," Mariel said.

"That's what I am discovering, too. 'Tis fearful."

"Martinus has the elector's favor and is a doctor of theology at the university."

"But he calls the pope the antichrist. And the emperor supports the pope. The *emperor*, Mam."

"But the emperor also needs the German princes' support, and Luther's elector, John Frederick, is one. Emperor Charles V needs their money."

"But Martinus stands against all that I have been taught."

"Nay, not all. Perhaps you should talk to him."

"Oh, I do not think so. He intimidates me."

"The doctor is a good man, and he likes you."

"He writes strongly against Menno Simons' followers and calls them Anabaptists. I am surprised he even allows us in his house. Does he know the circumstances surrounding Papa's death?"

"Nay."

"As it should be."

"Many are not content to move as slowly as Martinus."

"Slowly? He criticizes so many of the church's sacraments," Anna said.

"His only error is that baptism is not one of them," Mariel smiled.

"But Martinus calls the brethren revolutionists."

Mariel frowned. "He is wrong. While it is true that some reformers bring political upheaval and even warfare, the brethren are peaceful."

"But you cannot agree with their beliefs," Anna argued.

"I do. And I'm glad you are searching. Perhaps you should talk to Martinus."

"I think I shall go for a walk. I need some fresh air to clear my thinking."

"And prayer, daughter."

Anna hurried from their bedchamber. Her mother's words had destroyed what little peace she knew. She pushed open the great entry doors of the monastery. A rush of air greeted her and she pulled her purple velvet hat down to shade her eyes. When she was barely past the lane, a familiar voice hailed her.

"Hello, Anna."

"Peter!" She flew off the path, through the heath, and into her friend's arms. She could scarcely believe he was here.

When he released her, he straightened her hat, which had been knocked askew. Then, giving her a reckless grin, he guided her back onto the path.

"What are you doing here?"

"Looking at a beautiful lady. Realizing how much I've missed her."

"I have missed you, too." Anna drank in the sight of him— his brown curls, broad shoulders, and the olive doublet that accentuated the green flecks in his brown eyes. How she had missed their warmth.

"Where are you going?" he asked, his voice deep with emotion. "May I accompany you?"

"I was going for a walk, and yes—if you answer all my questions."

"I am fortunate that you came out just now," he said. "I was standing here plotting my course of action."

"You could have tried the door."

"But this worked out much better."

"Did Willem send you to check up on us?"

Peter laughed. "Actually, Willem did provide the connections for my assignment. And he did, indeed, ask me to look after you."

"You have a commission here? How exciting! Tell me about it."

"I'm doing sculptures for the courtyard of a wealthy burgher in Wittenberg, Nicholas Eeghen. He is in trade and banking. Acquiring art has become a rich man's hobby, and they pay high prices."

"How wonderful." She hoped her voice did not reveal her disappointment that she was not the pressing reason he was in Wittenberg.

"It is exhilarating. But that's not the only reason I accepted this commission."

"Oh?"

They stopped walking. "The bailiff has been harassing me, and I thought it would be easier on my family if I removed myself."

Anna put her hand on his arm. "How terrible! I wonder if he still seeks Willem?"

"I don't know, but Willem was doing well enough the last time I heard from him." Peter looked down at his boots and up again. "But that is still not the whole reason I came." Anna silently drew in a breath and waited. "I could not stand the thought that I might never see you again."

Anna felt a surge of joy to hear that his feelings matched her own, but it was followed immediately by a nagging fear.

"This is where you say, 'And I you,' " Peter prompted.

"It was hard to leave Visserswert. I am glad you're here, Peter." She glanced around and noticed how far they had walked. "Perhaps we should start back."

They turned around, and she asked, "How is your family?"

"They fare well and send their greetings. Esther says you owe her a letter."

"I see you still wear your grandfather's dagger."

"Ever your protector." He bowed.

"Are you rethinking your views then?"

"Nay. I reflect on the Holy Scriptures," he said. "My soul is quite content to seek out a peaceful life, but my hand still aches to wield a blade. Alas, I am caught betwixt the two."

"Where are you staying?"

"At the home of Nicholas Eeghen."

As they approached the monastery, Anna invited him in. "You must come in and see Mam."

"Nay. I am not sure I'd be welcome inside."

"Why not?"

"Martinus Luther is set against the brethren."

"Aye. He calls them heretics."

"Is that what you think of me, Anna?"

"You know I despise the faith that caused my papa's death."

"Your hatred still runs deep, then?"

Her eyes shot sparks, but she said calmly, "I tried to tell you so before."

"I did not understand, then. But I am beginning to. If you continue this way, your bitterness will destroy your very soul."

"You will not come in then?"

"Nay."

"Then I will say good-day to you," said Anna. When Peter did not try to persuade her to stay, she started toward the Black Cloister. But she did not miss the look of hurt in his eyes.

Peter watched her leave, head held high and back straight, violet skirt flouncing from side to side. When the big doors closed behind her, he let out a sigh. *I am so stupid! Ach, what came over me? Such pride!*

He turned from the building and strode quickly through the small courtyard. Opening the gate, he headed across the open meadow toward the heart of the city.

What did I expect? That she would throw her arms around me in wild abandon? His tumultuous emotions began to subside with the exertion of walking. *Nay, I could only dream of such a thing. Those days are past. We are no longer children, and she is just as headstrong as always. I shall just have to prove myself. I shall persevere. One day she will realize that Peter Cremer's arms are strong enough to safely hold her, that my faith—the same as her papa's—is the true way. Ach, I am impatient. For today, it is enough to see her lovely face.*

Inside the Black Cloister, Anna took purposeful steps toward Luther's study. Her conversation with Peter had only intensified her struggle with this religious issue. A student sat outside the doctor's closed door, working on some papers. He looked up and smiled.

She drew a steadying breath. "Would it be possible for me to have an audience with Dr. Martinus Luther?"

The student scrambled to his feet. "I shall see."

Anna did not need to wait long.

"He will see you now."

The student opened the door, and Anna entered the study. Inside, she paused to look around.

"Anna, please, be seated." Martinus waved his arm exuberantly in the direction of a chair.

Anna picked up some papers from the chair and seated herself, letting them rest on her lap. "I am sorry to bother you," she said, her heart still quaking from the disagreement with Peter.

"Not at all. What can I do for you?"

"I have been reading some of your writings and wondered if we could talk."

"Ah. You are searching for truth. Commendable."

"Please. I do not mean to be disrespectful, but I am trying to understand why 'tis all the rage to disregard what has stood for holiness for so many years. How can a religion that has served our ancestors be evil? Are we to believe they are not in heaven because all that has been ordained was in error? I cannot believe such a thing."

Martinus seemed surprised at her fervor and spoke with deliberate calmness. "Anna, I once believed as you do. I was a pious, obedient young priest. But as I searched the Scriptures, I realized that the more I tried not to sin, the more I did. I could not reach perfection. Then I realized that was exactly why Christ died for me."

"I understand that. That is why we celebrate mass, is it not?"

"In a sense. When we partake of the elements, it should be done to remember his sacrifice, not to earn grace from our actions. It is not penance that acquits the sins. So many of the rituals we perform are merely man-made. Christ does not require them. He alone can forgive sin. He alone can provide the sacrifice."

"Of course. That is what the church teaches," she said, with calm deliberation.

"Nay." Martinus shook his head. "The church teaches that you can purchase requital for sins, that you can buy your relatives out of hell. Then they take the indulgence money and fund a war against the Turks or purchase a new master-piece of art."

Anna gasped, but the doctor continued. " 'Tis not scriptural. It is not our sacrifice of money; 'tis Christ's sacrifice of blood. *We* can do nothing. It is by faith we are saved."

"I understand your point. But is it not more harmful than good to attack the church? What if people lose their faith altogether through such confusion and strife?"

"I can only speak the truth. The rest remains in God's hands. Now that we can print the Scripture, we can see where men have twisted God's Word over the years to suit themselves. Sometimes those in power have imperfect motives. Sometimes they bend the truth. Eventually, things become contorted. This cannot please God. In prophecy, he predicts such heresies."

"What of Munster? What of the Peasants War? Everyone has heard of these uprisings."

"I only wish to reform, not to dethrone governments or incite wars. Those like Menno Simons' followers are saber-rattlers. Such crusaders are dangerous to society. They are radicals, who hinder the reform I strive for and only wish to conquer and destroy."

Anna knew that believers like her papa were not saber-rattlers. Why, hadn't Peter said he was trying to give up the dagger? But she and Luther were at odds, and she could not reveal her association with Peter, so she rose from her seat. "Thank you for your time. I appreciate your explanations."

"I pray you will continue to ponder such things and that God will show you his truth."

She stood and replaced the papers on the chair, then left Martinus' study. Outside his door, the student looked up.

"Thank you," she said to him, then walked away, feeling like she had not cleared up anything. Peter's sudden presence had certainly stirred up her defensive nature.

Chapter 17

Time passed. Peter did not call again. The day of the Wittenberg Fair came, and Anna could hardly contain her excitement. As she arrived with Thedric, he remarked that her enthusiasm shone in her glowing cheeks.

She smiled and chatted with him, flattered to be on the arm of such a handsome and prestigious Wittenberg man. As he guided her through the bustling streets crowded with farmers, bankers, booksellers, pack animals, and oxcarts, she inhaled the many scents that filled the air.

Every seller of wares from anywhere near Wittenberg was displaying merchandise. Anna's pouch, which contained a few coins from her papa's savings, tapped rhythmically against her waist. They passed a beggar, and Thedric pulled her close. They shopped at a stand with scarves and head-pieces, and Anna slipped the silks through her hands, caressing the flowers and the sequins. Thedric helped her to choose a lovely feather fan. Then they worked their way through the press of university men and students and continued their shopping.

Anna nearly tripped when she suddenly saw Peter. He stood but an arm's length away, trying out a rapier at a nearby booth. The steel cast glints of light reflected from the sun.

Thedric followed her gaze. "Is something wrong?"

" 'Tis just someone I know." Anna wondered whether she should introduce the two men. Peter had not yet seen her. As she deliberated, a woman she had not noticed before tucked her hand into Peter's arm and leaned close to him. A sharp, unpleasant feeling swept through Anna.

Peter whispered something to the young woman and Anna's consternation increased. They seemed to be admiring the sword. The woman touched the hilt with reverence, and she and Peter shared an intimate look.

Anna jerked her gaze away. With a tight smile at Thedric, she said, "Let's go on, shall we?"

"Of course." Thedric placed a possessive arm at Anna's back and guided her through a throng of peasants and past a cluster of monks.

For a long while, Anna was caught up in her own little world. *Who is that woman with the long, golden tresses and beautiful clothes? Where did Peter meet such a creature?* The unpleasant feeling had turned into a dull ache. It seemed that everything ached—her head, her heart, and her body.

"Would you like to rest here awhile and watch the jugglers?" Thedric asked with concern.

"What did you say?"

Thedric gazed at her oddly. "Would you care to watch the jugglers?"

"Aye." She knew Thedric sensed her change of mood, and she struggled against her emotions.

It was a lovely day. The fair was captivating. She would not let Peter spoil such a wonderful excursion. She owed Thedric her kind attention.

He spread out his cloak in an open grassy area, and set their packages down, then assisted Anna. It felt better to sit and rest. Thedric's charming manner soon soothed her.

"Look!" he pointed.

A group of jugglers in pointy hats and tasseled clothes entertained the crowd, juggling fruit and other objects. They were talented performers, with hilarious acts, and gradually Anna forgot all about Peter.

"Excellent!" she clapped.

"I am glad you are enjoying yourself," Thedric said.

"Oh, I am! I cannot remember when I've had such a good time."

Thedric beamed and clasped her hand in his own. "Nor I."

The crowd milled about and constantly pressed in on them. Anna was caught up in the colorful costumes of nobles and knights and somber robes of church dignitaries who paraded past.

Thedric pulled out a handkerchief and wiped his brow. "We've enough time to get something to eat and find our spot for the play."

The play, *The Conversion of Saint Paul*, was unlike anything Anna had ever seen. It began with a multitude of burghers in colorful uniforms escorting the actor who played St. Paul.

"This is beautiful. How does it happen that you are not in the parade?" Anna asked. She knew he was a guild member, and Thedric had previously explained that the guild was in charge of the grand production.

"I am in the play," he replied, his black eyes gleaming with mischief. Anna gave him a puzzled look. "I have a small part—very small, and quite . . ." He paused to find the correct word. "Shocking." His wide smile was infectious.

"Pray, tell me about it."

"Nay. 'Twill be better kept as a surprise."

Anna felt excited at the prospect. "But how can you be in it if you are here with me?"

"That is the bad part. I shall have to leave your side for a moment." At this confession, he took her hand and brushed it with a kiss. "But when 'tis done, I think you will agree 'twas worth it."

She lowered her eyes and studied her hand. "I cannot wait to discover the surprise."

The sound of violas, lutes, dulcimers, and drums commanded

their attention for a musical presentation. After that came a colorful parade. When it finally passed, the actor playing God was ensconced in heaven—a round platform erected above the stage. Thunder broke loose from heaven.

Thedric pointed out that the thunder was created by rolling stone-filled barrels.

"Superb!" Anna clapped.

Thedric laughed at her spontaneity and enthusiasm. " 'Tis time now. Pay close attention. I shall return shortly."

Anna watched Thedric disappear into the crowd. When she turned back, she gazed unexpectedly into familiar brown eyes.

"Peter!"

"It *is* you," Peter said, with a smile. He started to speak, but hesitated. Anna sensed his discomfort. He glanced over his shoulder. The young woman appeared, and Peter introduced her as Berta, Nicholas Eeghen's niece.

Berta smiled, and Anna tried to be cordial. "Of course. You are staying at her uncle's."

Embarrassed, Peter nodded. "It appears you have an escort as well." He gave a nod at Thedric's discarded cloak.

There was an awkward silence. "Thedric is a friend of Martinus Luther's. He has gone to participate in the play, but he will shortly return. In fact, I am supposed to be watching for his part. Please join me."

"We will keep you company until he returns," Peter said. He helped Berta find a place to watch the next scene.

Anna fought to keep her mind off Berta's blonde curls and to concentrate on the play. She had already missed a large portion of it. A flaming rocket was launched from the firmament and landed close to the actor playing St. Paul. At the same time, a bush went up in flames. Anna gasped and jumped to her feet, as did the entire crowd. The apostle Paul's breeches had caught fire!

"Oh, nay," she giggled and bounced on tiptoe to see over the heads and shoulders of others who had risen to their feet.

" 'Tis out! They got it out. He is fine!" Peter shouted.

Anna put her hand over her mouth to suppress her laughter. The apostle fell from his horse, and the crowd burst into another fit of laughter. Somehow, in all the confusion, Anna found herself pressed close to Peter. Berta was separated from them by several feet.

Peter looked at Anna with regret. "I am sorry I did not call again. About the things that I said when last we met . . . Can you forgive me?"

"Forgive you?" a male voice repeated in a cold tone.

"Thedric!" Anna reeled and clutched Thedric's arm. Still breathless from the excitement of the play, she said, "That was wonderful!"

She was sorry that Peter's presence had ruined Thedric's surprise, but even more sorry that Thedric's return had ruined Peter's confession.

"I must find Miss Berta." Peter sounded displeased. "I will take my leave now."

"Wait," Anna said. She explained to Thedric that Peter was an old friend from Visserswert, here on an art assignment. The two men eyed each other warily. Then Berta appeared, and Peter introduced her as well.

Thedric said he knew of Nicholas Eeghen. The whole scene was uncomfortable, and Anna was glad when Peter and Berta made their excuses and departed.

Anna fought back her emotions and gave Thedric one of her best smiles. "Now that was quite a surprise!" she said, referring to the play.

Thedric grinned. "For me as well."

"What exactly did you do?" she asked.

He drew her close and pointed to the area behind the stage. "I lit the rocket, right over there."

"Oh, my goodness. Wasn't that dangerous?"

"Aye," he chuckled. "I believe it was." His gaze turned

serious, even intense. "I believe, however, it was even more dangerous to leave you unescorted."

"Nonsense. Peter is just an old friend."

"Sometime, I would like to hear more about him. After seeing the expression on your face when you first saw him, I believe there is a story to tell."

" 'Twould be a boring tale." Anna placed her small, white hand on Thedric's doublet, over his chest. "And today is not a day for boredom."

"Indeed not," he said, covering her hand with his own. "Today is a day to be cherished." He released her and reached down to retrieve his jacket. "As are you, milady."

Anna tried her best to be carefree, for Thedric's sake, but she could not put Peter out of her mind. Why had she not considered that he might come to the fair?

Anna remembered Peter's apology. *If he really wanted to say he was sorry, he could have come to the doctor's home earlier,* she told herself. Then she sighed. *Today I am here with Thedric. I should be more attentive. Otherwise he'll wonder why, and I really do not wish to discuss Peter with him.*

Thedric was telling her about the Frankfurt Book Fair in the harvest season. The Frankfurt Fair was bigger than anything they had seen today, he said. It was hard for Anna to imagine. In the past months, she had experienced so many new things. The trip to Valkenburg had been just the beginning.

"It has been a big day, and you are getting fatigued." Thedric gazed down at her with concern.

She gave him a bright smile. "Aye. But it has been wonderful, really. This is probably the most exciting day of my life."

"And mine. But I can see you starting to wilt," he said. "Come, 'tis not far to the carriage. I shall have you home in no time at all." He patted her hand.

As they turned to go, they saw merchants and farmers starting to pack up their wares. A wagon loaded down with bolts of cloth crossed in front of them, and several geese squawked and flapped their wings to escape the wheels. Anna squealed and jumped backward from the honking fowl. Thedric clutched her arm and guided her to safety, his eyes twinkling.

Anna laughed. "They frightened me, 'tis all. You've been such a gentleman, and I shall never forget this day."

"Nor I, Anna. I pray there will be many more like them."

Anna said thank you to Thedric again as they said their farewells at the Black Cloister. When she climbed the circular stairway, she realized just how fatigued she was.

Her bedchamber was empty. With a small groan, she relaxed on her bed. It felt good to be off her feet. She closed her eyes to relish the comfort, and memories of the day flitted through her mind. Thedric had been a perfect gentleman. *It matters not,* she told herself. *I am not in love with him, and I will soon be leaving for Antwerp.* Her thoughts darkened. *And leaving Peter here with that woman. Oh, dread! I wish I had never set foot in Wittenberg! Perhaps then, Peter would not be here either.*

Chapter 18

Peter knocked at the Black Cloister's great entry doors, and Kathrina happened to answer it. "May I help you?"

Peter rubbed his palm against the hilt of his dagger nervously. "My name is Peter Cremer. I am a friend of Anna's. Is she here?"

He felt Kathrina's probing gaze. "Anna is on an errand, but she should return shortly. Do you wish to wait?"

"Would her mother, Mariel, be here?"

"Aye, she is. Please follow me." Kathrina led Peter up the stairway to the parlor and excused herself.

Mariel was quick to receive him. "Peter! 'Tis so good to see someone from home. How are your parents?"

"Fine." He lowered his voice. "Except the Duke of Cleves-Julich is intent upon sniffing out the brethren."

"I am sad to hear so. Oh, that we could all just live in peace and worship God as we choose!"

"It seems they do so in this house." Peter looked around at the walls and ceiling, with their ornate carvings.

"Aye, but even so, Martinus fears little is happening to make the reforms that are needed."

"But it is a start."

"This is true," said Mariel. "We must have faith and courage."

"I am so glad to hear you speak this way. I only wish that Anna felt the same."

"I fear she carries more struggle in her heart than I can

understand. I only wish her papa were here to explain the way of faith to her. The Lord knows I have tried." She sighed, then smiled warmly. "Anna told me that you are here on an art commission."

"Aye. It is the sort of work I've always dreamed about."

"I am so glad for you."

"I have Willem to thank for it. He met Nicholas Eeghen through his trade."

" 'Tis the least he could do. You have always been good friends, and your family has done so much for us. We could never repay . . ."

Peter knew without looking that Anna had entered the room.

"Kathrina said we had a visitor." She saw Peter and hurried forward to offer her hand. He brushed it with his lips.

Not long after they were seated, Mariel made an excuse to leave the young people alone. Kathrina had mentioned that Peter called specifically to see Anna.

"I thought it was not safe for you to come here," Anna said when they were alone.

Peter looked about hesitantly. "I could not stay away. I have something important to discuss with you."

"Very well." They leaned closer to each other.

"I started to tell you at the fair—I am sorry about the other day. I was just angry. I did not mean to hurt you."

"I am sorry, too, about the misunderstanding," Anna said.

"I wish it were merely a misunderstanding."

"I cannot tread the path you have chosen."

"The path your papa chose, as well."

"Why must you bring Papa into this?"

"Because you spurn the faith for which he died."

Anna wondered why no one could understand her feelings. The pain she felt from her papa's death, from Peter's words, overwhelmed her. Her stomach lurched, and her head began to ache. "Papa's death was horrible! You saw it. I cannot go through that again. I cannot watch my friends and family be tortured."

"But your papa thought his faith was worth it. He out-smarted them all. Do you not remember how he saw the angels? Christ was with him in his last hour, and as horrible as it was for us, your papa went to heaven with a song on his lips. Miles was the victor."

Anna could only stare at Peter in disbelief. He continued, "You are looking at it from the human standpoint. Miles would want you to look at it through your spiritual eyes."

"Such nonsense. Spiritual eyes! Human eyes!"

"What about your heart, Anna?"

"My heart bleeds. It never stops."

"Somehow we must persevere through these hard times."

Anna saw the yearning in Peter's eyes. He took her hand in both of his. "God will make a way for us."

"You speak of hearts. Does your heart cherish the name of Nicholas Eeghens' niece?"

Peter withdrew his hand. He reflected a bit, then ventured slowly, "Berta is only a friend. But what of this Thedric you introduced? Is he more than just a friend?"

Anna felt her cheeks grow hot. "Nay, Peter. Just a friend." Her voice softened. "But not as close as you."

He leaned forward, put his fingers to his lips, and gently touched them to her forehead. "I'd best be going before rumors circulate through this household." Slowly he drew away and rose to his feet.

"Will I see you again, Peter?"

"I shall come again. But I hope the master does not ask too many questions about me."

Anna saw him down the stairs and to the door. He was still carrying his grandfather's dagger. The scene at the fair flashed into Anna's mind, but she tossed it aside. Nay, she would not think about that other woman right now. "Take care then, Peter."

"Take care, Anna."

As soon as he walked away, she felt lonely.

At the evening meal, Elder Cranach asked Anna, "Did you enjoy the fair?"

"Oh, I did. I have never seen a play before. It was delightful."

Lucas Cranach's eyes twinkled. "I am glad you and Thedric enjoyed the day."

Anna's face grew hot. She was flattered he would do matchmaking on her behalf, but she wished he would not meddle in her personal affairs. She took a bite of food and glanced across the table.

Martinus Luther's piercing gaze met hers. "There is nothing wrong with love and marriage. Marriage is an honorable thing."

Mariel's mug clanged against the table.

"If you please," Anna said.

"The attraction between Anna and Thedric is healthy." Martinus waved his knife in the air. "Natural as breathing."

Anna lowered her eyes. "I'd rather not discuss something so personal."

The doctor chuckled, and the elder gave a smug smile. Mariel coughed.

The following morning, Anna took one look at Kathrina's tired eyes and knew something was amiss. Her mother must have realized it, too, for she asked, "Is something wrong?"

"Martinus is not feeling well today, and he refuses to leave his bed."

"I am sorry."

"Martinus has so much to accomplish, but his body will not cooperate." Kathrina bowed her head. "He speaks of his impending death so matter-of-factly."

"We will pray that he does not lose heart, will we not?"

Anna felt her mother's gaze. "Most certainly."

"What can we do to help?" Mariel asked.

"I had planned to work at the farm today and then in my brewery," said Kathrina. "But I should sit with him."

"We can sit with him, can we not, daughter?"

Anna did not welcome her mother's offer, but she quickly reassured their hostess. "Aye, ma'am. 'Twould be an honor."

Kathrina's eyes were filled with gratitude. "If it would not be too much trouble."

"Nay, not at all. May we take him a tray of food?" Mariel asked.

"That would be just the thing. I shall fix it now, before I leave."

Anna went to relieve her mother of bedside duty when the sun was nearing its peak. She creaked open the door to the master's bedchamber.

Mariel looked up from her sewing and motioned her in. "He's sleeping now."

As her mother rose to take her leave, Anna settled in near Luther's bedside. His eyes fluttered open, and he smiled.

"Come to sit with the dying?"

"Nonsense. Do not say such falsehoods."

"Nay, I fear my time is near. But I am ready to meet my maker. Are you?"

" 'Tis dreary to speak of such things."

"I feel compelled to speak of them. I had a dream just now. First, I saw an army of riders dressed in black, red, and gold. They were intent on routing the land of heretics. They rode mighty dark horses that sounded like thunder."

Anna paled. "That is frightening."

He raised a weak hand. "Nay, because they faded away, and then I saw another army. 'Twas a glorious one. An army of golden angels, with wings and riding white horses. A splendid sight. I heard a trumpet, and I knew 'twas God's army—that God is in control."

Anna studied the wooden floorboards beside the doctor's bed and envisioned such an army.

"Are you ready?" For a sick man, his voice was strong.

"Aye," she said.

"I was never more miserable than in the days I attended the Augustinian monastery."

"Pray, why?"

"I could not find the peace of salvation. I tormented my body with fasting and prayers and confessions, yet I was never clean. I spent nights weeping, thinking all was hopeless with my soul. And then, one bright day, I discovered we are saved by grace, by faith in Christ, and all was well with my soul."

As Luther spoke, the sun continued its path across the sky so that light from a high window spilled onto the bedcovers around his face. Anna watched in awe and wondered whether the doctor was an angel or a heretic.

"Do not fight the spirit of God when he seeks to draw you close, child. You shall never find peace until you make your peace with God."

"Aye," she whispered.

"Come closer."

Anna rose and went to his side. He patted her hand. "I need to rest now."

She nodded and went to his window. Like so many others in the monastery, it looked out over the garden below. The doctor's favorite pear tree stood just below. Beyond that was the board fence. To the east was a little chapel, where Anna had gone each day to pray.

Was God's spirit speaking to her, as Martinus suggested? Was that why she oftentimes felt so miserable? Or was God mocking her, spewing her out of his mouth, because of all the blasphemies around her? The thought that pressed her day and night, the one she refused to harbor, returned. Was her papa with God now? Did the angels really come for him as Peter had said? Or was Papa wrong? Had he lost his soul?

It was too painful to consider. Her beloved papa. Anna's soul ached, her heart felt bruised and sore, her mind . . . she must not think. She tore her eyes away from the pretty chapel and looked back to the bed. The doctor's breathing had deepened. He was asleep. She hoped he would not dream again.

Chapter 19

That afternoon, when Kathrina returned to the Black Cloister, Mariel was cooking.

"Mmm, it smells delicious in here."

"I cooked up a pot of soup for the evening meal," Mariel said.

"I am so relieved. I did not intend to return so late." Kathrina bent close to the large kettle hanging in the fireplace and sniffed gratefully. " 'Twill be good for Martinus."

"You look tired. Why not take some and go to your husband? Spend the evening with him. We can handle things here. It will be simple fare, but filling."

"Oh, bless you. I am fatigued." Kathrina washed her hands in the basin. When she was done, Mariel had already filled two hollowed wood bowls with thick, steaming soup.

The door of Martinus' room creaked open, and Anna looked up. Kathrina smiled as she entered. "How is he doing?"

"He sleeps. His medicine is getting low."

"We must send someone to Lucas Cranach's apothecary. Perhaps one of the students?"

"I can go."

"Are you sure?"

"I would be delighted."

Anna went to get her headdress and informed her mother that she was going into the city. She left the monastery grounds and crossed the flower-dotted meadow that lay between the cloister and the city. The fresh air was invigorating. She walked down Collegien Gaffe and past the dormitories for the students. Behind them, a small river flowed through the city. The bell towers of the old town church, the *stadkirche*, rose above the center of the city, where the market was held. But Anna did not take the footbridge across the river toward the stadkirche. Instead, she continued down Collegien Gaffe.

As she was nearing the apothecary, a head popped out the door of a shop.

"Good day, milady!"

Anna's mouth flew open. Then she smiled as she recognized Thedric. "Good day to you. I am on an errand. I had no idea I was near your shop."

The printer wiped his hands on a large apron. His hands were blackened by ink and his hair was disheveled, but he smiled broadly. "I must apologize for my appearance."

He met Anna in the middle of the street. "May I join you? That is, after I have given you a tour of my shop."

"If it does not take too long," Anna replied. "Kathrina is waiting for her husband's medicine, and I must return before dark."

"Careful." Thedric guided her around a pile of pig dung. The pig itself was rooting in some food scraps a few feet away. Anna eyed it warily, but the animal paid no heed as she finished crossing the cobblestone street. The print shop was in a low, wooden building with a pointed, gabled roof.

They entered a large room where several men worked at a press. One pulled on a long pole, another set type, yet another sorted papers. Anna saw endless stacks of paper, books, and scrolls. There was a dog curled up in a corner, and he cocked his head at her.

She mentioned her errand again. "The doctor feels low today. I was on my way to the apothecary."

"I am sorry to hear so. I hope his illness is not serious. I hoped he could finish the pamphlet he has been working on."

Anna felt a twinge of anger. "His health is more important."

"Of course. I did not mean to imply anything else. I am only anxious to do the work of such a well-known person."

"I imagine 'twill be good for business."

"You are taunting me now. Come, let me show you around." The smell of ink and paper reminded Anna of Martinus Luther's study, only here it was much heavier.

The print shop was intriguing, and Anna's anger soon melted away. She looked at the publications and samples covering the wall and was amazed at the printers' work. Then her eyes fell on a heraldic coat of armor, like the one the bailiff had worn. It sent a pang of terror through her being. A coat of armor on Thedric's wall!

A young lad, sweeping the floor, smiled up at her. "Are you an apprentice?" she asked. She turned her back to the coat of armor, but a feeling of foreboding came over her and stayed.

"Aye. Let me introduce you to my shop workers," said Thedric. After the introductions, he disappeared into the back, leaving Anna in the front room to watch the press and wait.

Anna felt more ill at ease by the moment. When Thedric returned, she saw he had removed his apron, and his dark hair was freshly groomed.

He beamed at her. "If you are ready, I'd best get you to the apothecary and back to the Cloister."

"Thank you for the tour."

They left the shop, picked up the medicine at the apothecary, and started the short walk back to the Black Cloister.

Thedric kept Anna's hand tucked tight in his arm. She felt uneasy and wished she could withdraw it without appearing rude. She had been curious to see Thedric's print shop, but now she was sorry to have encouraged him.

"I've been counting the hours until I could see you again. Little did I know you would pass by my own doorstep."

Anna frowned. "I hope I did not interfere with your work."

Thedric chuckled. "You are such a delightful creature."

As they neared the flower-dotted meadow, Thedric leaned close. "May I ask you a personal question?"

Anna quickly disengaged her hand from his arm, and covered up the action by plucking a blossom. He studied her.

Looking up, she saw he still awaited her reply. "If you wish," she said.

"Do you have any other suitors?"

Anna stumbled slightly, and Thedric reached out to steady her. Avoiding a reply, she raised the flower to her nose. His meaning was quite clear.

Finally she said, "Please forgive me, Thedric. You are a handsome gentleman, and I cannot help but enjoy your flattery and attention. I have enjoyed your company, as well, but I fear I must be forthright."

"Pray, do."

"I have no intentions of forming an attachment. My stay in Wittenberg is a short one."

"That matters not. Plans can be changed."

"Nay. I soon return to the coast, where my brother Skylar lives. I intend to make a new life there."

"Why must you make a new life?"

"Since my papa died, my old life has been upended."

"You loved him very much."

Anna nodded and stared at her flower. Thedric reached out and gently removed it from her hand. He twirled it in his fingers, then tucked the white petals into her hair. "This blossom makes a sweet contrast against your dark headdress," he observed, as they walked on. "How did your father die?"

Anna darted an apprehensive look at him. An inner voice warned her to keep quiet. But maybe if she told him, he would quit his pursuit of her. "He died because he gave an Anabaptist preacher a ride in his boat."

"But surely he was given the opportunity to explain his actions?"

"He would not recant. He had taken the man's religious beliefs for his own."

Thedric's lip curled disdainfully. "He was a heretic?"

To hear him speak the words unsettled her. "He was a good man. He was cruelly mistreated," she said.

Thedric gave a mild curse, then apologized. "No wonder you fear living here at the Black Cloister with Martinus."

"I did not know the doctor was a great reformer. I should have realized, but so many things have been a blur since . . ." Her voice died out. "Since papa died."

"I am beginning to understand. Your heart is filled with fear. Since your papa's death, you lack a man's protection, someone to care for you."

"Nay, that is not true. I have two dear brothers."

"But it seems they have abandoned you. They are too busy with their own affairs to see to the needs of their sister."

"Nay, you do not understand."

Thedric stopped walking and turned to her, and his dark, serious eyes searched hers. "I know 'tis soon to speak of such things, but you have just reminded me that our time together is short. So I will spell it out—I can provide for you. And in a few years, I will even be a rich man. We could have a good life together. You need not fear."

Anna touched his arm. "I pray you, stop speaking of such things. It seems improper. We hardly know each other."

"Your heart needs time," he acknowledged, "but we shall speak of this again. Come now, milady. We have reached our destination."

Silence hung between them. Somehow Anna knew her destiny did not include this man beside her, who even now wore a self-assured smirk. It would not be easy to disengage his affections. He was far too forthright and domineering.

Too worldly, too smooth. She should not have let things go this far.

She recalled Thedric's concern at the print shop, not for Martinus the man, but for Martinus the writer of controversial pamphlets. It angered her once more.

"There is something I do not understand," she said. "Why are you so interested in Martinus' writings?"

"Printing them would help me build a richer clientele," he said matter-of-factly.

When they reached the cloister, Thedric lingered outside the arched entry doors. "It has been my pleasure, Anna. I will call again soon."

Anna knew she should invite him in to dine, but she felt a desire to leave his presence. "Kathrina says you are always welcome in their home. I am sure Martinus will welcome your call as soon as he recuperates."

"And you?"

She tried to put him off with a teasing tone. "You are too forward."

He chuckled, but his eyes betrayed a touch of anger. "Perhaps."

"Thank you for your kindness today. I own I am lacking in manners, but I have become quite tired. I would invite you in, but I fear I shall retire early."

He gave her a bow. "Another time, then."

Chapter 20

In the days that followed, the doctor's health improved. His spirits lifted as well, as he ambled leisurely about the Black Cloister and rested in his gardens. But Kathrina confessed to Mariel that she sensed a restlessness in her husband. Martinus was too weak to return to work, but he needed intellectual stimulation. She had an idea, and Anna entered the parlor just as she was explaining it to Mariel.

"I shall entertain guests to celebrate Martin's returning health. We have not done much to amuse you during your stay. This shall be for your benefit as well."

"Your hospitality is abundant," Mariel replied, "and your home offers many diversions. But a celebration does sound intriguing."

"Just so. What is your opinion, Anna?"

"It sounds delightful. What can I do to help?"

"Let's start by making a guest list."

Invitations were soon delivered. Among the many invited were Lucas Cranach, Thedric the printer, and Peter the stonecutter. Meal preparations and entertainment plans were underway.

The day of the celebration dawned clear and pleasant. Students helped set up tables outdoors and spread blankets for extra seating. Martinus greeted the guests from a comfortable chair beneath a large shade tree.

Anna helped set out the food. There were new peas cooked in milk and ginger, cooked greens, onion cheese pie, *blawmanger*

—a rice dish, stewed chicken, pickled meat *brewet*, pork tarts, seed cakes, spiced pears, and apple-raisin pudding. Kathrina had plenty of her own brew ready.

After the feasting, the guests lounged while some of the students played music. There was singing and laughter.

Later, Anna searched the crowd for Peter. She found him testing his skills at bowling. She watched quietly until he had taken his turn.

"You will have to roll straighter than that," she said, her blue eyes twinkling.

Peter smiled ruefully. "You speak no falsehood there. But I am set to conquer." He rubbed his hands together in anticipation.

On his next turn, he held the ball with both hands and ran forward, much like the previous time. When it rolled off to the side of the lane, Anna giggled.

"Go ahead, mock me!" he teased. He gave another gallant try and the ball rolled straight this time, scattering the pins in all directions.

"Hurrah!" Anna thrust her arm into the air.

Peter gave a bow, then looked directly at her.

Anna felt herself drowning in the warm brown eyes with flecks of green. Then she thought of Berta and came back to reality. "When you are done here," she said, "there's someone I would like you to meet."

"Let's go now," he said.

Thedric had been watching Anna's and Peter's antics from across the lawn. His dark eyes narrowed and his jaw clenched as he saw the two stroll away together.

"If you see something you want, you should not give up. Your time is slipping away." Martinus stood behind him.

"It seems the harder I pursue, the more she pushes me away," Thedric answered.

"You have talked to her of love, then?"

Thedric's dark face showed some ruddy color. "Nay, but of a future together."

Martinus sighed. "I believe this maid would rather hear talk of love."

"She is like a dove, ready to take flight. Her heart is full of fear."

"I had thought her unrest was due to God's dealing with her, but perhaps you are right. What is her fear? Do you know?" Martinus asked.

"Her papa was a heretic, executed for his beliefs."

Martinus grasped Thedric's arm with his knotty hand. "Miles? I heard no word of this. Surely not!"

"She told me he was an Anabaptist."

"Follow me." Martin walked back to his chair and slowly lowered himself into it. "Speak softly, and tell me all."

Thedric felt alarm at Luther's reaction. "That is all I know. Anna experiences some apprehension in your home, since you are a reformer. Regardless of her father's beliefs, she is a staunch follower of the pope."

"I wonder. The young man with her today—my wife tells me he is from Anna's village."

"She seems to have affection for him," Thedric added in a jealous tone.

Martinus' face turned a deep red. "Would you do me a favor, son, by finding my Katy and sending her to me?"

The doctor's behavior was confusing. "Are you feeling poorly?" asked Thedric.

"I just need to speak to her."

"Of course. I shall find her right away."

Across the lawn, Anna's heart raced with anticipation as she led Peter to Lucas Cranach. The older man turned and smiled when he saw Anna.

"Lucas Cranach," she said without hesitation, "I would

like to introduce the friend I once mentioned. This is Peter Cremer, the stonecutter. Peter, Lucas is a well-known artisan."

Peter strode forward and offered his hand. The older man took it in a strong grip. "May I see your work?" Peter asked.

"I would be honored. Follow me."

Anna and Peter browsed through Lucas' display, which had been set up for the guests. Then they conversed with him for a long while. As the two men continued talking, Anna excused herself to help Kathrina clear some of the food tables.

When another guest approached, interrupting his conversation with Lucas, Peter meandered through the display, savoring every piece.

"We meet again." The voice sounded vaguely familiar.

Peter turned to see the dark and handsome Thedric, Anna's printer friend from the fair.

"Hello," Peter nodded.

"How long will you be staying in our fair city?"

Peter detected animosity in the man's voice and felt the urge to goad him a bit. "Quite a long while. My work is far from complete."

"The last time we met, I questioned Anna about you. She assured me you were naught but a friend. I was glad to hear it."

"What a coincidence. She said the same of you, only more recently," Peter said.

"You are a liar."

Peter's hand touched his dagger. Thedric stiffened, and his gaze turned ominous.

Peter struggled to speak calmly. "If it were not for a mutual *friend*, I would make you take that back. But I have no need to prove anything. My standing with Anna is secure. I wonder about yours." Then he turned and strode away.

Thedric stood and fumed in silence.

Chapter 21

 On the morning following Martinus' party, Mariel surprised Anna by entering their bedchamber briskly. "Anna, good! You are dressed!"

"Mam?"

"Martinus has asked for an audience with us."

"When?"

"At once! Kathrina has already withdrawn to his study."

Anna frowned. "I wonder what could be so important this early in the morning?"

"I know not, but come. We shall see."

Inside Martinus' study, Kathrina waited rigidly in a straight-backed chair. Her lips were pinched together so tightly that they looked mortared shut. Her eyes were downcast.

"Please have a seat," said Martinus.

Anna felt a foreboding as she and her mother sat down.

"Thedric has told me some shocking news that concerns both of you."

Mariel squirmed in her chair. Her voice wary, she said, "Pray, tell us."

"He informed me that Miles was executed for heresy, that Miles held Anabaptist beliefs. Is there truth to this tale?"

Anna felt the floor spinning. The air seemed to be growing thin. She heard her mother answer the doctor's probing questions as if through a thick, lowland fog.

Mariel squared her shoulders. " 'Tis as you say."

Anna sprang to her feet to keep her mother from confessing,

as her papa had. "But we do not adhere to any of the brethren's beliefs," she said quickly. "Surely you recall as much from our talks."

Martinus fiddled with his inkhorn, his gaze fixed on Mariel. "Do you adhere to the brethren beliefs or not?"

"Mam!" Anna warned.

"I must speak the truth, daughter. I do."

"I see," the doctor said. "That is that." He frowned. " 'Tis only a matter of time until you are tracked here, and I shall be accused of aiding you." He flashed a big hand. "Do not misunderstand. If yours were a cause I supported, I would not hesitate to help you. But you must consider the predicament this presents." His fist smacked the desk. "The Anabaptist radicals work against the very reforms that I wish to accomplish."

"We are sorry," Anna said. She cast a glance at her mother. Mariel's face was ashen.

"You shall have to cut your visit short," the doctor concluded.

Kathrina did not argue with her husband, but her expression betrayed her disagreement with his harsh announcement.

"It would be best if you left at once, this very day," Martinus said.

"But my good husband . . ." Kathrina interceded.

Martinus stayed his wife with a gesture. "Katy, do not." She bent her head.

"I am disappointed in your beliefs, Mariel," he went on. "I trust you did not intend to undermine my work." He rose and opened the door.

Kathrina followed Anna and Mariel out of the study and gave Mariel a weak embrace. "I am so sorry, my sister. Please forgive us. I must stand by my husband, but I love you dearly. Let me know what I can do to help you in your preparations." She let out a sob and returned to the study, closing the door behind her. Anna and Mariel stood in a state of bewilderment.

"Mam, I am so sorry," Anna said. "I should never have confided in Thedric. What a traitor!"

"What shall we do?" Mariel mumbled, as she followed Anna toward their bedchamber.

"We must find Peter," Anna said without hesitation.

"But how?"

"If you can do the packing, I will go and find Peter to make arrangements for us."

"Can you find him?" Mariel asked.

"I know a little of the city. I believe I can find the Eeghens' dwelling. Peter told me it is close to the Coswiger Tor, the city gate." Anna rushed to the window to check the position of the sun. The morning was still young.

She gave her mother a kiss on the cheek. "Be brave and try not to worry." Mariel gave her a weary nod.

Anna hurried from the cloister and across the meadow of flowers. When she neared Thedric's print shop, she kept to the shadows of the gabled rooftops. All her senses warned her to avoid the man at all costs.

To her dismay, when she was just across from Thedric's shop, the door swung open. She broke into a full run. Her shoes clattered on the cobblestones, stirring up a gaggle of geese. She looked over her shoulder. Thedric was nowhere to be seen.

She crossed a footbridge and entered the heart of the city. At the stadtkirche, the bells in the tower began to peal, and her heart lurched again.

She pressed on, dodging an oxcart and maneuvering around piles of pig dung and refuse. When the cart had passed, she returned to the center of the street, which was paved. In the distance, above the steep gabled roofs of merchant dwellings and shops, rose many steeples and towers. Somewhere, beyond those roofs and steeples was the Eeghens' dwelling, where Peter was commissioned. Anna only hoped he would be there today.

Colorful signboards hung over the doors of taverns and tradesmen's symbols identified shops that opened to the street. The fronts of their stalls were lowered to display the merchandise. She crossed another wooden footbridge on huge stone piers and veered away from the marketplace. From here, she could see the outer wall of the city. In place of the cobblestones, the road became white sand.

As she drew near the city wall, the tiled roofs of wealthier homes came into view. It wouldn't be long now. She reached the grandest one, with its own small stone wall. It matched Peter's description. She passed through a gate and up stone steps to a large main entrance.

Breathing in deeply, she knocked at the door.

A servant appeared.

"I seek Peter Cremer, the stonecutter."

The servant's eyebrow twitched. He directed her to a receiving parlor and, within a short time, Peter appeared. His face showed pleasant surprise. The servant's eyebrow twitched again, and he left them.

Peter's sturdy presence gave Anna instant comfort. She rushed into his arms. "Oh, Peter! Something dreadful has happened. The doctor has ousted us from the Black Cloister!"

"How can that be?" Awkwardly he patted Anna's back. He could feel her trembling. "Tell me all."

Anna allowed Peter to gently lead her to a couch. He sat beside her, turning to her with earnest attention. Quickly she told the sad tale, concluding, "And so we need to get word to Willem to come for us."

"Leave everything to me," Peter said, squeezing her hand. "Wait here, while I make some arrangements with the Eeghens."

He left the room, and a servant appeared with some refreshment, which Anna accepted gratefully. Soon Peter returned with the mistress of the house. After proper introductions, she invited Anna to spend the night in their home.

Peter arranged to take a cart to the cloister to pick up Mariel and their belongings. "Thank you so much, Peter," Anna breathed. "What would we ever do without you?"

When he was gone, a female servant showed Anna to her temporary bedchambers and encouraged her to rest. Looking at the comfortable bed, Anna realized how exhausted she was from the strain and her brisk walk across the city. Gratefully she collapsed onto the soft mattress.

PART THREE

The Anabaptists

Chapter 22

Anna awakened to find Peter had returned with Mariel. The Eeghens were kind and hospitable, but if she had not been desperate, she would never have sought shelter from strangers—much less Berta's family. The prospect of witnessing Berta and Peter's blossoming friendship was unpleasant. Indeed, Anna suspected it was something more than friendship.

Through the rest of that first day, Anna stayed close to her mother and repeatedly whispered, " 'Tis only temporary, until Willem comes for us." Then Mariel's white, pressed lips would curve slightly, and she and Anna would exchange a meaningful glance.

The following day, Anna set out to explore the elaborate mansion, which towered several stories high. The Eeghens' home seemed as impeccable as their behavior. She paused at a stairway landing to reflect. Even Berta treated them with genuine kindness, not realizing her actions stung like seawater on the raw flesh of Anna's heart.

Anna stroked the smooth, wooden handrail as she continued ascending the stairs. Her private thoughts fled when she heard Berta's voice.

"Anna!"

Anna's foot faltered and she clutched the banister. She could hear the young woman's footsteps on the lower part of stairway. Her spine stiffened.

"I am so glad I found you," Berta chirped breathlessly. "I

usually take Peter some refreshment at this hour. Would you care to accompany me?"

Anna whirled slowly round and arched her brow. "Refreshment, now? We've only just broken the fast."

"Peter rises when the rooster crows." Berta smiled up at her. "Why, he has probably done hours of work already."

Anna worked hard to conceal her displeasure. With blood pounding in her ears, she squeaked, "I should like that."

As they descended the stairs, Anna fastened her eyes sullenly on the lacing at the back of Berta's dress. The girl retrieved a tray along the way, and they passed through a long, dark hall that led to a side door. There was no need for Anna to speak, for once they were outside, Berta's one-sided conversation drifted back like a suffocating aroma. Soon they entered another building.

Peter sat on a low wooden stool, his body hunched forward as he smoothed and chiseled a large chunk of marlstone. Berta called out a greeting.

He looked up, then scrambled to his feet. His eyes were bright with expectancy. Then they met Anna's, and his face filled with surprise. "Oh, hello. I got word off to Willem."

"So quickly?"

"An acquaintance of ours took the message."

"Oh? Whom do I know in Wittenberg?"

"His name is Guido."

"Nay." Anna shook her head. "I do not know of him."

"You would recognize him if you saw him." Anna struggled to place the name. "He is a messenger," Peter explained, "who travels among the believers of different cities and villages."

"Then I am sure I do not know of him. But please convey my appreciation to your friend the next time you see him."

"Perhaps someday you can tell him yourself." Peter stepped forward and took the tray of food from Berta. "What delicacy are you treating me with today?"

The young woman giggled. "Only something to give you strength and ward off hunger pains."

"You are a blessing."

Blushing, Berta motioned to Anna. "Come see Peter's handiwork. It is a statue of a lion."

Anna had to swallow a rising bitterness. But she followed, and when her gaze rested on the sculpture, she was compelled to step closer to the magnificent piece. "Why, 'tis lovely."

Peter slowly turned. "Your approval means a great deal to me." His gaze was so intense it sent the blood creeping up Anna's neck. They stood staring at each other for several moments. Then, suddenly, he jerked away.

Anna's face grew pale as quickly as it had reddened. How foolish of her to react so openly and embarrass Peter that way. And what must Berta think?

"Thank you." Peter was staring at her again. "Both of you. Now, if you will excuse me."

Berta shrugged and grasped Anna's arm. Anna was thankful, for her feet seemed to be permanently planted in the dirt floor. "Men are such strange creatures, are they not?" Berta whispered.

Several days passed. Traveling arrangements had been set for Anna and Mariel, but Anna was not pleased. The Eeghens, more indifferent than sympathetic to the Anabaptist cause, believed it best that Anna and her mother journey to their niece Berta's home in Emden. Her family was of the believers' sect and would surely take them in. Emden would also provide an excellent port for Willem's ship. Peter's friend Guido was to accompany them to Emden. Berta would be cutting her visit short, but she did not complain. In fact, Berta continued her friendly gestures to Anna, though Anna did not want them.

One evening before their departure, Anna entered the parlor and found Peter conversing with another man. "Oh, forgive me," she apologized. "I did not realize the room was occupied."

Peter's head shot up when she entered the room. "Come in, Anna. This is someone special I'd like you to meet."

Anna tilted her face slowly upward to take in the man's great height. Why, he was a tree! When her gaze finally reached his face, she noticed a thin scar. It ran from his temple, beside one of his blue eyes, down the curve of his face until it met his square jaw.

"This is Anna van Vissers," Peter said. "Anna, may I present Guido Dirksz? I was telling you about him."

"Pleased to make your acquaintance, again," the stranger said.

"Pardon?" said Anna. He must be mistaken. She would not forget such a man.

"We met briefly, once before."

"Pray, forgive me—I do not remember it. But I do want to thank you for taking a message to Willem."

Guido bowed his head. " 'Twas my pleasure."

Anna studied Guido curiously. "Where did we meet?"

"I fear it was at a time you may not wish to recall. I was foolish to mention it," he said with a chagrined expression.

"You have my curiosity now. And you do look familiar in a sense. Pray, tell me."

"Very well. 'Twas in Valkenburg."

The two men exchanged a look of concern while Anna's mind searched for the buried memory. This was the Anabaptist who had helped Willem in Valkenburg, the one who had found her in the street! He had held her until Willem and Skylar came. This was the man she had cursed. "I do remember," Anna finally admitted, her face heating. "You were at Papa's execution."

"Aye. I am a friend of Willem's and of Peter's."

She turned sharply away. "Peter, I would like to speak with you in private."

He gave her a marked look of displeasure, and gripped her

arm uncomfortably as he escorted her from the room. Peter shut the door behind them.

"That was rude," he said, still squeezing her arm.

She jerked it away. "I do not like him! He is . . . too big. And 'tis not necessary for him to travel with us. I am sure Mam and I can manage on our own."

"Willem would not like that. I have charge over you."

"You do not have charge over me."

Peter's brows drew together and his eyes narrowed. "Nay, I cannot allow it. Your attitude toward Guido is childish and ungrateful."

Anna clenched her jaw so tightly that her teeth hurt. "You may make up whatever excuses you wish for your friend's sake. I am going to my chambers." Snatching up her skirt, she marched away.

"Suit yourself!" Peter called after her.

Anna stepped into her sleeping chamber and slammed the door. Her chest heaved, and she threw herself across the bed. Memories of her papa's execution returned, as vivid as the day it had happened—her beloved papa being led to the ladder, his smile, the way he had turned away, never to look in her eyes again, or say her name, or confess his love. And then they had tortured him to death.

Anna desperately wished to escape the pain. It was the same intense desire to flee as that day in Valkenburg. And that was when the detestable Guido had found her. *I shall not travel with that man*, she told herself. *I will not!* She thought of Peter's anger toward her. *He is not in charge of me. I shall not listen to him!*

Finally a plan began to form in her confused thoughts. She would find the serving girl's dress. 'Twould be a perfect disguise when she went to the docks to book her own passage to Antwerp. Why should she and Mam go to Emden and stay with strangers, when they could go directly to her brothers in

Antwerp? The docks could not be that different from the ones she had visited with Papa.

She would go immediately. She wiped her eyes and rose from her bed. A trunk with her belongings sat against the wall. As she crossed the room to get it, a soft knock sounded on the door. She scurried back to her bed and sat on the edge, her heart racing.

"Who is it?"

" 'Tis I, Berta. May I come in?"

"I'd rather be alone. I am not feeling well."

"Please."

Anna groaned inwardly. "Very well." She eased back to a reclining position. The door creaked open.

Berta peeked in and took timid steps to Anna's bedside. "I will have one of the maids come and help you off with your clothes and let your hair down. I am sure you will feel much better."

"Nay. I can do it myself. 'Tis just the megrims." It was not a lie. Her head was throbbing.

"You poor thing. Your eyes are all swollen. You have been crying."

"Nay."

Berta perched gently on the side of the bed. "There is no shame in admitting it. Here, you need not even move. At least let me take your hair down." Anna felt a gentle tug and soon her hair spilled out over her pillow. Berta walked to the other side of the bed, her skirts swishing, and pulled back the covers.

Next, she removed Anna's shoes. "Here. Just slip under the covers." Anna did as she was bidden, all the while keeping a watchful eye on Berta. The young woman crossed the room and closed the drapes. The ensuing darkness soothed Anna's aching head.

"Would you like me to send someone up with some herbs for your headache?" asked Berta.

Anna peered from beneath the covers. "I need nothing."

"A tray of food?"

"Nay."

Berta gave a sweet-sounding sigh. "Very well, then. I hope you feel better by morning. I am sorry for all you've been through. 'Tis no wonder that . . ." The girl's bosom rose and fell. "I am sure I could never be as brave as you have been." Berta walked across the room and opened the door.

Just before she slipped from sight, Anna called out. "Berta."

Berta's golden head peeked back in, "Aye?"

"Thank you."

"Rest well."

Anna lay still. More voices sounded from the hallway, and another knock shook the door. "Anna, may I come in?"

"Aye, Mam."

"I just heard that you were ill. Is it the megrims?"

"Aye."

"Poor child. You've had such a hard time." Mariel stroked Anna's forehead. "Shall I request a tray of food?"

"Nay. I just want to sleep through the night. I am sure by morning I will feel fine." A pang of guilt pricked Anna's conscience, and she nearly confessed her plans. But her tongue did not betray her. She would tell Mam of the change in plans after she had made arrangements.

Mariel bent close and kissed her cheek. "Good night then, love."

"Good night, Mam."

The room grew quiet, except for the sound of Anna's own heart. She battled with guilt. She could not fault Berta's kindness, but then Berta was not the one whose life had been inflicted with pain. And after all, Berta had Peter. She could afford to be charitable to Peter's castoff friend for his sake. With new resolve, Anna tossed off the covers and started across the room.

Chapter 23

Anna wrinkled her nose at the peasant dress, which she held at arm's length. She had forgotten its ugliness and its smell. Well, it mattered not. She pulled the rough fabric over her head, and it settled like a sack over her slim body.

She combed her hair into a knot at the base of her neck, and counted out several guilders. These she slipped into a pouch at her waist. They would serve as a down payment, but the rest of the passage fare would have to come from Mam later.

The small oil lamp resting on the bedside table would light her path. She snatched it up on her way to the door and peeked out. The hallway was clear in both directions, so she eased out and closed the door behind her. She managed to reach the side entrance Berta had used earlier without being detected.

Outside, she scanned her surroundings in all directions. It was a long walk to the docks, but the weather was pleasant. She needed only to follow the road past the town kasteel and the kasteel church to the Coswiger Tor. Then there was the moat to cross. After that, she would be at the docks. Her course mapped out in her mind, Anna started toward the road. She was just about to pass through the Eeghens' enclosure wall when an angry voice accosted her from behind. Anna flinched.

"It *is* you! Halt this instant!"

Instead of heeding Peter's command, Anna bolted. In a few moments, though, his hand grabbed her arm and swung her around. "Agh!" she gasped.

"What are you doing?" Peter's eyes were dark, narrow slits. "Let go of my arm this instant!"

"Not until you explain why you are dressed in that absurd dress and where you are sneaking off to."

" 'Tis not your affair."

"It most certainly is my affair."

They glared at each other. "You are spying on me," Anna said. "Why are you not eating with the others?"

"I was bidding farewell to Guido."

Anna jerked her head around and searched the grounds for the other man. "You need not worry. He's gone," Peter said. "I saw you from afar—your actions looked suspicious. Then I recognized your walk."

"I am going to the docks to find passage to Antwerp. Now let me pass."

"I have already made your traveling arrangements."

"I do not like them. I shall not go to Emden with Guido. I shall go to Antwerp to find my brothers. Please move aside."

"Nay, I will not."

"You may come with me if you like. But you shall not stop me."

"Anna, do not force my hand."

Anna stared at the ground. She could not outrun Peter for he was much too strong. She must either outtalk him or distract him.

"Come, let's go back to the house and talk about this." Peter nudged her elbow as if to guide her.

"Nay, Peter." She jerked her arm away. "I will not go back until I have been to the docks!" She took a step forward.

Suddenly, without warning, Peter snatched the oil lamp from her hand and swept her up in his arms. He began carrying her toward the house. Anna beat on his chest and pushed away from him with all her might, but she could not stop him. He only held her more tightly and walked faster.

"Put me down, you beast!"

"Be quiet!" Peter hissed. "You'll have the whole house outside. I shall only put you down if you are willing to listen to reason." He continued toward the main entrance.

Anna could not be seen like this, struggling in his arms like a child. "Fool. Do not use the main entrance."

"You will listen?"

"Aye," she agreed, reluctantly.

Peter dropped her to the ground but did not release his grip, guiding her around to the side of the house. The oil lamp swung precariously from his free hand. Anna's face grew hot with fury as he lectured her.

"You cannot travel alone. Guido's plans allow him to safely escort you as far as Emden. You will be safe there with Berta's family until Willem can come for you. To travel all the way to Antwerp alone would be costly and dangerous. If it were not so, I would already have made such arrangements." His voice took on a pleading tone. "Why can you not see reason, Anna?"

"I am frightened. I do not like it here, and I especially do not like Guido. He is a heretic. He reminds me of Valkenburg. And besides, he is . . . big."

"Listen to me. Berta's family will take good care of you. Willem knows them. That is how I got this commission. I am sorry if meeting Guido upset you, but you have nothing to fear from him. 'Tis true he is big, but he is harmless as a dove."

"You do not understand."

"Very well. If you will not abide with the plans I have made for you, then I shall have to accompany you to Antwerp myself."

Her eyes lighted with pleasure. "You would do that?"

Peter's eyes grew soft. "I would give my life for you."

His steady, somber gaze wrenched Anna's conscience. "What about your commission here?" she asked.

The muscle in his jaw moved slightly. "It matters not."

She sighed. "Nay, I would not ask that of you." She hesitated and squinted her eyes. "Are you sure Guido is to be trusted?"

"You have my heartfelt promise."

"Then I suppose I shall have to go with him."

"Thank the Lord," he breathed. "Let's get you back inside, where I shall confiscate that rag of a dress. Where did you find it anyway?"

"In Valkenburg. It is marvelous, is it not?"

"Valkenburg! You were sneaking out in Valkenburg?"

"Nay. I planned to, but I never got the chance."

Peter groaned. "Come. If we hurry, we can get you up to your chamber while the others are still eating."

When they reached her sleeping chamber, Peter instructed, "I shall wait outside the door. Hand me the dress when you are ready. And do not keep me waiting long. It would not help your reputation."

Anna rolled her eyes and closed the door. Several minutes later she cracked it open again and handed him the dress. "I am going to miss it."

"As I can well imagine," he said, his brown eyes twinkling. "Good night."

"Peter, I am hungry."

"Then I suggest you find a maid. I certainly cannot tell any-one I've been to your sleeping chamber."

"What about you? Are you not hungry?"

"Aye. I am sure Berta will find me a tray. And something tells me you will not go hungry either."

She scowled. "Be off, then." He gave a slight bow and left.

Anna's appetite had disappeared at the mention of Berta's name. She decided that rest would do her more good than food, so she retired early.

When she awakened the next morning, she felt fresh and clearheaded. The megrims were gone. But she made sure she was not available at the time Berta took Peter his morning refreshments. Anna did not care to see him or have any desire to watch the two of them ogle each other. But about midday, Berta tracked her down in the flower garden.

"Are you feeling better today?" she asked in a sympathetic tone.

"Aye."

"I've an idea," Berta whispered. She cast a look about to make sure they were alone. "Peter told me about your fascination with the docks."

Anna wondered if Peter had told Berta about last night's episode, but the girl's expression revealed no ridicule, only sincerity.

"Indeed?"

"And I know that your papa was a ship owner and that your brother sails." Berta seemed to be waiting for a response.

Anna nodded skeptically, "And?"

Berta leaned close. "I know a spot along the river where there is an old abandoned vessel, shipwrecked. I go there sometimes to be alone." She shrugged. "I just thought you might find it interesting. We could take a picnic, if you would like."

Perhaps Berta hopes to acquaint me with the docks so I will run off again, Anna thought. It was hard to resist such an adventure, however, no matter what Berta's true intentions proved to be. "I would like that," she said.

"Good." Berta clapped her hands. "I will make the preparations. The cook can pack us a lunch. We shall need some sturdy boots . . ." She broke off making her list and said, "I will meet you back here in a few minutes."

"Very well," Anna said with a ghost of a smile.

A manservant accompanied them through the narrow streets until they reached the river. Then they walked in and out along the weedy, tall grassy banks. Just as Anna was getting tired, Berta said, "There it is! Is it not romantic? My brother and I used to come here to play pirates."

The land jutted out into the river then cut back into the forested bank. It was just as Berta had described—a deserted patch of cove, hidden and intriguing. The ship itself, Anna guessed to be about a hundred years old. The small craft had run ashore, and its rotten timbers were strewn around the area. But small portions of the craft remained accessible, its rotten floor planks revealing great, ragged holes.

"Be careful," Berta warned.

Anna climbed onto the craft and a flock of birds took wing from the far side, flapping their wings like rumbling thunder. Both girls shrieked, then giggled at themselves. They tested each step, then eased themselves onto their stomachs to peer through the gaping floorboards. The dark, cavernous space below deck smelled musty.

"Incredible," Anna said.

"I am sure there's nothing down there. People who grew up in these parts have been all over this ship," Berta said. "But I still like it."

" 'Tis the perfect place for a child to explore," Anna agreed. "Where is your brother now?"

"Emden. He is married and has a family."

The girls sat up and dangled their legs into the hole. "Have you lived there all your life?"

"Aye. And you?"

"I lived in Visserswert, a small river hamlet, until Papa's death." She looked out across the water. "This is a nice place. Thank you for bringing me here."

Berta perked up and pointed. "There is a small sandy spot over there. Are you ready for lunch?"

"Aye. 'Twould be nice."

They shared their lunch and watched the small vessels that occasionally passed on the river. Anna became aloof once more, though Berta tried to engage her in conversation. Still, they whiled away several hours before Berta gave a sad smile. "I suppose 'tis time to go back."

That night, in her chamber, Anna wondered about their expedition. Why would Berta share her special spot? She had not questioned Anna about Peter or made her feel uncomfortable. She had been only sweet and kind.

Guido came to sup the following evening. Anna knew Peter was attempting to better acquaint them and set her at ease. Her place at the table was next to Peter. Guido and Berta were seated across from them. The other three kept up a conversation, but Anna did not speak unless someone asked her a question. Guido avoided her eyes, which was fine with her.

It pained her, though, to watch Berta and Peter together. The two shared a sweet camaraderie. She fought to keep an emotional distance from Peter.

As she considered her problem, a new idea took root in her mind. *Perhaps I should join a convent. Of course. 'Tis the only safe place in the world. And to think Mam ran from such a haven. Might Willem know of a convent in Antwerp?* Anna guessed no one else would take to her idea, so she kept it to herself for now.

After the meal, they retired to the parlor. "Your ship leaves day after the morrow," Peter said. Anna wished she were already on it, though she dreaded the trip. She merely nodded.

Peter and Guido were soon engaged in a game of chess, which Anna found stimulating to watch. Then she discovered it was Berta who had taught Peter the game. She could well imagine the evenings they had spent together.

Berta interrupted Anna's self-pitying thoughts with friendly conversation, and in spite of herself, she began to enjoy the evening.

Across the room, her mother talked freely with Nicholas

and his wife. She seemed content. It had been hard for her, leaving Kathrina in such a distressing manner. If Anna had been able to foresee the future before they went to Wittenberg, she would not have set her mother up for another heartbreak. She was relieved to see her in such good spirits, and looking well at last, aside from a new set of lines about her eyes and mouth. Anna marveled at the way she had carried on after Papa's death, not merely surviving but seeking fulfillment. Anna knew Mariel's courage came from God, yet thoughts of God frightened Anna.

If only she could turn back time. But, nay, time moved forward, not backward. *So be it,* she thought. *Let it move quickly, so I can endure the voyage with the giant and the stay at Emden. Then Willem will come and take us to Antwerp. If I do not like it there, I shall join a convent.*

Chapter 24

 The following midmorning there was a tap on Anna's bedchamber door. She gave her hair one last stroke with the comb and turned. "Who is there?"

"Berta. May I enter?"

Anna rolled her eyes and clasped both hands over the comb on her lap. Her hair flowed freely over her shoulders and back. "Aye."

"I've been looking for you. What are you doing?" Berta's gaze swept across Anna as she entered the room.

Fingering a lock of hair, Anna said, "I was going to put my hair up. 'Tis so hot."

"Aye, and not even midday yet. Here, let me do it for you."

Anna shrugged and relinquished the comb. Berta made several strokes through the abundant brown locks. "Your hair is beautiful—such a shining, dark gold."

Anna did not reply. She supposed she should return the compliment. Anyone could see that Berta's own golden hair was beyond beautiful. Berta began to braid. "I am going to pack today. After all, our ship leaves in two days."

"Most of my things are already in my trunk," said Anna. There was an awkward silence. "I am sorry you have to leave early because of our situation."

"Do not let it trouble you. I hope you like Emden."

"Oh, 'tis only temporary, you know. But I hate to intrude on you and your family. Mam and I appreciate what you are doing for us."

"Think nothing of it. Peter is my friend, you are his friend, and that is that. Actually, I am looking forward to going home. I will miss Peter, though. Will you not miss him?"

Anna jerked, and her hair pulled painfully. "Aye."

Berta patted the finished coils of braids and moved to face Anna. "How is that?"

"Fine."

⚜

Thedric hung his apron on a peg in the back room and walked through the front of his print shop. "Keep things going. I am stepping outside."

His journeyman raised an inky hand and waved.

Out in the street, the sweltering humid air was oppressive. Perspiration collected instantly on Thedric's brow. He mopped it away and surveyed the area lazily. His friend Lucas Cranach was shuffling along on the other side of the street.

"Good day, Lucas!"

The older man looked over, and his shoulders sagged slightly. He hesitated a bit, then turned and came across the street. He kept his head bent toward the ground until he drew close. Then he looked up with a concerned expression. "How are you?"

"The shop is smothering," Thedric said casually. "I came out to see why. Such weather."

Lucas wiped his brow. "Aye." He studied Thedric a moment. "I was sorry to hear about Anna and her mother. I meant to drop by earlier to see how you fared. I feel responsible, having played the matchmaker."

Thedric shook his head, struggling to comprehend. "Wait. Sorry to hear what?"

Lucas gaped at him. "You do not know what happened?"

The hair on Thedric's arms bristled. "Nay."

Laying a consoling hand on the young man's shoulder,

Lucas spoke in barely more than a whisper. "Martinus found out that they are Anabaptists. Miles, Mariel's husband and Anna's father . . ."

Thedric nodded with impatience. He knew who Miles was, for pity's sake.

"Well, it seems Miles was executed for heresy. Burned at the stake." Lucas leaned close. "And here Kathrina had flung the gates wide open for the two women. Took them in like little chicks. Well, Martinus was incensed that he'd been duped. 'Tis like harboring the enemy in your own camp. So he threw them out on the street! I imagine they are fortunate he didn't report them to the elector."

Thedric narrowed his eyes in disbelief. "Threw . . . threw . . ."

Lucas released his shoulder and stepped back a pace. "Aye, threw them out. And I always liked them, too. I was fond of Mariel. Why, years ago she stayed in my home. I knew Miles. And the daughter, Anna. What a lovely young woman. I even introduced you to Anna. I am feeling embarrassed now, I must say." Lucas rubbed his long white beard. "You look a bit shocked, son."

Thedric ran his hands through his hair. "Aye. Shocked, indeed."

"I am sorry to be the bearer of bad news."

"Do you know what happened to them? Where did they go?"

"Nay. I've been wondering that myself. 'Tis like the earth opened up and swallowed them."

Thedric narrowed his brows. "Are you off to the Black Cloister now?" Lucas nodded. "If you hear anything . . ."

"I will let you know." Lucas patted Thedric on the back. "But 'tis best to forget her." He strode off as if in a hurry to get someplace.

Martinus threw them out? 'Tis my fault. I cannot believe he actually threw them out. Two women, alone . . . Then as if he expected to catch a glimpse of them, Thedric scoured the street in all directions. What he saw was a person who might know the women's whereabouts.

With jaunty steps, Peter left the smithy, examining his newly forged chisel. He was eager to try it out. He had nearly completed his commission for Master Eeghens, and now that Anna was leaving, he was anxious to finish it. He hoisted himself up and leaned over Master Eeghens' wagon, placing the chisel behind the bench. Just as he swung himself into the seat, a voice called out.

"You!"

The insulting tone startled Peter, and he eased himself back to the ground and turned toward the voice. He might have known! It was Thedric the printer—the scoundrel. He placed a hand on his hip, just above his dagger, and waited for the other man to draw near. He still had bitter feelings from their last meeting. But even more, he was angry because this man was responsible for betraying Anna and her mother. He did not care much for the printer's haughty attitude, either.

Peter squared his shoulders. "You wish to speak with me?"

Thedric stopped several feet in front of him. "I need to find Anna. Do you know where she has gone?"

"You expect me to help you, after you betrayed her confidence?"

"How dare you reproach me?" fumed Thedric. "You have no right to accuse me of anything. You know nothing about what happened. Do you know where she is or not?"

Peter lifted his palms in the air in front of him. "As you said, I know nothing."

Sighing deeply, Thedric said, "Look. I mean Anna no harm. I only want to discuss the situation with her."

Peter shook his head in disbelief, turned his back on the printer, and climbed onto the wagon. His arms trembled with anger. "Get up!" he said to the horses.

Just before the wagon lurched forward in a small cloud of dust, he saw the printer step backward and heard him give a curse.

The sound of wagon wheels and creaking harness interrupted Anna and Mariel's conversation. They had sought refuge from the heat under a large willow tree at the side of the Eeghens' house.

" 'Tis Peter, returning from the smithy," Anna said, giving a little wave. She watched him rein in the team and pull up beside the house. "I will go see what he's about, Mam." She dusted off her skirt and walked over to the wagon.

One glance at his face made her ask, "Trouble?"

Peter shrugged. "I just had a conversation with your betrayer."

"You talked with Thedric?" She crossed her arms. "And what did he have to say?"

The reins still taut in his hands, Peter propped his elbows on his knees. "He asked where he could find you."

Anna's arms slipped down to her sides. "I still cannot believe he betrayed me. You cannot know how that hurts."

"I did not give him much of a chance to talk. But if he is looking for you, he probably wants to make things right."

Anna shook her head and looked out into the distance. "I'd rather just leave this place. Get as far away from here as I can."

"I only hope your ship sails before he bothers you."

"You did not tell him where I am staying."

"Nay. But, if he has any sense at all, he will figure it out. If he does show up . . . well, do not fall for any of his nonsense." Peter gave a nod, as if he had said his piece. Anna smiled weakly and stepped away from the wagon. "Get up!"

"What was that all about?" Mariel asked, from beneath the tree.

"Nothing to worry about, Mam."

Chapter 25

 On the morning of their departure, Anna swept a sidelong glance at Peter. His brown hair bounced rhythmically on his broad shoulders as he led Anna, Mariel, and Berta through the city wall by way of the Coswiger Tor.

She felt a pang of sadness. Who knew when she would see Peter again? Things had not progressed much between them since the last time she sailed away. If anything, their relationship had abated, now that he had met Berta.

They crossed the moat, and the reflection from Peter's dagger threw shards of dancing light across the wooden drawbridge. When they stepped onto the quayside, the air was filled with sailors' grunts, oaths, and shouts. But one man towered above the crowd.

Guido raised his hand and motioned. They threaded their way toward him through the tangle of activity. Peter reached out and snatched Anna from the path of an ox-drawn cart that was scraping and bumping along. "Anna," he said. "I hope you can set your mind at ease and remember that you can trust the giant."

"I shall remember. And if there is a problem, you will be sure to hear of it when you meet us at Antwerp."

Peter chuckled and they fell into step again. "I have no doubt of that. But I trust when I meet you again, you will receive me with gladness of heart and not complaints." He grew serious and gave her a look that penetrated to her soul. "It is not easy to send you across the sea."

She took a few steadying breaths. The air smelled of fish, sweat, river sludge, and fresh tar. "As always, you take your responsibility to Willem too seriously. Our voyage is not dangerous. You said yourself, we shall probably hug the Dutch shoreline."

Peter's brows arched and made a furrow under the stray lock of hair on his forehead. "There is always danger with such a voyage." He cast a glance over the river. "I may meet you at Emden, depending on how soon I can finish my commission. Otherwise, I shall come to Antwerp." They stopped walking, and he clasped one of her hands in his. "I shall miss you."

"I wish you many good days and nights, Peter the sculptor." Anna saw his blush of pleasure and quickly added, "I am only sorry I cannot see your finished sculptures. But I know Master Eeghen will be greatly pleased."

A flock of river fowl scattered and shrieked as Guido approached. Peter released Anna's hand, and their eyes turned to the big, blond man. Guido greeted them, bending to bring his sparkling blue eyes to their level. " 'Tis time to board."

Anna looked apprehensively at the three-mast rig that would soon weigh anchor and gave Peter an anxious look. He drew her into his arms for a quick embrace. She could feel the tension in his lean, hard body. Fighting to keep her tears at bay, she gave him a wavering smile. He released her and turned toward Mariel and Berta. Anna clenched her teeth to keep from sobbing. When at last all the farewells were said, the three women followed Guido up the gangplank. With one backward look at Peter, who wore a bereaved expression, Anna stepped onto the ship.

Guido's form was blocking her view. Anna muttered nervously to Berta, "I cannot see a thing beyond the giant. He could be leading us into a donjon for all I can tell."

At that moment, Berta lost her footing and grasped at Anna's arms. "I never was good aboard ship." When she had regained her balance, she added, "You do not seem to have a problem."

"I often sailed with Papa."

"As did I," said Mariel. Anna smiled up at her mother, who murmured, "Fond memories."

Guido led them to the rail, and they watched the diminishing quay with Peter's rigid form and behind him the Wittenberg steeples. The capstan turned, chains rattled, anchors were heaved, and sails unfurled. The ship glided slowly toward the center of the river Elbe, where it came about to catch the gusts of wind that would push them down river.

After they had wound serenely through a measure of German river lands, the ship's master descended from the poop deck to greet them. Hard work had sculpted the captain's flesh and bones into mounds of muscle. A smile flashed in his weathered, craggy face. "Captain Sachs, at your service. I hope you find my ship agreeable."

"Most agreeable, captain." Guido introduced the women and explained, "The captain has been good enough to offer you his cabin."

" 'Tis only one night. Glad if I can bring you ladies a bit of comfort."

"Why thank you, Captain Sachs. 'Tis more than we expected. We are truly in your debt," Mariel said.

"Not at all. Now if you will excuse me." He dipped his head.

The women watched him stride across the deck and with a flurry of gestures give orders to his crew. "Captain Sachs is a good man," Guido said. "Shall we investigate your quarters?"

They followed him up a flight of steps, where he opened a big oak door. The compartment was tight with three women in it. Guido stooped and peered at them through the open doorway. "I'll be just out here, if you need me."

"Guido, where will you stay?" Mariel asked.

He pointed at the deck. "Right here." He grinned down at

them. "You will have to move me before you can open the door."

Anna's eyebrows rose. Somehow this giant's presence just outside their door was not that reassuring, though she was sure he meant it to be. "That is kind of you," Mariel said, and eased the door shut.

Anna looked around the small room. There was a tiny bed, built into the curvature of the ship's hull. A table and two chairs sat in the center of the room, and there was a shelf with books and personal possessions. On the stern was a tiny window, positioned so high that all Anna could see was blue sky and an occasional white fluff of cloud. She pulled out a chair just as Berta's hand shot out to steady herself against the bulkhead.

"I do not feel so good."

Anna and her mother exchanged a knowing look. "Please, you must lie down on the bed," Mariel offered. Berta nodded and stumbled toward the bed.

"You have been seasick before?"

Berta nodded with a groan. The next few hours were spent cleaning up after Berta and assuring her that she was not going to die. Anna was disgusted with the girl's weak stomach. Why, they were not even out to sea yet! Mariel must have sensed her feelings, for as soon as Berta fell asleep, she suggested that Anna stretch her legs and get some fresh air.

Anna went to open the door, and was frustrated when it would not budge. She remembered Guido, and gave an impatient little knock, staring at the bulkhead until the door eased open. She gave him a look that would have squelched the most courageous man and squeezed past him to make her way down the steps.

At the Eeghens' home in Wittenberg, Thedric knocked on the door. It soon opened, and a well-dressed woman stood before him. "Thedric Bettendorf, calling for Anna van Vissers."

The woman seemed to carefully select her words. "Anna has returned to her home."

"And do you know where that might be?"

The woman faltered, then shook her head. "Nay."

Thedric smiled. "I am a friend."

"Truly, I do not know where she makes her home. I only know her brother lives in Antwerp."

Thedric could sense the woman was hiding something. He scowled. "Antwerp. Sorry to trouble you."

"No trouble at all."

The door closed. Thedric stepped away from the entrance and gazed about the massive premises. One path led to the main entrance of the enclosure wall. Another path veered westward. He chose to examine this one. He had not gone far when he saw Anna's sculptor friend in the distance.

"Ah ha. 'Tis the sculptor."

Peter flinched and spun around. "So, the printer pays a call."

"I am looking for Anna."

"She is gone."

"You seem to despise me. Do you want her for yourself?"

Peter returned to his work. "Her brother placed her in my care."

"The brother that lives in Antwerp?" Thedric did not miss the startled expression that crossed the sculptor's face.

"You will get no information from me."

Thedric stepped forward, his body charged with anger. "If it is as you say and you are merely her protector, you have no reason to withhold information from me. I mean her no harm. I love her."

Peter laid aside his chisel, his own body poised to fight, and took a step toward Thedric. "Why, you worthless cur! You are not fit to touch the hem of her garment."

"Ah, 'tis as I suspected. You mean to have her for yourself."

Peter's eyes darkened and narrowed. "I may never marry her, but I would give my life to keep her from the likes of you."

With a taunting smirk, Thedric asked, "You wish to fight for her? Let's settle this, here and now."

Peter threw his head back and laughed. "Hah! I see you do not know her well. She would do her own choosing."

"And I would choose to bloody your face." Thedric's fist flew out and struck Peter smartly on the mouth.

Peter reeled backward at the unexpected blow and spit out a mouthful of blood. He appeared stunned at first, then cast Thedric a look full of hate. Thedric stepped forward and the two men began to move in a circle, their arms spread.

Thedric could think of nothing but his evil desire to remove Peter's say over Anna. He lunged toward Peter's face and landed another blow to one eye.

Peter's head jerked back, but he quickly recovered. Taking an aggressive step forward, he shot a quick blow to Thedric's chin. Thedric swayed, then righted himself and rushed at Peter, his head low, driving him backward.

Peter fell to the ground, but managed to roll sideways as Thedric hurled his body at him. Then, lunging to miss a kick, Peter teetered to his feet to protect himself against flailing fists. Some hit the mark, but Peter delivered a smashing hook that caught Thedric full on the mouth. The man tottered backward and slid on his seat. Then he leaped to his feet.

Peter watched Thedric's wild eyes as he spread his hands and circled his opponent again. When Thedric sprang forward, Peter caught him on the jaw and Thedric slid to the ground. His feet thrashed for just an instant before his eyes closed. Peter knelt over him and gave his face a sound slap to revive him.

Thedric groaned.

"Had enough?"

Raising himself to his elbows, Thedric spat, "Enough of the likes of you."

"And I you," said Peter. He jerked Thedric to his feet and pushed him toward the pathway.

Thedric staggered away, then turned to leer at Peter. "You'll never have her. 'Tis as you say. She will do the choosing."

⁂

On the main deck, the fresh air invigorated Anna. She made her way to the spot along the railing where they had stood at their departure. Her eyes took in the changing scenery—green and lush in this summer season, nourished by the river Elbe. She hugged herself, savoring the moment. If she closed her eyes she could hear the deep voices of the sailors, the creaking of the rigging, and almost imagine she was at sea with Papa.

"You sail well."

Guido. Her eyes flew open. " 'Tis not like we are at sea."

"It matters not."

"My papa had a ship."

"I know."

"What do you know of my papa?"

Guido's voice was soft as a kitten's purr. "Willem has spoken of him."

"Oh. I forgot for a moment that you know my brother." She gave him a piercing look, then sighed. "I have never been on a fishing boat."

"This one is bigger than most and more comfortable."

"When will they fish?"

"Not until they reach the sea. That is why the captain takes passengers on this leg." Guido shrugged. "Actually, the captain is a rare sort. He might take us even if it were not profitable for his pocket."

A kasteel came into view on the crest of a tall hill. "A German prince," Guido said, pointing.

Anna nodded. The sudden appearance of the majestic fort moved her mysteriously, bringing back the awful emotions of her visit to the donjon in Valkenburg. Her eyes began to burn, yet she could not pull them away from the spectacle. " 'Tis beautiful. He must be powerful and rich."

"In this world," Guido said.

She tilted her head. "Do you live in another?"

"The world is made of many different kinds of kingdoms."

"Indeed?" *He dares to preach?* she thought. "I shall return to my cabin now." Guido turned abruptly to accompany her, but she stopped just as abruptly and looked up at him. "I do not need a shadow."

Anna saw the hurt flicker across Guido's face. The sunlight and shadow accentuated his scar, making his expression appear even more tragic. He hesitated, then gave her a nod. Pushing back a prick of guilt, she turned and walked away, thankful she did not hear his footsteps following her.

When she opened the door to the captain's cabin, her mother smiled at her from across the room. "Hungry?"

"I believe I could eat something."

They made a lunch from bread and smoked meat that Mariel had brought aboard.

"Let us ask Guido to join us," said Mariel.

"He would not fit in here. Anyway, I do not believe he is out there," Anna replied.

Mariel crossed the tiny room and cracked the door to see for herself. "Nay, daughter. Guido is here." Anna felt the back of her neck grow hot.

"Would you like to eat?" Mariel asked their protector. Soon she was passing bread and meat through the door.

⚜

Peter washed himself at the barrel of water by his work shed. A shadow fell across him, and he jerked up his head. It was Master Eeghen, who let out a curse when he saw Peter's face.

"How did that happen?" But before Peter could respond, Master Eeghen remembered his wife's words about the printer's visit. He asked, "Who won? You or the printer?"

"I did. But it proves naught," Peter said, his voice edged with bitterness.

"The matter is not settled, then?"

"I did not even think. It never crossed my mind that I did not have to fight. Sometimes I wonder how weak my faith is."

"I would not know about a thing like that. But a man who carries a dagger will probably be called upon to use it. He may be called upon to die by it."

"I wish my life to be ordered by God and not man nor blade," Peter replied.

"Let's go put a slab of meat on that eye," said Master Eeghen. He started Peter toward the house. "How long until you are finished here?"

"I should finish tomorrow."

Master Eeghen wagged his head. "That is good. I am pleased with your work. But I think you need to follow after that woman you've set your heart upon."

Peter's head flew up, a startled look in his one good eye.

Master Eeghen burst into laughter. "You are a sight!"

Chapter 26

The next day the fishing boat put in at the Hamburg port, on the northeast bank of the river Elbe. With its outlet to the North Sea, Hamburg was a huge free trading center, protected by the Hanseatic League and surrounded by German lands.

Guido, always close at hand, took charge when it was time to debark. He led the women across an unfamiliar set of docks, threaded by canals, much busier than the docks at Wittenberg. They hurried to keep up with Guido's long strides as they made their way by exotic red brick warehouses. The little towers and balconies made the buildings look more like small kasteels than warehouses.

Guido stopped in front of a three-mast cargo ship called the *Félicité,* or *Fortunate.* "This is it. Wait here, and I will make arrangements." Anna and the others nodded and waited on the busy quayside.

Guido stepped up to a knot of sailors straining beneath heavy loads and headed for the *Félicité*'s gangplank. "Could you tell me who is in charge here?"

Two of the sailors kept going, but one with long, blond hair tied in a red neckcloth gave Guido a sidelong glance. He called over his shoulder, "Bos'n's over there."

Guido was just thanking the sailor when a lad stepped unknowingly into the sailor's path. He shouted a warning, but the lad did not move. Swinging back to continue up the gangplank, the sailor hit the lad broadside with his brick-hard body. The boy sprawled across the gangplank, and the sailor lost his footing as well. The large barrel rolled from his grip and clattered down the gangplank, barely missing the boy.

The sailor swiveled and raked his eyes over the errant lad, now on his hands and knees. His eyes widened as the barrel bounced past him. Then the sailor stomped forward and grabbed him by the scruff of the neck. Jerking the boy to a standing position, he slapped him across the face with his hard hand. The lad flew backward, landed with a thud on his back, and skidded to the edge of the gangplank.

Guido lunged forward, certain the boy would roll right off the gangplank into the water. But he stopped just short of it, lying still as death.

The lad was conscious, but stunned. Guido knelt and gently pulled him to a sitting position. Suddenly, breath returned to the boy's lungs. He gave several wild gasps and scrambled to his feet. Blood streamed from his nose and mouth. He mumbled something at Guido and took off in a stumbling, running gait, up the gangplank and past the sailor who had slapped him. He disappeared inside the ship.

By this time, the commotion had attracted the bos'n, who strode toward Guido and the sailor. The sailor glared at Guido and went to retrieve the barrel. Hoisting it over his shoulder with a grunt, he started back up the gangplank.

The bos'n drew close to Guido. He smirked, "Is there a problem?"

"Nay. But I seem to have gotten the lad in trouble." Guido looked back at the ship, where the lad had disappeared.

"Do not trouble yourself. 'Tis just the captain's boy. Better get out of the way here, now. My men have work to do."

"We've passage aboard your ship and need some help with the women's trunks."

The bos'n gave a nod and shouted, "Lend a hand here! Get these people aboard."

Guido returned to the women. "The ship leaves port early morn. We shall spend the night aboard." He gave the ship a wary glance. "Let us amuse ourselves in Hamburg and stay out of the crew's way in the meantime."

Anna opened her eyes. A thick blanket of gray hid her surroundings. Only the tiniest glimmer of light softened the darkness. The orlop deck, where they had bedded on straw, was below the ship's waterline, and its ports were closed.

It could be morning and still be dark. Judging by the deep roll of the ship, they were close to open sea, if not already there. Berta groaned, speaking incoherently. Mariel's bedding rustled.

Guido must also have heard the stirring, for suddenly a dim light shone from the other side of a makeshift wall. From behind the canvas and trunks came his deep voice. "Are you hungry? I have some food here."

They made a small meal of biscuits. Afterward, Berta complained of nausea and returned to her bed. Anna watched as her mother knelt with the girl and stroked the soft curls from her hot brow. Guiltily, she remembered the night at the Eeghens' when Berta had thought Anna was ill and had lovingly cared for her.

"Mam, why not let me stay with Berta, and you go above?"

Mariel gave Anna a look of surprised approval.

"I would be glad to take a turn with you on the main deck," Guido offered.

"Thank you, Guido." Mariel gave Berta a gentle pat and rose to her feet. "I think I will get some exercise."

When her mother and Guido had departed, Anna crawled into her own bed, close to Berta. In the golden glow from brass lanterns, Anna could see the girl's downcast eyes. "I am sorry to be such a bother," she said, weakly.

Anna gave her a sympathetic smile. An awkward silence prevailed. "What is that scraping noise?" Berta asked.

"Hm? Oh." Anna stopped sifting the contents of her pocket and pulled out her hand. In the hollow of her palm lay several seashells. With her free hand, she drew the lantern close to show them to Berta.

"Pretty," she said. "Did you find them at the Hamburg harbor?"

"Nay." Anna returned the shells to her pocket. "They are a remembrance of Papa."

"You carry them with you at all times?"

Anna shrugged. "Most always, if convenient."

"Tell me about your papa," Berta said.

The girl's face was pale and wan. Thinking a diversion would help keep Berta's mind off her illness, Anna shared some brief stories about her papa. At first, Berta's eyes brightened with interest, then began to droop with weariness, and closed altogether. Her breathing grew heavy with sleep.

Anna rolled onto her back and stared at the low ceiling overhead. Sounds of moving feet and rigging drifted down through the deck. She closed her eyes and tried to imagine what it would be like when Willem came for them.

The next thing she knew, she was startled awake. Her mother's eyes stared into hers. "I am sorry to disturb you," she whispered.

"Nay," Anna said, rubbing her eyes, "I did not intend to sleep."

"How is she?" Mariel gave a nod toward Berta.

"She kept her food down, but barely."

"Poor thing." She eased down onto the straw bed. " 'Tis your turn to get some fresh air."

Anna nodded and ran her hands through her hair, trying to look respectable. Then, tottering on her sleepy legs, she pushed open the canvas. *Good, the giant's gone.* With cautious steps, she walked the length of the dark orlop deck until she came to the steps and hatch that led to the main deck.

Holding her skirts with one hand and the rail with the other, she climbed out and squinted into the bright, open sky. The smell of salt removed the last vestiges of sleepiness from her head.

The main deck was astir with activity. Anna edged across the deck toward a rail to watch quietly. The *Félicité* was sailing on the wind. A breeze swept across the bow and wafted her hair away from her face. From behind she heard a deep, resounding voice. "Ready about."

They were changing tack. Anna placed her hand on the rail to keep her balance as the ship shifted direction. She fastened her attention on the ship's crew.

A beak-nosed, hollow-eyed seaman gave a boisterous bellow. "Ready!"

The crew uncleated the leeward jib sheet and luffed the forward half of the jib sail. With proficient ease, a deckhand cast out and let the sheet run through his hands. Another pulled in the slack in the other jib sheet, winding it around a winch.

Anna gripped the railing and watched the bow of the ship turn and pass through the eye of the wind. Her hair whipped hard across her face. Masts and rigging creaked as the sailors worked to trim the sails. Once the activity settled down, Anna turned her gaze outward, beyond the rail. She could see no land, only sea and sky. She almost envied Willem his seafaring job. She could not fault him for his love of the sea.

Time passed. Finally, Anna withdrew from the railing. She saw movement from the corner of her eye and was not surprised to find it was Guido. He nodded, but she pretended not to see. She had a mind to do a bit of exploring. Taking care to avoid Guido's gaze, she moved past him toward the ship's quarterdeck and poop deck.

"Halt there," said a voice. "I would like a word with you." Anna's heart gave a lurch. She stopped.

"Captain," came a second voice.

"I would talk to you concerning the boy," the captain replied.

Anna let out a sigh of relief and relaxed. For a moment, she had thought the captain was speaking to her. She turned around and walked the other way, so as not to disturb the captain.

"I've no use for him," she heard him say. "He is stupid beyond belief. There is no help for him. I just want to be rid of him. Will you do it, Salty?"

Anna's steps faltered. She knew she should not eavesdrop, but her curiosity was aroused, as well as her pity. Surely the boy the captain referred to was the one involved in the incident with Guido. She had observed the scene that day on the quayside, though she had not spoken of it. But her heart had been wrenched at the boy's treatment.

"Aye, captain. I can send him on a fool's errand at the next port. Or would you rather we just drown him?"

The captain's tone was cruel and dismissive. "Matters not. 'Tis your problem now."

"Aye, captain," said the bos'n cheerfully.

Nausea squeezed Anna's stomach. It was as if the bos'n enjoyed his evil assignment. Suddenly, a memory came to her of the bailiff's taunting voice. But the sound of approaching footsteps brought her back to the present. *The captain—he is coming my way!*

She wheeled and fled as if escaping the devil himself. Her feet pounded down the deck toward the hatch. But just as she reached it, she ran directly into a solid body. "Ach!"

It was Guido. He reached out to steady her. "Whoa."

Anna looked up at him wildly and whispered, "I need to speak with you." Then she broke free from his grip, scrambled through the hatch, and scurried down the stairs. At the bottom, she waited for Guido, her chest heaving. Through the tunnel of light, Guido's boots appeared. Finally, the rest of him came into sight. Anna sighed with relief that neither the captain nor the bos'n was following him.

Guido stood before her in the shadows. "Did someone bother you?" he asked with concern.

"Nay." Anna swallowed hard. "But I overheard the captain talking to his bos'n, the one called Salty."

"What did he say to trouble you so?"

"Remember the boy that tripped the blond-haired sailor? The one with the barrel?"

"Aye." Guido bent his head to listen more closely.

"The captain ordered Salty to kill him."

Guido's hand softly gripped her shoulder. "Are you sure?"

She bristled, not from his touch, but at the tone of his voice. "I know what I heard."

Guido withdrew his hand and leaned closer. "Tell me. Please be exact."

Anna repeated the conversation she had just heard. Her voice became more desperate. "What should we do?"

Guido spoke with gentle reassurance. "Everything we can. I shall keep my ears open and keep a close watch on the lad. But it will not be easy because he is most often in the forecastle or busy in the captain's cabin."

"But is that enough? We must help him."

"We shall pray that God will spare the lad. Will you stay put down here if I prowl around a bit?"

"Aye." Anna nodded.

Guido left at once. His boots were quiet on the stairs. If anyone could sneak around and get information, Guido could. Nevertheless, Anna worried over the boy as she returned to her tiny quarters where Mam and Berta slept.

It seemed ages until Guido returned. Anna hurried to his side of the canvas. "What did you discover?"

"Everything is quiet up there. The boy is nowhere to be seen."

"Do you think they have already killed him?" she gasped.

"Nay. I did strike up a conversation with the sailor that belted him on the gangplank that day."

Anna nodded and anxiously searched Guido's face in the lantern light.

"The boy is deaf."

"Oh!" Anna pressed her fingers to her mouth and closed her eyes. When she opened them, she said in a quivering voice, "Poor boy."

"Aye. 'Tis good there is a God to see us through the hard things in life."

Anna gritted her teeth. "God . . ."

" 'Tis all right to question God, only . . ."

"Only what?"

"Only never stop seeking him. God is in this. I am sure of it. You were meant to overhear that conversation. God will be the boy's savior." Guido lightly touched her arm. "Do not fear."

Anna nodded. "Please do not follow me. I need to be alone."

She did not have to go far. In a dark corner, she sat on the edge of the *shallop*—a small boat stored in the orlop deck— and sank her face into her hands to think. Gently she rocked, as Guido's last two words washed over her. *Do not fear. Do not fear. Do not fear . . . If only I could trust God.*

Chapter 27

At sea, the hot, humid weather curled Anna's hair and caused it to stick to her face and neck. She and Guido lounged against the ship's windward rail on the main deck, mopping perspiration. They had stationed themselves there to watch out for the boy, but the sky had claimed everyone's attention.

Streamlets of sweat ran down the deckhands' tanned faces and necks. Open shirts and baggy trousers clung to the sailors' taut, muscular bodies. Regularly they tilted their faces, their eyes trained on the horizon.

Suddenly, what they had expected appeared in the distance —swift-moving, green-black clouds. The beak-nosed bos'n hollered, "Squall!" Bare feet scurried across the deck. Bodies scampered up the ratlines.

Guido pointed to the churning sky, with its fat and towering clouds. "We had better get you below deck right away."

Anna could hardly tear her eyes from the coming storm, but the deck was a perilous place to be caught. According to Papa's stories, a storm could sweep able seamen overboard in the blink of an eye. She followed Guido toward the hatch, all the while dodging sailors and keeping an anxious eye out for the deaf boy.

The sky had become a terrifying ribbon of night, hovering over the distant water. A gust of wind whipped up her skirt, and she fought to control it. A sea bird squawked and landed on an overhead yard. Grit and sand from the deck swirled around them. Anna shut her eyes.

Guido grabbed her hand, more firmly this time, and pulled her along, down through the hatch, and toward the others in their group.

"What is happening?" Mariel asked.

"A storm, Mam," Anna gasped. She grasped the canvas to steady her footing, for the ship had started to pitch.

"Will you stay put if I go up and watch out for the lad?" Guido asked.

"Should you go up there? 'Tis so . . ." Mariel began, while Berta only gaped at them all with big, round eyes.

"I have a feeling the boy is in danger," Guido said in a rush of words.

"Please. Be careful," said Anna.

Guido gave her a smile. "Aye." Then his expression became serious. "Now, stay put. No harm should come your way. Once I am gone, put out the lanterns. Rough seas can start a fire." He gave them an authoritative nod and hurried away.

"What boy?" Mariel asked in confusion.

Anna reached for the lantern and began to explain.

Guido prayed as he scrambled up the steps to the main deck. *No telling what kind of trouble the lad will get into at a time like this. Lord, please keep the women safe while I look for him.* When he popped his head up through the hatch, he was caught off guard as the wind sucked the air from his lungs.

The crew struggled to take in the sails and secure the running rigging. Men hung precariously from the swaying tops. Guido grabbed the nearest mast and scoured the darkening decks for a glimpse of the boy. The rain arrived in a fury, buffeting and blinding. Thunder cracked. The storm became a strong fist, beating the sea into a mighty turbulence. Guido clung to the swaying mast. *Where is he? Maybe Anna overheard wrong and the crew meant him no harm. Maybe the captain has tucked him away in a safe place.*

Below, in the orlop deck, the women struggled to keep objects from toppling and rolling onto them as the boat tossed. Water began to seep through the cracks in the overhead deck, down through the hatches, running in streamlets toward the bilge.

"I have never been in a storm before . . . on a ship, I mean," Berta stammered.

" 'Twill be a fine thing if our protector gets himself killed up there," Anna said.

"Anna!" Mariel said in a sharp tone.

"Well, for once I would appreciate his presence!" Anna shouted above the noise of the rain, creaking timbers, and ravaging wind.

"One good thing is that squalls pass quickly," Mariel said, as she grasped the girls' hands. "We must pray."

The ship seemed to be at the mercy of the storm. Waves crashed and foamed, the ship rising and plummeting, tossing and pitching. Guido had to remind himself that the storm was not in control. God was, and even though the sea heaved like a shaken blanket, every soul aboard was under the Maker's watchful eye.

He circled the slippery mast, squinting and peering through the deluge. The taste of rain was salty as it slid down his face onto his lips. He was of a mind to give up, when he finally caught sight of the boy. The bos'n was gesturing at the lad, who was hesitantly advancing toward the seaman. The bos'n's sinister expression sent a chill down Guido's spine. One jerk of the man's strong arm could send the lad flying into the soupy tempest to his death. Guido let go of the mast and staggered against the wind toward them.

The bos'n worked a windlass with one arm and stretched out the other, reaching for the boy's neck. *I will not make it in time,* thought Guido. *He is out to hurt the lad. The only chance I have of reaching him . . .* Instinctively, with a mighty lunge, he threw himself at the boy. He tackled him and smashed him down against the deck, free from the grasping bos'n, but on the way down the boy's temple struck one of the handspikes. Guido eased himself off the boy's limp body. A puddle of blood, diluted by the rain, encircled the boy's head. Guido jerked his gaze to the bos'n.

An instant of fury shone on the man's face, then satisfaction. "You killed the boy!" he shouted over the roar of the wind.

Guido could only hope it was not true. The bos'n turned his satisfied gaze back to the windlass and paid no more attention to Guido. The boy lay still but breathing. Guido slid his hand beneath the boy's limp neck and lifted him in his arms. At first he thought the force of the wind would knock them back down to the deck, but he bent his body protectively over the boy and pressed on toward the hatch.

The boy felt still as death in Guido's arm. With his free hand clutching the railing, Guido worked his way down the steps. When his feet hit the tilted orlop deck, he proceeded with care through the darkness, staggering—not from his load but from the ship's pitching. He could hear the women's murmuring and followed the sound of their voices. As he drew near, he realized they were praying and felt heartened. Then as gently as he could, without losing balance, he knelt down before them.

"Guido?"

"The lad is hurt. May I lay him on a bed?"

"Here!" Mariel quickly offered.

"What happened?" Anna asked, "Is he dead? Oh, I wish we had some light."

"I do not think so. Here, hold him so he will not roll off the bedding. I shall be right back." Guido crawled through the darkness and felt his way to his own bed. The canvas that usually separated their beds was torn down from the ship's tossing. He found his bedding and ripped off a piece of cloth. Folding it into a small, square bandage, he half stumbled, half crawled back to them.

"Hold this against his head." Guido felt for the sticky blood and placed the cloth against it. " 'Tis all we can do until the storm subsides."

"Did the bos'n do this?" Anna demanded.

"Nay, I did."

"What?"

"Salty was luring the boy to harm. I could not reach him in time. I lunged and smashed the poor lad against a handspike." Guido's voice was sad and strained. "Seems I am the boy's worst enemy on this voyage."

"That is not true, and you know it. You most likely saved his life," Anna said.

The boy struggled. Together, they managed to hold him steady. Guido lifted the boy's hand to feel the cloth on his head. He seemed to understand they were trying to help him, and his body relaxed. Gently, Anna caressed the boy's cheek while Mariel prayed.

Almost eerily, the ship suddenly became steady. The noises decreased. As quickly as the storm had come upon them, it passed. Guido rose abruptly and fumbled with one of the brass lanterns. Soon a yellow glow shone over the small, huddled group.

"Now, let's have a look at that wound," Guido said. He used gestures to communicate with the boy. "What is your name?"

"Matz."

Anna and Guido exchanged astonished looks. As Guido inspected the cut, he talked to the lad. Soon they discovered that Matz was not completely deaf, and he could also read lips.

"The wound is not so bad. Could use some lacing, though. Keep this cloth on it while I go above and find a surgeon."

"Let us get the boy a drink," Mariel suggested. While the women cared for the boy, Guido left in search of the captain.

Up on the main deck, the hands were busy trimming and tacking, trying to get the ship back on course. The captain was on the poop deck. Guido started toward him, but they met each other on the quarterdeck.

"Heard you killed our boy," the captain said in an accusing tone.

"That is what I've come to talk to you about. 'Twas an accident, but the boy will live."

The captain's bushy brows shot up. His mouth opened to display a wide gap in his teeth, evidence of the scurvy, then snapped shut again. His eyes narrowed, and he studied Guido intently.

"Do you have a surgeon aboard?" Guido asked.

"Nay." The captain shook his head. "Only a chest of ointments."

"May I take a look at it?"

The captain gave the crew an appraising glance, then shrugged and motioned for Guido to follow. When they reached the captain's cabin, Guido waited outside the door. Soon the older man reappeared, with a small chest in his hands.

Guido peeked inside and saw a needle and thread. He began to leave, then turned back. "Do you need the boy?"

The captain narrowed his eyes but did not reply, so Guido went on. "I heard rumors he was not suited to his job."

" 'Tis true enough. The boy is dimwitted."

"Perhaps his deafness just makes it seem that way . . ."

"What business is it of yours?"

"I feel responsible. Is there any chance I can take him with me when we dock?"

The captain leaned back against the bulkhead and crossed his arms, his eyes calculating. He cleared his throat. "You like the lad . . . you want him?"

"Aye."

"It will cost you."

"The price?"

The captain rubbed his chin. "The boy came with some others I bought off a crimp. Kept his father out of debtor's prison. I would have to get me a new boy." He cleared his throat. "Forty shillings."

Guido felt the blood rush to his face. It was an exorbitant price! But he knew better than to argue. "I can get it in Emden," he said, with an edge of sharpness, and turned away from the captain. *I had better walk away now, lest I hinder the boy's chance of escape,* he told himself.

When Guido returned to the injured boy with the chest of supplies, he could see Anna's relief. He wished he did not have to tell her what was in store for the lad. In the short time since Guido had met Anna, he had been saddened by the pain she carried. He eased down beside the others. "Who will help me?"

Berta said, "I would like to, but I am in no condition."

"My eyes are better than Mam's. I will do it," Anna said.

"Very well." Guido turned his face so the boy could not read his lips and whispered, "Do you want to do the sewing or hold the boy down?"

Anna's eyes flashed, and she gulped. "Sewing?"

Guido nodded and waited.

"You are probably a better seamstress," Mariel whispered.

Anna shifted her incredulous stare from Guido to her mother.

"I shall help you all I can." Guido's eyes were pleading. He could almost see the inner war Anna was waging. Finally, she pinched her lips together and nodded. He gave her a wide, appreciative smile. Next, he opened the medicine chest and leaned over Matz to try to explain what they would do.

Anna tried to set her mind on the task and not on the patient.

She clenched her jaws as she worked with her hands. Guido was excellent at restraining and reassuring the patient. As they labored together, night fell silently over the ship.

By the time the wound was closed, everyone was exhausted. Guido rehung the canvas wall between his bed and the women's beds, then he carried the boy to his side of the canvas. The last thing Anna remembered was the rustle of bedding before she fell into a deep sleep.

⁕

The next morning, across the North Sea and up the river Elbe, Peter boarded ship, preparing to take much the same route Anna's ships had taken. His commission finally finished, he was on his way to intercept Anna at Emden or to travel on to Antwerp, if need be. He gave a quick tug on his hat, which he had pulled low over his face in hopes of hiding some of the vivid bruises.

He carried one piece of baggage. His sculpting tools had been loaded earlier. Before he stepped off the gangplank, he turned and cast a final look over the good city of Wittenberg. He wanted to impress it on his memory. From where he stood, he could see the towers of the kasteel and the kasteel church. The city was full of fond memories, and his work had been satisfying. But, as Master Eeghens had suggested, his heart must follow Anna.

As his eyes swept the quay and the people gathered around, his thoughts suddenly darkened with a feeling something was amiss. But he could not attach the feeling to anything. He could not deny the knot in his stomach and the prickly feeling in his spine, but there was nothing to do but board the ship.

Thedric stepped out of the shadows into the light of the quay. His dark eyes searching, he observed Peter until he was out of sight. With a smirk, Thedric stepped quickly. He would inquire after the ship's destination. With a new gleam in his eyes, he mentally rehearsed his plans.

Chapter 28

Anna stepped onto the gangplank and looked back at the ship. The *Félicité* had docked safely in Emden's busy harbor, but Matz had taken a fever. Now they had no choice but to leave him on board the ship while they disembarked.

The captain had promised Matz would be safe as long as Guido returned with the required payment, but Anna did not believe he would do anything to help Matz's recovery in the meantime. And there was no telling how long it would take Guido to collect the necessary funds to purchase the boy's freedom.

"The sooner we leave, the sooner I shall be able to come back for him," Guido said, addressing her thoughts and nudging her forward onto the bustling quay. Anna felt a twinge of anxiety as she looked at the unfamiliar city stretching before her, and she glanced backward. From this distance, the *Félicité* looked much like any other ship in the harbor, its crew crawling over it like ants on a rotten apple. "Stay close," Guido warned.

Since the dramatic events on their voyage, Anna now accepted orders from Guido without question. She hurried to keep in step with him, her mother and Berta trailing along. Anna lifted her eyes and studied the quay again. A familiar face popped out in the crowd. The stooped woman swathed in a gray cloak tilted her head in a telltale way. Anna could not contain her excitement.

She reached out and clutched Guido's shirtsleeve.

"Stop!" Guido's steps faltered, and he stared at her, puzzled. Anna pointed. "Over there! That woman. We must get to her!" His gaze followed Anna's finger. But there was no time for explanations. The woman might easily disappear into the surging throng.

Anna jerked hard on his sleeve. "Hurry! We must not let her get away!" She broke away from Guido, weaving in and out of the crowd in pursuit of the old woman.

Guido grabbed Berta and Mariel by the hand and charged down the quayside. "Wait! Come back!"

" 'Tis Rosmunda!" Mariel exclaimed.

The healer woman had stooped to pluck a wild herb growing by the quayside. "Rosmunda! Please wait! I must speak with you!" Anna shouted.

Rosmunda's head popped up, her dark and narrow eyes darting from side to side. Then they fastened on Anna and softened somewhat. She left her half-filled basket to struggle to her feet. "Anna of Visserswert!"

Anna grasped the woman's bony fingers. "Oh! What good fortune that I have found you," she said, breathlessly.

"What is it, child?" The woman's fish odor swept over Anna. " 'Tis good to see you!"

Footsteps clattered, and Guido's shadow fell across them. Moments later Mariel and Berta encircled the old woman. Rosmunda looked up warily at Guido, who observed her with quiet curiosity.

"Rosmunda, this is Guido Dirksz, our escort," said Anna. "And this is a friend who lives in the city, Berta. Rosmunda is the healer woman from Visserswert."

Guido's expression cleared. "And you've asked her to help Matz?"

"I was about to." She looked into Rosmunda's troubled eyes. They resembled two seas with adjoining tributaries—wrinkles running in many directions around them. Now they squinted.

Anna cleared her throat. "I see you have your herb basket with you."

"Aye."

"As I was saying, we need your able healing hands. We've a friend—a boy, the captain's boy. He is still on the ship. He has a head injury. We laced it up, but he's come down with a fever."

"Who laced it up?" Rosmunda's bony finger pointed at Guido. "Him?"

Mariel beamed. "Anna did."

The old woman studied her. "You did it?"

Anna nodded. "But now he has a fever and the captain is not doing a thing to help him. If only you could! He is such a sweet lad. His name is Matz."

Rosmunda rubbed her chin. "I guess I do owe something. And this captain, is he an agreeable sort?"

Anna cast a look at Guido. "If you agree," he offered, "I will see to it that the captain is not a problem."

"Aye. I shall do it, then."

"Oh, thank you." Anna turned to Guido. "Can we take her back to the ship now?"

Guido nodded. "I shall take her and talk to the captain." His eyes took in their surroundings. "But let us find a safe place for the rest of you to wait."

They chose a vacant spot in the shade of a nearby linden tree. Guido gave them some strict orders and promised to return in a short while.

Within the hour, Guido returned with a hackney already loaded with their belongings. When Anna saw him, she jumped up from her grassy seat. "What did the captain say? Did Rosmunda stay with Matz?"

"The captain said he could not fault our determination. And, aye, the healer stayed with Matz. She will tend to him each day as needed until we can get him removed from the ship. God is answering our prayers."

"*Your* prayers."

"Perhaps God is answering all our prayers," Berta said. Anna blinked and stared. Berta had been so quiet of late, suffering from the seasickness, that her opinion was unexpected.

"I believe he is," Mariel added. "There is nothing more we can do. Now we must trust God for Matz's care. 'Tis a miracle he sent Rosmunda."

The hackney waited, its driver standing on the sandy roadway and leaning against it. When they got in, the space was cramped, and Anna's nerves were on edge. But as they left the quayside and drove onto one of Emden's cobblestone streets, the singsong rhythm of the horses' hooves helped to soothe her.

She wished the ride could last forever. She dreaded what lay ahead. More changes. She envied Berta's ever-brightening expression.

Berta's home was a lovely stone house. Her slim mother, also golden-haired and beautiful, seemed surprised but exceedingly joyful to see her daughter. Berta quickly explained the van Vissers' situation, and the Emden Eeghens welcomed them at once.

Berta's father proved to be a quiet and thoughtful man, and strong. He easily carried in the women's trunks, the muscles in his broad shoulders and thick arms matching even Guido's. The man's eyes shone with warmth and grace. They had the same light Anna had oftentimes observed in Guido's and Peter's eyes.

"I am pleased to meet Willem's family," Berta's father announced.

"We are surely in your debt," Mariel said.

Berta's mother put an arm about each of the van Vissers' waists. "I am so pleased to have my daughter returned to me

early that I believe I am in *your* debt. Come now, have something to eat."

Anna had a hard time fitting in with another household of
strangers. To accept such hospitality again only reminded her
of her homelessness and the reasons for it.

The next night, Guido stopped by. His eyes twinkled and
the scar that ran down his face gave a little twitch. It could
only mean he was bringing news.

"Willem's ship should be here in a few days."

"How do you find out such things?" Anna demanded with
a smile.

Guido shrugged. " 'Tis what I do."

Berta's father then drew Guido into conversation. But later,
when the others were talking among themselves, Anna studied
Guido a moment and asked, "What exactly do you do?"

He leaned forward in his chair and whispered, "That is a
secret."

Anna snapped her mouth shut and felt the blood rush up
the back of her neck. *Most likely an Anabaptist secret.* Her
emotions confused her. Guido was the epitome of kindness,
but he was undeniably a heretic.

He grinned at her. "I see that troubles you."

"But of course it does. Still, I thank you for bringing us the
message. I am anxious to proceed to my brother Skylar's
home."

"As am I," Mariel said, joining the conversation. "It seems
these past fortnights have been in vain."

"Or like God has abandoned us." Anna said in an undertone.

Mariel heard her and corrected, "Nay, daughter. That is
not what I meant."

"In all things, God works for the good of those who love
him," Guido said. Anna gave him a quelling look. He grinned
and shrugged. "It is Scripture."

"Since you seem to know everything, how does Matz fare?"

"He is improving under Rosmunda's care." Guido chuckled. "She is a character."

"But what will become of him?"

"I have gathered up the required payment." He tapped the pouch at his belt. "I will get him off the ship as soon as I leave here."

"Really! Where will he go?"

"One of the brethren is going to house Matz. At least until he has recovered. Then it will be up to Matz to decide if he wishes to return to his father. If so, the believers will gather the money necessary to send him home."

"But what if his father is cruel? What if he only sells him off again?"

"It will be up to Matz. Perhaps after he is settled, you can visit him."

"Oh, aye!" Anna nodded.

Chapter 29

The following day Anna accompanied Berta into the city to deliver a message from Berta's mother to her father.

" 'Tis good to be on land again," Berta said.

"I am glad you are feeling better. I suppose you are glad to be home?"

"Aye, 'tis true enough. You should like Papa's shop. It is the kind of place your papa probably frequented."

"Is that how Willem became acquainted with your family?"

"I am not altogether familiar with Papa's business, but Peter did mention the connections."

"Did he? I am sure the two of you had many wonderful discussions." As soon as the words had left her lips, Anna regretted them.

Berta's steps faltered and she stared at Anna, who felt even more ashamed. Suddenly a gleam appeared in Berta's eyes. She wagged her finger at Anna. "Why, you are jealous! You are in love with Peter."

Anna desperately sought to deny it. "Most certainly not!"

Berta shook her head. "All this time I could not understand why you were so cold to me."

Struggling to explain, Anna said, "Peter and I are only friends. I feel inclined to watch out for him."

"Nay, 'tis more," Berta chuckled. "How could I be so thickheaded? Pray, believe me. There is nothing more than friendship between Peter and me."

"Well, then. That makes us all just friends, does it not?"

"Not if you and Peter are in love."

"I just told you . . ."

"Anna." Berta gave her companion's arm a slight pat. "He is in love with you too, you know. Now the question is, what are we going to do about it?"

Anna shook her head. "If Peter is attracted to anyone, 'tis you." Her voice broke, but she continued. "I saw you at the fair together. You looked so intimate, and you are so lovely, and . . ."

"Enough," Berta raised her delicate hand. "I am saying *you* are the one he favors. I am sorry you thought I had other intentions. I only wanted to be your friend."

Anna felt choked with shame. "You are the kindest person I know. Even when I did not want to like you, I did. And you are not only kind, but fun."

" 'Tis settled then. One can never have too many friends. And I have to admit that when Peter told me about you, I was anxious to meet you. You sounded so brave."

"Why would you say such a thing?"

"Peter told me how you stowed away in your brother's cart. My, how I would love to have an adventure like that!"

"It did not seem an adventure when my papa's life was at stake."

"Of course not. Please forgive me. I was not thinking."

" 'Tis all right. I understand. You are much like my friend Esther."

"Peter's sister? Tell me about her."

"She lives in Visserswert. We have known each other forever. She is a believer, like you, and she is never afraid of anything. She always speaks her mind."

"You do not seem the type who would fear anything either."

"I fear that God has abandoned me."

"You must come to our meeting."

An unpleasant wariness crept up Anna's spine. "What meeting?"

"That is the message I have for Papa. A believers' meeting. Everyone will be there. Guido is coming."

Anna gave a sarcastic laugh. "That does not surprise me."

"Say you will come. Do it for me."

"Nay," Anna said, shaking her head. "I went to one such meeting with my friend Esther. It made me queasy."

"I promise not to leave your side. Besides, where will you go when everyone comes to our house?"

Anna moaned. "Being your friend is not going to be easy, is it?"

"I will help you overcome your fear. Now, let us discuss that other thing."

Rolling her eyes, Anna asked, "There is more?"

"What are you going to do about Peter? He could soon arrive. We shall have to come up with a plan."

"I cannot be in love with him. My heart aches at the sight of him, and my stomach feels tied in a knot. We quarrel all the time. I would hardly call that love."

Berta giggled. "On the contrary. From what I have observed, 'tis exactly what love is like."

"It cannot be. We are of different beliefs."

"Aye. That is a problem we need to resolve. I shall pray about that." She patted Anna's arm. "Look! We are almost there. See that long building? It belongs to the rope maker. Look, beyond is the canvas mender. You must take a peek."

Anna allowed Berta to pull her along. The canvas mender had wondrous sails that billowed in the wind. The sight took her back to the ports she had visited with Papa. This was exactly the type of place where he had loved to mill about. She felt a soft pat on her arm and remembered what they were about. "Oh, forgive me. I was lost in thought."

"Your papa?" Berta asked.

Anna nodded.

"I am sorry if I made you sad. Maybe you do not like it here."

Anna reached out and grasped Berta's hand. "Oh, but I do! I never want to forget my papa. The sights here, the smells—they just bring back so many memories."

"I understand. Come, then."

Berta guided her to a tiny shop. When they entered, her eyes filled with pride. "This is my papa's shop."

Inside, the small room was furnished with tables and stacks of heavy paper. A large flat-bed press filled the center of the room. Several prints were hanging up to dry.

Berta skipped over to her father, who was hand carving swirling lines to represent the sea. "Papa. Good news."

He laid down his sharp metal tool. "Daughter! What a pleasant surprise. And you have brought our guest." He extended his hand. "I am glad you could come, Anna."

"My papa would have loved your map shop."

"Her papa was a sailor," Berta added.

He nodded with interest. "So Willem told me."

"Of course," Anna said.

"What is your good news, child?"

Berta's blue eyes danced. "Menno Simons is in the city."

Anna felt as if the air had been whacked from her lungs. Through a haze, she heard Berta and her father discuss the news. Unconsciously, she backed away until she reached the shop's main entrance.

"Anna?"

"If you do not mind, I would like to wait outside."

Berta gave her a strange look and shrugged, then turned back to her father.

Anna closed the door behind her and leaned against it. *Nay. It cannot be true. Menno Simons, here?*

The rest of the day passed in a blur. That evening, the Eeghens and their guests had settled in the sitting room when the wind picked up and howled like a pack of wolves. It reminded Anna of the recent storm at sea. She was not surprised when Guido appeared at the Eeghens' door in the midst of it.

Berta's mother helped him off with his wet cloak. After a period of friendly conversation, Anna picked up a lantern and excused herself. She stepped into the adjoining room to get a drink of water. As she put the cup to her lips, a voice startled her from behind.

"You are somber tonight." It was Guido.

Anna set down the cup and turned. "I have much on my mind."

"Do you want to talk about it?" he asked.

She sighed. "I am sure you know that Menno Simons is in the city."

"Aye, I have heard."

"Have you met with him?"

Guido paused for a long while. Finally he said, "Aye."

"How can a noble man like you be involved with the likes of him?"

Guido smiled. "I thank you for the compliment. However, I fear if I answer your question, I shall start a quarrel or lose your good opinion."

"Nay. I truly seek the answer."

"Menno Simons teaches about Jesus, the Son of God."

"Of course. I know who Jesus is."

"But there is a big difference between knowing who Jesus is and allowing him to be your Savior and Lord."

"You sound like all the other believers."

"What you said about me—if it is true, 'tis only because Jesus lives in me. Christianity is not about following all the right rules. It is about inviting Jesus to live in your heart and direct your steps."

"My papa was a man like you."

"And Jesus lived in him. Perhaps if you come to the meeting, 'twill help you find the answers."

"I went to a meeting once. It only angered me."

" 'Twould please me if you came to the meeting." He smiled. " 'Twould please Willem and Peter, too."

She smiled. "And Mam. And Berta."

"Will you think it over?"

Anna sighed and changed the topic. "How is Matz?"

"He is in the excellent care of Rolf and Ludovika. Rosmunda visited him. Would you like to see him?"

"Aye. Will you take me?"

"Tomorrow."

She looked up at him. "I thank you."

Chapter 30

 The following day, the weather turned and the sun shone. True to his word, Guido came for Anna, and they walked to the home of Rolf and Ludovika. By the time they reached the door, Anna was hot and thirsty.

Guido gave the door a light rap, and a woman with small, deep-set blue eyes came to greet them. Her round face lit up with pleasure. It was easy to see her affection for Guido.

The woman's second chin jiggled up and down. "Do come in. Never had so much company as since the boy came. Everybody we know, it seems, drops in to meet our Matz. Come in now." She turned her back and entered the house, expecting them to follow. "I did not know how dreary our days were. Before Matz came, I mean."

As soon as she paused to take a breath, Guido quickly interjected, "Ludovika, this is Anna van Vissers. She is the young woman who helped save the boy."

Plump Ludovika turned around and searched Anna's eyes with her bright blue ones. "Then 'tis you I have to thank for the boy. What a pleasure it has been to have him! He will be so excited to see you. But just look at you. You are red as a berry. Need you a drink? Of course you do. Follow me." She waved her fleshy little hand. "I heard tell what an able sailor you be. But I can see you are a brave one. And 'tis you I have to thank."

Anna was finally able to interrupt with a word or two. "Nay, I've done nothing out of the ordinary."

"Nonsense," Ludovika said, shoving a tankard at Anna, and getting one for Guido as well. "Drink up. 'Tis glad I am you came to see the lad."

Her thirst quenched, Anna thanked Ludovika and she and Guido followed her outside to the back of the house. A small tributary, one of many that emptied into the sea, cut through the property. "There he is. Just look at him. He has been exploring out here all morning. Go ahead and have your visit, but do not leave without a good-bye." Ludovika hummed a tune as she walked back toward the house.

When she was gone, Anna quietly observed Matz, who was poking a stick around in the muddy water. His back was turned, but she could see that his accident and fever had left him thin and frail. Guido nodded at her, and they moved forward. He reached out and tapped the boy's shoulder.

Matz jumped and wheeled around, his stick splashing into the water. A wide smile quickly replaced his startled expression.

Guido winked. With a swift movement, he fetched the stick from the river and handed it back to the boy. "Greetings! I brought you a visitor."

"Hello," Matz said. He looked down at his bare feet.

Anna drew him into a quick hug, then said in a cheery voice, " 'Tis good to see you looking so well!"

Matz's thin hand brushed across his wound. "It is healing. I do not remember much, but I know you laced me up."

Anna glanced at the wound, then touched his arm. "Are you happy here?"

The boy nodded violently. "Oh, aye. Happy as I have ever been." Then his face darkened, and he poked the ground with his stick. "But the captain will be angry if I do not get back to the ship."

Guido crouched down at eye level with the boy. "I've been meaning to talk to you about that. Would you like me to arrange it so you do not have to go back?"

The boy's head bobbed up. "You could do that?"

Guido gave Anna a sidelong glance. "Aye."

The lad's eyes narrowed. "What about my father?"

Anna inched closer. "What is your papa like?" The boy cocked his head and looked confused.

"What is your papa like?" she repeated. Matz shrugged his narrow shoulders. "If you had your choice," she went on, "would you stay here or go back to live with your papa?"

He began to stammer. "I . . . I do not understand. Sometimes I . . . I do not hear things right."

Guido, who was still crouching, used two fingers to illustrate the choice. "Which one? Stay here? Or go back to Papa?"

Matz tilted his head. "I could stay here longer?"

Ludovika chose that moment to return. "Will you not come in and have some bread? I know Matz is hungry. He never refuses food." She walked up to him and ruffled his hair. "Do you, lad?"

She heaved a great sigh. "Such a joy it is to see him consume it, too. Come along, now," she said, as they all followed her. " 'Tis much too hot out here." She slapped her neck. "And these bugs eat you alive down by the water. I do not know how you can stand it, Matz. Just like Rolf. That is my husband," she said, casting Anna a quick look. She threw open the door. "In with you."

The lad propped his stick against the door and entered. As Ludovika started to follow, Guido blocked her entrance. "I would have a word with you."

She looked up at him, questioning, and Anna had to stifle a chuckle. Guido made a huge, impenetrable barrier. The door closed, and Anna found herself alone with Matz. "Let's sit down." She gestured toward a chair.

When they both were seated, she placed her hands on her knees and leaned toward him. "This is a fine home, do you not think so?"

Matz nodded. He stared at her intently. But before he could reply, the door burst open and Ludovika rushed inside with outstretched arms. In an instant, she was bending over the boy, tears trickling down her cheeks. "Matz, I want you to know that you can stay here forever. I never had a son. Rolf and I would be proud to have you. Of course, if you ever want to see your papa, it can be arranged. But we will not let him ever send you away again. Matz, did you know your name means 'gift of God'? That is what you are. You must have had a saintly mother to name you so rightly."

Guido motioned to Anna from the door. Quietly, she got up to follow him, leaving the woman and boy to themselves. Once they were outside, Guido said, "I did not want to interrupt that scene."

"You mean you *could not* have interrupted," she corrected with a giggle.

They burst into laughter and started toward the Eeghens' home at a pleasant pace. When Guido could speak without laughing again, he said, "He is bound to understand some of it." This put them into another round of giggles.

Anna felt more encouraged than she had in weeks. "It has turned out well for Matz."

"Aye, the Lord is good. We cannot change the world. That is for God to do. Some people are wicked and refuse to change. But we can do our part by showing love to those whose lives cross ours." Guido smiled. "Now, I am done sermonizing and have a question for you."

"What?"

"Will you come to the meeting?"

Anna thought about all that had happened that day and even before. The husband and wife who had taken Matz were believers. All the believers she had known were loving and willing to help those in need. She thought of Peter's family and how they had taken in her family. Then there was Berta and her family. And Guido, like Peter said, was a trustworthy friend. A lump formed in her throat. "How could I not?"

When Anna and Guido reached the Eeghens' home, Berta rushed towards them. "You are here at last! Come. We have a surprise!"

The only thing Anna could think of was that Menno Simons was inside the house. She stood still. "Berta, please tell me first."

"Someone is here." She pointed. "In there."

Anna cast a hesitant look at Guido. He shrugged his shoulders. "Who?" she asked.

"You are wasting time. Just trust me," Berta urged.

Reluctantly, Anna followed Berta to the other room. But as soon as she took one step inside, joyful laughter burst from her mouth. "Willem! Oh, Willem! You have come at last!"

Willem jumped up from the table where he had been talking to their mother. He rushed toward Anna, swept her into his arms, and swung her round and round. She buried her head into his strong shoulder, taking in his scent and enjoying the security of his hearty embrace.

"My little sister. How fare you?"

"Oh, well," she said breathlessly. "Now that you have come at last."

"What is this 'at last'? You have only been here a few days."

"I know. But now I know that all is well."

"But of course it is." He put her at arm's length. "Let me have a look at you." He made a big show of looking her over, from head to toe, until she felt her face grow hot. He scrunched up his mouth and finally said, "You look beautiful, but feisty as ever."

She smacked his chest. "Willem!"

"Children," Mariel said, "come sit with me."

"Join us." Anna motioned to Guido and Berta.

They all settled around the table, and Mariel rested her hand on Willem's arm. "Now that you have eaten, tell us what news you bring."

Anna listened expectantly to her brother's words. "Skylar has had a hard time of it."

Mariel's face paled. "I felt that something was going to happen. Pray, tell us."

"Hilda's mother grew ill and died," Willem began. "And then the baby came early. Hilda is all right, but the baby was too small and did not live long. Hilda is downcast. Everything happened so fast. It has been quite a shock for Hilda and a strain on Skylar."

"Oh, nay," Mariel moaned.

"They are hoping you can come with God's speed. They need you, Mam."

"Of course. I want to go to them."

"Good. My business here will be short. I would like to leave in just a few days."

"But a few days may be too long," Mariel objected.

"A few days will not matter much."

"We shall be ready," Mariel said.

Guido asked, "What is the religious atmosphere in Antwerp?"

Willem's hands continued to gesture. "Explosive. Unstable, at the least. I am afraid I have bad news there also. Do you remember the Frenchman, Ansel—the fish seller?" Those from Visserswert nodded. "He died a noble death."

"What happened?" Anna asked with dread.

"He set up a business and had become a believer. He was baptized and was such a changed man that he went about witnessing to everyone of God's grace and of what Christ had done for him." Willem's voice broke. "He was bold, and they arrested him for his beliefs, for his baptism. The authorities drowned him. But during his short stay in our city, he touched many lives. He made a difference for the faith."

"It turned out he was a brave man, then." Anna's voice trembled.

Willem looked at her with surprise. "Aye."

Berta said, "I did not know the man, but I wish I did."

⚜

Ships of all sorts and sizes—ocean-going vessels, yawls, and rowing boats—clustered around Emden's harbor like bees at a hive. When Peter's ship docked, he stepped off the gangplank and gazed over the rocky quayside. The town crane loomed over the water, unloading barrels. Across the way, men crowded around a customs office.

Peter's first concern was to find Eeghen's mapmaking shop. He scanned the row of shops—cooper, blacksmith, tavern, and moneychanger. A man clattered past, dragging a wine cask on a trolley, and Peter stepped backward to give him room. The midday sun beat down, and he pushed up his hat to wipe his neck. Then he stepped back onto the sandy stone roadway.

Thedric kept to the shadows. He stopped long enough to flex his shoulders and crook his neck from side to side. His muscles were stiff, and he felt dirty. He was tired of his furtive role, dodging behind cover every time Peter drew near. It had been especially inconvenient on board ship. But all that really mattered was that the stonecutter would soon lead him to his heart's love.

Then Anna could decide for herself who she would have. If she did not choose him, Thedric would resort to extortion. He must have her. He would not leave without her. He leaned against a willow tree and observed the stonecutter, pausing before a mapmaker's shop.

❦

Mariel placed stacks of folded clothing into a wooden trunk. She stopped to wipe away some tears, then reached for another stack of personal items.

Anna stepped inside the bedchamber. "May I help?" Mariel stiffened, and Anna said with surprise, "Why, you are crying."

Her mother sank onto the bed and placed her head in her hands. Anna had observed her courage and resolve for months. Suddenly, she realized her mother was only flesh and blood after all. She crossed the room and put a hand on her shoulder. "What is it, Mam?"

Mariel shrugged. " 'Tis just that everything caught up with me."

"Are you worried about Skylar?"

Mariel nodded, her face bent toward the floor, and allowed the words to pour out. "I knew he needed me, yet I selfishly went about my own way. I truly felt God wanted us in Wittenberg. But for what?" She looked up at Anna from beneath long, wet lashes. "Naught but pain has come of that visit. If only your father were here."

"I miss him too." Anna fell into her mother's arms and they clung to each other. Finally, Anna drew back. "Kathrina will always be your friend. Martinus' beliefs cannot destroy that."

"You are right, daughter. I am sorry. We must look for the good in the situation."

Anna strained to find more encouragement for her mother. "The boy on the ship might have died had we not been there for him."

" 'Tis the truth. I must not be selfish."

"Nay, you are not selfish. You have a kind and giving spirit. 'Tis not your fault that you could not be in Wittenberg and Antwerp at the same time."

Mariel released a quivery sigh. "I pray that when we go to Skylar's, we will all find healing."

"God is everywhere, is he not?"

Mariel gave Anna a surprised look. Then a smile brightened her face. "Aye, he is."

"Guido believes God is here in this place."

An even brighter light came into Mariel's eyes. "Keep looking for him, child. Perhaps there is more than one reason God led us to Wittenberg."

Chapter 31

 The next morning Anna and Mariel were just descending the stairs when male voices sounded from the front entrance. Anna's heart gave a little lurch at the familiar voice. Peter! She hurried down, Mariel trailing behind.

"Look who I found wandering down at the docks!" Berta's papa announced.

Anna smiled widely, while Mariel welcomed Peter with a hug.

Next, Master Eeghen introduced Peter to his wife. "Peter is the sculptor my brother commissioned."

"How nice to meet you."

Peter thanked her and stepped past the others. His gaze rested on Anna. He stepped closer. *Why, his face is battered!* she thought.

"Hello, Anna."

"Hello, Peter."

The bruises on his face stood out vividly. The others crowded close and vied for his attention, but Anna held her tongue. She could not get past the bruises. For an instant, she saw a look of vulnerability flicker in his face. Even so, his strength permeated her being. She forced herself to look away, lest someone see the adoration in her gaze.

"I bring letters from Wittenberg." Peter passed them out. "One for Berta's family, from the Wittenberg Eeghens, and one for Mariel."

"Why, 'tis from Kathrina!" Mariel tore hers open and eagerly read. Thankfully, Anna saw tears of joy on her face. Kathrina must have made amends of some sort.

Peter worked his way to Anna and whispered, "I missed you."

"What happened to your face?" she whispered back.

Peter flinched and reddened. "I shall tell you about it later."

When they were alone, she would extract the truth from him, she told herself. "Tonight?"

He nodded and said in his normal voice. "I must find Guido. He promised that I could lodge with him."

"I know how to contact Guido," Master Eeghen said. "He is just a stone's throw from my shop. I shall take you whenever you are ready."

"I am a bit anxious to get settled in."

"You will come back for the evening meal, will you not?" Berta asked.

"Do, please," her mother urged.

"I would be honored." Peter lowered his voice and said to Anna, "I shall see you tonight."

He started toward the main entrance and gave her a backward glance as he stepped outside.

Peter wished he could stay to drink in the sight of Anna. *She is more endearing as each day passes,* he thought.

How humiliating that she had asked about his bruises! He had felt the women's curious gazes. Master Eeghen, of course, had questioned him at once, and it had been hard enough to admit the truth to him. He dreaded telling Anna and hearing her reaction. Would she consider him weak? Or would she loathe him for Thedric's sake?

Berta walked with Peter and her father to the end of the walkway. "Where are your things, Peter?"

He turned around and met her inquisitive eyes with a smile. "I left them at your father's shop."

Master Eeghen, a few steps behind, suddenly stopped. "That reminds me. I left my pouch inside. And I've a word to say to my wife. Please, excuse me."

As soon as her father was gone, Berta's eyes narrowed accusingly. "I need to scold you about something!"

Peter frantically searched his mind. What could he have done to invoke her anger? He could not think of anything. "What have I done?"

Berta stepped close and held up her finger. "First, you invited Anna into my uncle's household and did not even tell me you were in love with her. You said she was a friend. Hah! A woman needs to know a thing like that. I could have avoided many difficulties with her if I had known. She was terribly jealous of me." She thrust two fingers in the air. "And second, how could you let her leave Wittenberg without telling her you loved her?"

Peter was bewildered. He had no idea what to say, but Berta's flashing eyes demanded some reply. "What are you, a matchmaker?" he asked defensively.

"I have seen the way you look at each other. She loves you too."

"You know nothing. I have told Anna of my feelings before. She will not have me."

"So you *do* love her. Just as I thought."

"Aye. But that does not settle anything."

"Tell her."

"You really think she cares . . . about me?"

"I know it. And you had better do something about it."

The door creaked open, and they heard footsteps. "Perhaps I shall."

Master Eeghen appeared and clapped Peter on the shoulder. "Let us be off, then." Stepping into the street, they fell into companionable silence. Peter could not stop thinking about Anna. *Can it be true? Does she love me? Lord, I have waited so long.* He heard a rumble of laughter beside him and glanced over.

"Young man. It seems you are in another world."

Peter cleared his throat and stared at the cobblestones. " 'Tis true enough. Pray, forgive me."

Thedric kept vigilant watch from behind a thick tree and shrubbery outside the Eeghens' neatly groomed house. When Peter exited with the mapmaker, he was startled. Then his spirits soared as Berta appeared. Her presence verified his assumption that Anna van Vissers was inside the house. That was enough for now. As Peter disappeared down the road, Thedric turned his thoughts to another problem, lodging. Creeping out of the concealing thicket, he abandoned pursuit of the stonecutter to attend to his own plans.

Late that evening, Anna slouched on a cushioned bench and cast a languid gaze across her bedchamber. A velvet curtain surrounded the bed. In the corner of the room, her trunk was packed, ready for departure in a few days.

She should be pleased over the prospect of settling in Antwerp, but her emotions felt about as high as a worm groveling through oxen muck. All afternoon she had anticipated Peter's return in the evening. She had hoped for a time of intimate conversation with him.

She had wished to tell him about the ship's voyage, to admit that Guido was gentle as a dove, and to explain about Matz. She would even have confessed the small bit of faith that had risen in her spirit. She had imagined Peter rejoicing when she told him that she was searching for God, for truth. But Willem had occupied Peter's time and attention, and that intimate conversation had never occurred.

Tomorrow was the believers' meeting. If only she could have talked privately with Peter before the meeting. Eventually, she grew weary of her dark thoughts. The bed across the room looked inviting. As she rose from the cushion and took a step toward it, a noise startled her. It was a light pinging on the window. Curious, she crossed the room to peer outside.

Peter stood below. When he saw her staring down at him, his hand paused in midair. He was holding a lamp in his other hand, and by its light she could see a sheepish smile on his face. They stared at each other a moment, then he motioned for her to come outside.

With a rush of happiness, she waved and fled from the window. By her chamber door, she paused to smooth her hair and straighten her skirt. All her weariness had vanished.

As she hurried into the corridor, the door to the next chamber opened and a blonde head popped out.

"Have a nice time with Peter."

Anna gasped. "Berta! *Shh.*" Of course! Berta's window faced the same direction as Anna's.

Berta giggled and disappeared behind her door again. Anna stifled a grin and continued along the passage that led down to the garden courtyard.

The garden was eerie with shadows and strange insect sounds. She stepped onto the main path and followed it around a curve. Suddenly a hand reached out and touched her.

"Peter! You frightened me."

"I had to see you right away. Come. Let's sit on that stone bench."

"Is something wrong?"

"Sit quietly, I beg you, and listen."

He seemed so intent that Anna seated herself and fought to contain her curiosity. "Very well, Peter."

He set his lantern on the ground, and it cast a golden glow that surrounded his face. His brown eyes gleamed as he leaned close. "Since we were children, I have indulged you."

Anna felt a prick of hurt that he should start with a scold when she had been so excited to see him. She tried to swallow her rising anger as he continued. "When you opposed Willem or ran your schemes, I did not interfere with your plans. I always adored you as a child. Then I was gone for those years, living with my grandfather. When I returned, I adored you in a new way. But this time, I cannot let you go your own stubborn way."

"What stubborn way is that?"

"I love you, Anna, and you will hear me out."

"You . . . you love me?" she repeated.

"I know you love me, too. Do not deny it. I see it in your eyes. Look at me and deny it. You cannot."

"I do not deny it." Even though she had longed to hear such admissions from Peter, she felt compelled to argue. "But that does not mean we would suit."

"See? You are stubborn. What is keeping us apart?"

"You know what it is."

"Tell me."

"I fear that if I give my heart to you, I shall lose you."

"Nay." His voice sounded impatient. "You would not lose me."

"How can you promise such a thing?"

"Because no matter what happens to us in our earthly lives, I shall always love you."

"And if something happens to you?"

"Such foolishness, Anna. You cannot live your life according to the worst thing that could happen."

Anna looked down at her clasped hands. "The worst has happened to me. I cannot forget how they took Papa to his death. To be separated in such a way . . . I would rather release you now."

Peter reached out and tilted her chin so that her eyes met his. "Your memory serves you wrong."

"How can you say so?"

"Did you not see the joy in your father's eyes? He spoke of angels—of beautiful, unimaginable things. He loved you, yet he was courageous. He was fulfilled in a way that we've not yet experienced. The angels opened heaven's door to all of us that day."

Anna squirmed free of his hold and asked in confusion, "Why must you always speak of angels?"

"Because I shall never forget your father's own words: 'I see the angels. The Savior comes.'"

"You heard him say that?"

"Aye. Did you not hear him?"

"Nay." She slowly shook her head. "I only saw what they were doing to him. I saw him turn away from me. He would not answer me."

"Because he was singing, seeing beyond us. You cannot blame him for not taking his eyes off Jesus, can you? Do you not see how wonderful it was? In his last moments, he was not even fully aware of what the cruel people were doing to him. He was covered in God's love, in Jesus' love. Anna, your papa had already left us."

She grasped Peter's arm. "Do you truly believe that?"

"Aye, I do. God is always there for us."

Gradually, she relaxed her grip and let her arm fall to her side. They were quiet for a time. Then Anna ventured, "You are so strong. Is there nothing you fear?"

Peter squared his shoulders. "That I will use my blade to cut someone down. I know 'tis not the way God would have it, yet . . ."

Ever so gently, Anna cupped his disgruntled face in her hands. "Is that what happened to your face? Were you in a fight?"

Peter nodded, looking much ashamed. Her hands fell away. "Do you want to tell me about it now?"

"Thedric and I fought over you," he mumbled.

Anna felt a rush of joy that Peter cared so much for her, yet she was sorry he and Thedric were enemies. "Thank you for sharing so deeply with me," she said softly. "You have so much courage, Peter. You only have to find how God would have you use it."

Peter took her hands and kissed one of her palms. " 'Tis a nice thing to say. I love you, Anna. Only God knows the future, but our love is forever." He caressed her hands and stared deeply into her eyes.

Anna was near to bursting with joy. "I am glad you came to see me tonight."

"I am, too." He leaned toward her, and Anna knew he was going to kiss her. She did not stop him.

Chapter 32

Thedric stepped into the dimly lit Old Crane Tavern. The large room, with its few windows and thick stone walls, was dark and dingy. Its cavernous fireplace was cold and empty.

A din of conversation filled the dank air, and every so often a raucous laugh rose up. He found an empty table in a corner, and a maid with flirting eyes and full lips came to take his request. Shortly, she returned with a tankard. He tipped the drink to his mouth, his eyes continually surveying the room and its main entrance.

After a time, the heavy door groaned open and a man entered. He stopped just inside the doorway.

Thedric rose to his feet and waved an arm. "Johan. Here!"

Johan closed the distance between them and firmly embraced his cousin. " 'Tis so good to see you. I was surprised to get the word to meet you here."

Motioning to the maid to bring more of the tavern brew, Thedric settled in to tell his cousin a tale. He thought Johan would find it most interesting.

Anna entered the Eeghens' sitting room and smelled a strong fish odor. She looked around at those assembled. Rosmunda? A feeling of uneasiness swept over her. There sat the old woman, with slumped shoulders. Her hands lay limp in her lap; her eyes were downcast.

"Is something wrong?"

"There you are, Anna. We have been waiting for you. Come, sit down," her mother said.

Anna seated herself apprehensively and looked over the group again—Mariel, Rosmunda, and a woman who was a total stranger.

Mariel cleared her throat and said in a gentle voice, "This is Rosmunda's sister, Lurlene."

Anna smiled politely and nodded. A long-suppressed memory had returned—she and Peter searching in the shed, Rosmunda asking for shelter and needing help to get to her sister's, trouble with the bailiff.

Anna's thoughts returned to the present. Of course, she remembered now. Rosmunda had mentioned Emden. So that was why Rosmunda was here in this city.

"Rosmunda? What is it you want to tell us?" Mariel urged.

At first the old woman did not reply. She sat, wringing her hands. Finally, she said, "I have come to beg forgiveness from both of you. I've done a terrible thing. I have killed a man." She choked up and could not continue.

Lurlene squirmed. Anna tried to imagine what might have happened. And why should it concern her? Suddenly she felt a stab of fear. Was it Matz? Had his fever returned? "Pray, tell us what happened."

"I am sure you are not to blame," Mariel urged, her face full of compassion.

Rosmunda struggled to her feet and paced back and forth across the room. Tears streamed down her creased face. "I killed your husband . . . your papa."

Anna frowned. What sort of madness was this? Was Rosmunda deranged? Warily, she eased back against her chair and glanced over at her mother. Mariel's face had become deathly pale. Anna bit her lip. Rosmunda was not in Valkenburg when Papa died. Rosmunda . . .

"I am the one who gave the bailiff Miles' name," Rosmunda mumbled. "But I did not know they would kill him. I wish it would have been me." She pressed her fist against her mouth, emitting a gruesome, inhuman sound.

Anna stared. The old woman stood in the middle of the room moaning. Lurlene got up and encircled her with her arms. Rosmunda's confession settled over Anna like the blackest cloud. *Rosmunda* had informed the authorities that Papa was a heretic. *She* was the betrayer who had caused Papa's death.

"*Why?*" Mariel asked in an anguished voice.

Anna's head swiveled from her mother back to the center of the room.

"The bailiff found out I had nursed Menno's wife and wanted me to tell him where Menno was. But I did not know. They hit me and would not leave me alone. They asked me over and over, 'Where does Menno stay?' All of a sudden it came to me that I heard Miles had taken him somewhere in his boat. I did not mean to tell them, but it slipped out, and I am so ashamed. But even then I had no idea what it would mean for Miles . . . for you. The nightmares I have . . ."

Anna jumped to her feet, her fists clenched. "As well you should have! I have nightmares, too, because I saw my papa . . ." She could not finish. The sobs choked her throat. Her rage and desire for revenge came strong and blinding. She could not control her thoughts or her actions. She fled from the room.

Anna holed up in her bed, sinking lower and lower into despair and confusion. Hours later, a knock sounded, and the door creaked open.

Mariel stepped in. She crossed the room and put her hand on Anna's back. "We cannot turn back time, Anna. Rosmunda needs our forgiveness."

Anna rolled over, one arm flung under her head, the other fumbling with the bedcovers. "How can we forgive her?"

"I already have."

Anna stared at her mother through her tears.

Mariel sighed and caressed her daughter's arm. "Hating Rosmunda will not bring back Papa. I believe if she had to do it over, she would respond differently. Rosmunda is miserable. She will never be able to survive without our forgiveness."

"Is that not what she deserves?"

"Aye. But none of us deserves God's forgiveness according to our deeds. Still, God offers it. I have invited Rosmunda and Lurlene to tonight's meeting."

Anna's eyes narrowed, and her voice hardened. "I promised Guido I would go. But if Papa's murderer is there, I will not go."

"It would be a shame to hurt Guido. He is innocent. Pray about it, Anna. Ask God to help you forgive. I shall leave you alone now."

Anna turned her face toward the wall until Mam left the room. The emotions raging within her brought back memories of the days after they had been cast out of their home. How she had wanted revenge! But then it had been impossible. Now she could avenge her papa. Rosmunda was only a weak old woman. Stupid woman!

As she thought of ways to get even, her mother's words came back to her. *It would be a shame to hurt Guido. He is innocent.* If she went back on her word, she would hurt Guido. Peter, too. She had wanted to please Peter. Mam was right about one thing. It would do no good to sulk in her bedchamber. It only made her hurt more. Why should one small woman keep her from doing what she wanted to do? She would go. Maybe she would even find a way to repay Rosmunda for her betrayal.

It was well after dark when people assembled at the Eeghens' home. Anna stepped into the room and searched the crowd for Rosmunda's unwelcome face. She did not see her or Lurlene. Perhaps they would feel too ashamed to come.

Peter and Guido entered the far side of the room. Anna moved toward them, weaving through the makeshift benches.

"Hello, Anna. I have good news for you," said Guido.

"Hello, Guido. I would welcome some good news."

"Matz wanted me to tell you, personally, that he is happy with his new family."

"That is good news." Anna turned to Peter. "I must tell you about the boy we helped on the ship."

"Guido told me. As always, you were very brave."

"Nay. But I am glad Matz has decided to stay with Rolf and Ludovika. I fear his father is a cruel man."

"I am glad he has a new home. And I am happy to see you here at the meeting." The look in Peter's brown eyes was so intense that Anna could feel it penetrating to her soul.

Someone touched her arm, and she looked away. It was Berta, smiling. How long had she and Peter stood gazing into each other's eyes? Even Guido had slipped away.

"Ready?" Berta asked.

"Aye. I shall talk to you later, Peter." He nodded and went to find Guido. Anna followed Berta to a seat near the back.

When they were seated, Menno, the preacher, entered the house. He looked weary but rugged, even resilient. Anna shuddered to think how she had spoken to him at that other meeting. As he worked through the crowd, she stole another look at him. To her dismay, he turned and his gaze singled her out from the others. It was a burning look of compassion, of command. Anna looked away, and the preacher passed on.

Berta gave Anna a reassuring pat as her father welcomed the believers in Jesus' name. Then a brother came forward to lead the group in song. Anna watched the people around her, and something within her longed to experience the joy that shone on their faces. The singing stopped.

Next, Berta's father introduced Menno Simons. Menno began by giving news from the area where he was ministering, just down the rivers Rhine and Maas. He mentioned the hamlet of Visserswert. "The brethren are harassed and threatened in that area. Yet they continue to be steadfast and faithfully meet together. Please remember them in your prayers. There are many good leaders now.

"Let us pray over this household. May God spare it from persecution by those who want to destroy our faith."

They paused to pray. Anna found herself earnestly joining in prayer for Berta's family, Guido, Peter, and Willem. Then her thoughts shifted to Rosmunda. Silently, Anna questioned God about the situation. When she opened her eyes she saw that many people had dropped to their knees. Others remained sitting. It was an informal meeting like the one she had attended in the field by Visserswert, nothing like the Torgau Kasteel Church, which she had attended while staying at the Black Cloister.

She found herself checking the hallway that led toward the main entrance, expecting at any moment to see someone like the bailiff who had entered her house in Visserswert. She shivered at the memory. Berta must have felt it, for she gave her a sympathetic smile.

Finally, the prayer was over, and Menno began to preach. His manner was both humble and powerful as he logically and clearly pointed out humans' need for salvation. Step by step, he led them through the Scriptures. Christ taught that once people believed, they were to be baptized. It was a symbol of forsaking the old life and putting on the new life. Christ forgave sins and transformed people. As Anna listened, a desperate loneliness enveloped her, and a deep longing disturbed her soul.

Miraculously, for the first time ever, she began to understand her papa's faith. As Menno described Jesus, Anna could see her papa. She thought about the other believers that she knew, about their loving actions. Anna saw Jesus in them, too.

But this loving Jesus was not merely human; he was also God, in control of the universe. His plan stretched way beyond today and this time into the future and spanned generations of people on the earth. She listened earnestly as Menno explained, and she understood as she had never understood before.

As these new truths coursed through her spirit, Anna felt compelled to test them against her old reasoning. Could the pope and bishops really be at fault or capable of human error? Were they not special people anointed of God? But Menno said he had been a priest, just as Martinus had. Not knowing it was God's Spirit that gave her this new understanding, she foolishly questioned. Why had no one explained this before?

When Menno gave a repentance call at the end of his sermon, Anna trembled.

Berta whispered, "Would you like me to go forward with you?"

Anna looked up. When she did, she saw Rosmunda and Lurlene walking to the front of the room. When had they come? Confused, she shook her head and wrestled with the decision she must make. Dark emotions welled up within her at the sight of Rosmunda. Then the others in the room faded from her senses again. In her spirit, Anna called out to God in fervent prayer.

She heard no voice, but became aware of a supernatural reassurance. Oh, how she wanted to believe Menno Simon's words were true. Lovingly, the divine presence urged her.

I believe you, she prayed. When at last she looked up, Berta grasped her hand. Rosmunda and many others were kneeling in the front, but Menno had left.

"Where did he go?"

"I know not. But Guido is up front. He is asking if anyone will answer God's call. Will you, Anna? Do you want to go forward?"

Anna looked at Rosmunda and struggled with the healer's request: *Will you forgive me?* The divine spirit that filled Anna's soul was warm and loving, meeting needs she had not known existed. Compared to God's peace, the hatred she harbored against Rosmunda felt trite and sinful.

"Aye." Anna rose to her feet, but before she could step away from the bench, the sounds of banging doors, heavy boots, and screams filled the room. Instantly, Anna knew what was happening. Beadles dressed in red, black, and yellow strode up the aisle. Anna recognized the awful bailiff, Johan. He headed straight to the front of the room. To Guido!

Two men grabbed Guido, one on either side. Johan snarled, "So, you are the renowned Menno Simons. Let's see you elude us this time." Then he turned to the group of believers with a sneer. "Say farewell to your leader. He is on his way to hell."

"He is not Menno Simons!" Anna screamed. But her cry was muffled by the loud confusion that filled the room.

Then Peter's voice rose above the others. "Thedric! So you are the scoundrel behind this. Come for your revenge, have you?"

Anna whirled around. Thedric strode past Peter as if he had not spoken. He kept coming, straight toward her. They stood face to face. Berta held her upright, but Thedric spoke as if they were alone in the room.

"My love, I have come for you. You do not have to be like them. I will take you away from this. Someplace safe."

Shame surged through Anna like a river of fire. To be singled out in front of all the believers. To endanger Guido and all the others. It was unbearable! She groaned and shook her head. "Please."

"I can see you are overcome. Take some time to think. You can find me at the Old Crane. Come and see me. We will talk." Anna stared at him, too horrified to speak. He reached out and touched her chin.

Peter had pushed his way through the group of believers to reach Anna. Thedric scowled and pushed him back. "Stay out of this or I will have your life!"

Peter fell backward, but quickly regained his balance. He stood tall between Anna and Thedric. The intruder only curled his lip and turned away. Peter lunged toward him.

Just as her world tipped, Anna cried out, "Nay, Peter! Remember . . ." Then the room went black.

Chapter 33

Did Peter cut him down with his dagger?" Anna's words were slurred as she looked up into her mother's anxious blue eyes.

Mariel gave a trembling smile. "Nay."

Anna raised her head a few inches and looked about. "Then what is Willem doing with Peter's dagger?" The room was still abuzz, with chaos everywhere. "Are they gone? What happened?"

Willem laid the dagger on a nearby bench and stepped forward. "Shhh. I am glad you are back." He looked at their mother. "Can we get her to her bedchamber?"

"Aye. Come this way."

"Nay! I must know what happened to Guido," Anna protested.

"What you need right now is rest. There will be plenty of time for talk tomorrow." Mam's face hovered above her, its expression protective. Perhaps Guido was even now being dragged to the donjon. She felt Willem's arms lifting her.

As he carried her, Berta and Mariel trailing behind, Anna looked up into her brother's blue eyes. "It is happening, is it not—what I feared?" She saw the pain as he quickly looked away.

Mariel pulled back the curtains and Willem laid Anna on the bed. She crawled under the covers. "The last time you tried to keep the truth hidden, I stowed away in a cart."

Willem and Mariel exchanged a look. Then Willem sighed

and stroked Anna's forehead. "The man that spoke with you, is he the printer you met in Wittenberg?"

Anna nodded. "Thedric Bettendorf."

"He and the bailiff took Guido and Peter."

Anna shoved herself up on her elbows. Panic spread through her body. "Peter? They took Peter, too?"

She knew it was true when Willem's hand clamped onto her shoulder. Silent tears streamed down Mariel's face.

"Ah, nay," Anna moaned. She slumped back on the bed, uttering moans of grief.

Finally, Willem said, "I must go back to the others and see what plans the believers make. Be strong." He left.

Mariel leaned across the bed to offer Anna comfort.

"Peter loves me," Anna moaned.

"I know, child. I know."

Thedric's last words came to Anna. *You can find me at the Old Crane.* Suddenly she felt a supernatural peace, the same as she had experienced during the meeting. *Is that what you want me to do, God?* she prayed silently. The peace remained. She had her answer.

The next morning, Anna opened her eyes and consciousness slowly returned. With it came the knowledge that Peter and Guido had been arrested. She struggled with her emotions, frantically searching her mind for a way to help them. It seemed hopeless until a small voice repeated Thedric's last words to her, *You can find me at the Old Crane.*

Remembering her plan, Anna threw on her clothes and hurried from her chambers. She was eager to see what was happening in the household and eager to explain her idea. On the bottom step of the stairs, she heard voices coming from the parlor. She was about to go in when she heard her name and paused.

"Anna will try to reason with Thedric. You know she will.

But we must not allow it. Perhaps I should go to him."
Willem, she thought.

"Nay. The bailiff might still be looking for you. It might even be a trap." *Mam.*

"If we do not allow Anna to go to Thedric, he will return for her." *Master Eeghens.*

"We shall have to guard her carefully." *Willem again.*

"Perhaps you should take Mariel and Anna and leave at once. Let the believers here do what we can. We must get word to the captives' families."

Anna backed away from the room and crept back up the stairs, retracing her steps to her bedchamber. She closed the door and paced. *I cannot leave Emden without Peter.* Peter's strong, handsome face, as it looked that night in the garden—yearning, hopeful, and full of love—filled her vision. How she wanted to believe they could have a life together. But her fears had come true. It was not to be. And gentle Guido. What would they do to him if they believed he was Menno Simons? *At once, Master Eeghens said. Take Mariel and Anna and leave at once.*

It was risky to delay. She must talk with Thedric immediately. If she hurried now, she might not be missed. Her thoughts raced. She could stuff clothes from her trunk under the covers and make it appear that she was still asleep. They would never wake her, knowing the pain she was in—at least not for several hours. The Old Crane was by the harbor, near Master Eeghen's shop. She could easily find it.

Anna's heart thumped as she stealthily made her way along the hall, down the stairway, and out the side door. Once outside, she broke into a run, keeping close to the shrubbery. She remembered sneaking out at the Wittenberg Eehgens' and felt desperately sad. That time Peter had stopped her. He had taken her up in his arms and carried her. He had made promises and said he would give his life for her.

She slowed her pace. She would give her life for Peter, if

only it would do any good. What good was a life of fear anyway? She was tired of it. Her steps faltered. Then her mind
leaped. Of course! She had only meant to reason with Thedric.
But she had the power to dicker for the life of those she loved.
She would give her life for Peter!

She walked briskly, not noticing the landscape. All she saw
was a plan unfolding. Surely this was what was meant to
happen! If there was a reason for everything that happened to
a person, then surely this was the reason she had been afraid
to love Peter. Perhaps everything had prepared her for this
one event, to save Peter. It was why she had gone to Wittenberg in the first place, to meet Thedric.

She continued to reason. Peter loved her and so did
Thedric. And Thedric had made promises. Her life with him
would be safe. He would pamper her. She would grow to respect him, maybe even love him. But most of all, she would
never have to fear for her life nor for his. And in return, he
would give Peter and Guido their freedom. She would not
have to face a new life in some unknown place. No monastery.

A sudden thought shattered her plans. What about her
family? If they would not allow her even to talk to Thedric,
how would they allow her to marry him? There was only one
way. She would have to convince them that it was what she
wanted, perhaps even what she had desired all along.

Is this God's plan? she wondered. Then she asked herself,
Is God's love not sacrificial?

The strong scent of sea air made her notice her surroundings. She was close now. She followed the familiar landmarks
until she saw the Old Crane. She paused, took a deep breath,
and opened the door.

As her eyes adjusted to the darkness, she searched the tables.
Thedric was not there. The tavern keeper raised an eyebrow
at her. She crossed the room to him, ignoring the gazes that
followed her. She felt a rush of embarrassment as she stepped

up to the bar. "Would you have a message for me? My name is Anna van Vissers."

"Nay."

"You do not recall a Thedric Bettendorf leaving a message about me?"

"Oh, aye." The keeper nodded. "The printer. He did mention that a woman might be arriving. Would you like me to get him?"

Anna gazed hesitantly around the dark room. Every reasonable thought urged her to flee from this place. "If it would not be too improper, and you could point me in the right direction . . ."

"Oh, aye. He is at the end of the hall."

The man's snide expression added to the humiliation and frustration she already felt. But there was no turning back now. She walked across the room with her head held high, looking straight ahead, then down the passageway the keeper had indicated. The hallway was quiet. She worked up her courage and rapped on the door.

"Who is it?" Thedric's curt voice frightened her. She backed away and turned, but the door flew open. "Anna!" Thedric stared at her with a look of disbelief. Then a light came into his eyes. "Come in."

She hesitated until he reached out to her. She placed her hand in his. Gently, he pulled her inside the room and closed the door. When she heard the latch close behind her, a chill ran up her spine. She was placing herself in a dangerous position. What if he used her to find Willem? The random, wild thought sent a shudder through her body.

Thedric glanced about the room. There was a bed with disheveled bedcovers in the center of one wall. A small toilette table took up one corner, and there was one chair. Thedric motioned toward it. "Please. Sit down, my dear."

The small courtesy eased her mind a bit, and she seated

herself. If she were going to persuade her family of anything, she must begin her acting now. She forced a faint smile.

"You still look a bit pale, but better than last night," he said.

"You frightened me."

Thedric sat on the bed, crossed his legs and placed his chin in his hand. He studied her intently. She waited, unsure how to proceed. Then he spoke. "I was going to call on you today to see how you fared."

"My family would not have allowed you to see me. That is why I came here. Although I am sure the tavern keeper is using his imagination."

"Do not worry about that. I shall see to your reputation. But I am sorry you had to experience that terrible scene last night. The bailiff is . . ."

Anna suddenly interrupted, "Your relative."

Thedric's brow shot upward. He tilted his head. "How did you know that?"

"I am not sure when I realized it. Perhaps just now. But that day in your print shop, I saw your coat of arms. It was similar to the bailiff's."

"Let me explain. I followed your friend from Wittenberg."

"Peter?"

"Aye. I knew he would lead me to you. I wanted to see you. When I realized my cousin was in the city, of course, I paid him a visit. It seems he has been looking for your brother and Menno Simons. I persuaded him to forget about your brother in return for taking him to the house where the believers lived."

"That was not Menno Simons. The man you took is named Guido. He is not a preacher."

"But he is a heretic, like your sculptor friend. Let me take you away from all this. Marry me! Let me protect you. Come home with me."

" 'Tis tempting, Thedric. But even though you say you

protected Willem, I do not know if I could live with the fact that you led the bailiff to my friends."

Thedric rose from the bed and hovered over Anna. "Do you think you could care for me? Nay," he reached out and touched her hand, "do not answer that. It matters not. My love for you is enough."

"But of course, I do care for you. I will even marry you if you will free Peter and Guido."

Thedric's eyes darkened. He rubbed his chin. "Help me to understand this. You agree to marry me, if I free your friends?"

" 'Tis as you say."

"I have to know. Do you love him?"

"Aye." Anna's head bent, and she stared at her feet. "But I cannot marry him. And I cannot marry you, either, if you do not see that they are released. I cannot live with a man who I resent."

"Please look at me." His eyes were narrowed, his brow furrowed, but his voice was calm. "I should be furious with you. But I believe you speak the truth. If I *could* get them released." Thedric began to pace. "And I do not know if that is even possible. I am merely a cousin to the bailiff. But as you say, this man is not Menno Simons. Johan could still hope that the believers will lead him to Menno." He stopped in front of Anna again. "If I were able to get them released, would you try to . . ."

"Love you? I would try to forgive you, to be a good wife to you."

" 'Tis enough," he said, his dark eyes alight. "We will be married right away. I shall call upon your family today."

"Nay. First, I must see the men released. It is my only request."

"As you wish. I will escort you home. Then I will look for Johan."

"I must return alone. My family does not know I am gone.

Until the others are released, my family will not accept you, Thedric."

"As your betrothed, I insist that I escort you. I shall wait outside to make sure you are safe. They will not know I am there."

Anna nodded and rose from her chair. Thedric grabbed his hat. He took her arm and escorted her from the tavern, stopping at the bar to properly introduce Anna to the keeper as his betrothed. The whole ordeal was most embarrassing.

When they stepped outside the tavern and started toward the Eeghens', Thedric said, "I want to apologize again for what happened in Wittenberg with Martinus. I had no intention of doing anything that would hurt you. I have many wonderful plans for us, my dear. You shall never regret your decision."

After that, everything seemed like a muddled dream, her grip on Thedric's arm, his future plans for their life together, their betrothal. Had she done the right thing? Nay, she had done the only thing.

Thedric kissed her hand and waited while she let herself into the Eeghens' house.

Inside, Berta saw her enter. "Anna! We thought you were asleep!"

"Nay, I went for a walk. I had to do some thinking." If Thedric was going directly to the hideous Johan to get Peter and Guido released, they could soon be bursting through the doors. She must begin her playacting, to persuade her family that she loved Thedric. *I will also need to persuade Peter,* she thought with a stab of pain. It was the only way he would ever release her. "Do you know where Mama and Willem are?"

"They are in the courtyard. I shall go with you."

Chapter 34

Anna stepped into the courtyard. It reminded her of the night Peter had met her there. But she must not think about Peter. She must release him so he could live. She was the same as betrothed to another. She would make sure Peter never found out the truth, or he would never accept her gift.

"Hello, Mam, Willem."

They looked up at her in surprise and greeted her. "We were just making plans."

"But I have my own plans."

Willem exchanged looks with Mariel.

"I have told you all along I do not agree with papa's beliefs —your beliefs. Just as I suspected, more evil has come from it. I have decided that if Thedric asks, I shall marry him. I want to be free of all of this. And I do care for him."

"But I thought you loved Peter," Berta said, in a sharp tone.

"I am fond of Peter. But as I told you earlier, we do not mesh. Anyway, who knows what is to become of him?"

"Anna!" Mariel said.

"I did not mean it the way it sounded. But Thedric makes me feel safe, secure. I did not tell you because I knew you wanted me to believe the same as you. But now Thedric has come to rescue me from all that. I wish to return with him. Will you not give me the desire of my heart? Please do not deny me this. We are meant to be together. He will only follow me to Antwerp."

"I will not go to Antwerp without you," Willem said.

"See how confusing everything is? I am so tired of running and hiding. Do you have something against Thedric?"

"How can you ask that? After he was behind the arrest of our good friends?" Willem exploded.

"Perhaps he could help us to get them released."

"He will not help us." Willem said coldly.

"And I shall not go to Antwerp with you." She turned her back to them and faced the house.

"Anna! Where are you going?"

"To my bedchamber." Anna strode from the courtyard.

The shutters were open and a slight breeze moved the tree branches. Anna lay on her bed and tried to calm her thoughts. What would life be like with Thedric? He was gentle and attentive, and he would someday be affluent. She had some friends in Wittenberg. How would Luther accept her? He would be glad to hear she had broken ties with the believers. Perhaps it would shame him that he had sent them away. Perhaps he would invite Mariel to come and visit again. Would the God that had come to live within her leave?

She could not picture Thedric's home. She had only seen his printing shop. It seemed tidy and functional. But the bailiff would be her cousin! A sick feeling engulfed her. She had not thought of that. She felt a panicky need to escape, to flee. Yet to save Peter and Guido . . .

A knock sounded on her door. "Who is it?"

"Mam."

"Come in."

The door creaked open, and her mother stepped inside. She seemed happier than during their talk in the courtyard. She came to the side of the bed. "I have good news—Peter and Guido were released! And Peter wishes to speak with you."

Anna bolted upright. "Thank God!"

Mam searched Anna's face, looking for signs of a change of heart. "Are you coming, then?"

"Aye. Go ahead. I shall be right along."

Mariel nodded and left the room.

Anna sat on the edge of the bed and dropped her face into her hands. It was done, then. Thedric would soon come for her. It had seemed so right before. Now her stomach felt queasy and her heart lurched. If only she did not have to fulfill her promise. But she did.

How could she face Peter? Only two nights ago, he had given her his pledge of love. She loved him deeply too. Why else would she sacrifice herself, if not for great love? Aye. She must break away from him. She must be strong. Cold. Even cruel. He would not release her otherwise.

"Anna!" Peter ran to her when she appeared at the foot of the stairs.

They embraced. She drew away, breathless. "I am so glad you are free!"

"Guido, too."

"Aye. Mam told me."

"Let us take a walk in the garden." Peter offered his arm.

Anna took it, knowing she would soon miss the protection he had always provided. "How were you released?"

"I am not sure. The bailiff said something about us not being who he thought we were, and Emden being out of the Duke of Cleves-Julich's territory. God gave me the strength to bear up in the donjon. Of course, Guido was a rock. The worst thing was my fear that I would never have a life with you."

They paused under a tree, and Anna released his arm. Peter leaned against the tree, one foot against the trunk. "I just want to drink in the sight of you."

Footsteps clattered on the stone walkway, and they both

looked up. "Anna, there is someone in the parlor." Berta arched an eyebrow at her. "And I would have a word with you."

Her thoughts scrambled, Anna urged, "Please wait around the corner. I need to say farewell to Peter." Berta nodded and disappeared from their sight.

Anna turned back to Peter, and he gave her a puzzled look. She steeled herself as she began her mentally rehearsed speech. "I shall always love you, Peter. I am delighted above all that is good and true that you are safe again. But there is no future for us. I am going to marry Thedric."

Peter's foot slid down the tree trunk and hit the ground. His head jerked in disbelief. "You are what?"

Anna's words became even more clipped. "I am going into the parlor to accept Thedric's proposal. We are no longer children. It is time for you to pursue the things you believe in. I am going to do that. If you get in my way, I shall never forgive you. 'Tis time to put childish dreams away." She turned to leave, then thought better of it and turned back. "Farewell, my love."

Peter's face went pale, then turned bright red. He opened his mouth several times to protest, then pinched it shut. His arms hung straight, his hands balled into tight fists. She wheeled away and stepped briskly past the hedge.

"Anna, wait!" Berta called. Anna slowed her pace. "You cannot leave Peter for Thedric! I will not allow it."

"Eavesdropping, Berta?"

"We both know you love Peter. If you only wait awhile, your fear will not seem so overwhelming." Anna picked up her pace again, and Berta gestured as she walked alongside. "Only think how God answered our prayers!"

They had reached the door to the house. Anna paused to face Berta, her hands folded in front of her skirt. She looked at the ground and said, "I am grateful for your concern, my friend. But do you not think I know my own heart? Now please, respect my wishes and do not speak of it again. Perhaps Peter could use a friend right now."

Berta's eyes sparked and her lips pressed together. "I am sure he can!" She wheeled away in anger. Disheartened, Anna wondered if she had lost Berta's friendship forever. But she resolutely straightened her skirt and stepped up into the house.

In the parlor, Thedric sat in a straight-back chair by the hearth. Mariel was on a nearby bench, pretending to do mending under the light of the window. Thedric stood and stepped forward.

"My dear."

"Thedric. 'Tis good of you to call." Anna extended her hand, which he took and squeezed gently.

They sat down, and Thedric began to play his part for Mariel's benefit. "I had to see you and explain. I must admit, I followed you to beg that you reconsider some things we had discussed."

Anna did not miss the intense looks Mariel was sending them. "Perhaps you should explain about last night," she said.

"Johan and I met at a tavern. I mentioned that I had come to Emden with intentions toward you. Johan is tracking down Menno Simons. He thought I would lead him to the preacher. You always seemed to hate Menno, so I did not think it would do any harm. But when your friend Peter got in my way, I could not stop myself. We've had a quarrel or two before. I am sorry. I suppose the authorities do not really have anything to hold him on."

"Nay. They have released him already. But it did frighten me."

"Can you forgive me?"

"Everything turned out well enough. Of course I forgive you. We are always to forgive others. Did you not try to teach me that, Mam?"

Mariel's face reddened. "Aye. But we must use common sense, of course."

Thedric leaned forward and whispered to Anna, "Your family does not think much of me, I can see. Is your word honorable? Will you marry me?"

Anna nodded and looked at the floor. When she looked up, his dark, earnest eyes held her gaze. "I just want this to be over," she whispered.

Thedric rose and crossed the room to Mariel. "I would like to have a word with you."

Mariel's hands went limp, and the fabric she held in her lap drooped. "You may speak."

"Your daughter and I wish to be married. We desire to have your blessing."

"I would speak with her brother Willem."

"Of course."

Mariel laid her mending on the bench and swept from the room, avoiding Anna's eyes.

"What if they do not agree?" Anna asked.

"Then we shall meet at the *Swift*. It will set sail shortly. We shall return to Wittenberg, and Martinus can marry us."

"I hope it does not come to that."

" 'Tis not my first choice, either. But I have come a long way for you. I do not intend to leave without you. If something happens that they refuse, and I should leave without permission to make plans with you, then meet me tomorrow at noon at the wharf by the *Swift*. Can you find it?"

"Aye."

"I shall make all the arrangements. Do I have your word on this?"

Before Anna could reply, Willem and Mariel entered the

room, but she felt Thedric's gaze upon her. She glanced up and saw that he expected an answer.

But Willem placed a hand on her arm. "May we speak with Thedric alone?"

Anna looked at Thedric and gave him a nod. His face relaxed visibly, and she left to go to the adjoining room and wait. It was not long until she heard raised voices. A moment later, a determined Thedric burst through the door. He cast a dark look over his shoulder, then gave Anna a quick smile and stalked out.

Next, Willem and Mariel hurried from the room. They stopped to face Anna, and Willem gave her an authoritative look. "I will not bless such a marriage. You would not be happy with him."

Anna narrowed her eyes. "Everyone around here seems to think they know what is best for me. I guess I should know my own heart!" She wheeled, ready to run up the stairs to her bedchamber, but a tall figure blocked her passage.

It was Peter. His eyes were darker than she had ever seen them, and they bored into hers accusingly. "I will not change my mind," she said. He stepped back so she could pass. As she did, her arm brushed his, sending a shiver through her.

She gripped the stair railing with tingling fingers and fought to control her feelings. She wanted to throw herself in Peter's arms and beg him to make everything right again. If only things could be like that night in the courtyard when Peter had confessed his love. But it would not be long now until his love turned to disgust. Her own love would finally lessen and turn to complacency. It would be better that way. She could not love one man and live with another. Or could she?

Peter felt a hand on his shoulder. "She told you, did she not?"

He nodded at Willem. "It feels as if she reached in and ripped my heart out. I know she loves me as much as I love her. She is a stubborn woman."

Willem's expression was grave. "I fear we need to watch her closely. She will probably run to him since we have denied her. You must wait for her, Peter. She will come around in the end. I am taking her with us—we leave for Antwerp tomorrow."

"I suppose you know best. I cannot think right now. I am going back to Guido's."

"What will you do, Peter?"

"I know not. Perhaps I shall go home to Visserswert."

"You could come with us as far as Antwerp."

"Anna would not appreciate that. I will think it over."

"I shall be at my ship, if you wish to contact me."

Peter raised a hand in farewell and left the house.

Chapter 35

Peter lay across the straw tick mattress and stared up at the thatched roof of Guido's one-room tenant dwelling. Anna van Visser's decision to marry the printer had ignited a seething anger in him. At the same time, it made him feel so sick that he had not eaten a morsel of food since he and Guido were apprehended. Now he had taken to his bed.

He hoped Willem could control Anna long enough to carry her far away from Thedric. But he carried little hope for his own future with Anna. In fact, bitterness had taken root in his heart, convincing him that even if she changed her mind, he would reject her. He was sure the damage she had inflicted on him could never be repaired.

There was an insistent rapping on Guido's door, and Peter staggered from his bed. He leaned against the door until the room stopped spinning, then fumbled with the latch. The door flew open and Willem bolted in.

"Peter! Are you ill?"

Peter made his way slowly back to bed. "Aye."

"This does not set well. I need your help."

Peter lay back and lifted his feet onto the mattress. "If it concerns that sister of yours, you shall have to find someone else." His sharp tone disguised his curiosity.

"So that is what ails you. Lovesickness. We've no time to bewail . . ."

Peter gripped the edge of the mattress and narrowed his eyes. "Did you come here just to belittle me?"

"You would abandon Anna in her time of dire need?"

Peter rolled his eyes at the question. When had Anna not been embroiled in some trouble and generally as the result of her own doing?

Willem threw his arms in the air and paced in a small circle in the center of the room. " 'Tis but a ruse. I suspect Thedric involved Anna in some scheme in which she agreed to marry him. In return, Thedric arranged for you and Guido to be released from the donjon."

Peter ran a hand through his disheveled hair, and remembered Anna's hurtful spiel to him in the garden. It would be forever engraved on his memory. *I shall always love you. I am delighted above all that is good and true that you are safe again. But there is no future for us. I am going to marry Thedric. . . . If you get in my way, I shall never forgive you. 'Tis time to put childish dreams away. Farewell, my love.* "Nay. She made it quite plain . . ."

"She lied to rescue you, do you not see? Anyone can tell that she loves you."

The simple statement shocked Peter out of his sickbed. He sat up, and his feet hit the floor with a thud. Rubbing the back of his neck, he shook his head again. "What kind of love would . . ."

"Sacrificial love, Peter. And you know Anna's impetuous nature, her reckless knack for entangling herself in trouble."

Peter's hand sliced through the air. "Enough! I will help."

Willem nodded with enthusiasm. "I made inquiries at the tavern where Thedric lodges. The keeper described Anna perfectly. She paid Thedric a visit on the morning you were released from the donjon."

Peter hit the wall with his fist. "That woman!"

Willem went on, "Next, I inquired about any ships destined for Hamburg. One of them weighs anchor at midday today—the *Swift*. I believe Thedric and Anna will attempt to board that ship."

"We must stop her!"

"Indeed!"

Peter staggered to a small, square window and threw open the wooden shutter. " 'Tis nearly midday now!" He reached for his dagger and began to fasten his belt, muttering all the while. "That scoundrel."

Willem blocked the doorway. "Peter, in your condition, 'twould be best to gird yourself with the Lord and leave your blade at home."

Is Willem referring to my physical weakness or my emotional upheaval? Peter wondered. It mattered not. He felt naked without his dagger. "You know I always carry it," he snapped, pushing past Willem and rushing out the door.

Willem had no choice but to follow. He laid out his plan as they went. "My crew stands ready at this instant. I intend to put Anna on my ship, willing or not. Agreed?"

"We will do it."

The two men raced toward the docks, where they located the *Swift,* bound for the Baltic and routed to drop anchor at coastal seaports, including Hamburg. The crew scurried over the ship, trimming the sails and loading cargo.

"Over there." Willem pointed toward an unattended horse and cart. "We can watch the ship's gangway from both directions and remain hidden."

As they lay in wait, Willem noticed one of his own ship's crew traversing the quayside. "I daresay that man is looking for me." Willem stepped out into the open and shouted the man's name. He wheeled about and started toward them.

"I shall go and see what he's about," said Willem. Peter nodded.

Not long after, just as Willem had predicted, Thedric and Anna appeared on the quay in the distance. As they drew closer, it was clear that the printer was exuberant while Anna looked downcast and hesitant. Peter was encouraged to see that Anna's heart was not in tune with her rebellious actions. He cast a sidelong glance at Willem. He was still detained. He was going to miss them!

Peter brushed a feverish hand across his dagger. Fortunately, there were no bystanders to interfere. When Thedric and Anna were in direct line with the cart where Peter hid, he lunged out with a cry. "Halt!"

"Peter!" Anna stared at him as if she were face-to-face with a ghost.

He withdrew his dagger and ordered, "Step behind me, Anna."

Thedric tightened his grip on Anna's elbow, but she jerked away and backed up several paces. "But . . . I . . . but . . ."

"She is coming with me. You will not interfere," Thedric threatened.

"This blade says you will walk up that gangplank alone." Peter stretched out his arm and pointed it at Thedric's chest.

"But, Peter . . ." Anna interceded.

A shriek rent the air from beyond. "There you be! Please, wait!"

Peter and Anna jerked their heads toward the voice. Thedric took advantage of the diversion and lunged forward, striking Peter's arm.

The dagger clattered to the ground, into an outcropping of sharp rocks. As Peter struggled to reclaim it, he scraped his hand on the stones, then nicked the edge of his blade, slicing his palm. Thedric managed to grab the dagger by its hilt and scoop it off the ground. Peter, still on his hands and knees, looked up to see Thedric brandishing the dagger above him. Hatred and revenge were on his face.

Thedric means to kill me, Peter thought, scrambling to rise. But he was too weak. Thedric raised the dagger high over his head with both hands, clenched his lips, and brought it down toward Peter's head.

"Nay!" a woman cried out as she hurled herself on top of Peter.

Thedric's face froze in shock, but it was too late to draw back. The dagger plunged into the woman's back.

Thedric cursed as he let go of the dagger. Peter gasped and pushed the woman off him, gently rolling her onto the ground.

Anna rushed forward. "Rosmunda!"

Peter bent over the woman's anguished face and asked, "Why did you do it?"

"I saw Anna pass by my house," she wheezed. "I followed . . . to ask . . . forgiveness."

Anna's face went pale. She knelt beside Peter and stroked the woman's wrinkled forehead. "I forgive you, Rosmunda."

"Thank . . . you."

"But why did you jump in front of the dagger?" Peter asked, still in shock that she had taken the blow meant for him.

"It . . . seemed . . . right." Rosmunda's failing voice grew so soft that Peter and Anna leaned close to her trembling lips. "Tell Miles . . . face-to-face . . . how sorry . . ."

"We must get help," Peter said, and rose. He searched the docks frantically with his eyes, but there was no help available. In fact, no one had yet noticed the skirmish.

"Nay." Rosmunda fastened her gaze on Anna. "Can I tell your papa that you will follow Jesus?"

"Aye," Anna nodded. She choked back strangling tears. "Tell him."

Rosmunda let out a ragged wheeze. Her body jerked once, then went limp. Anna draped herself across the healer's body and wept. Nothing could help her now.

Peter turned to face Thedric, who had been silently observing. They stared at each other and then at the dagger, which remained pinned beneath the woman's body in a puddle of scarlet blood.

"Anna!" Thedric hissed. "Get off the old fool. We must board ship at once."

Anna glared up at him through her tears. "I cannot marry a murderer."

Thedric's eyes narrowed. "I was only protecting you. As you yourself saw, it is the stonecutter's dagger. He came at us like a madman." His voice softened into pleading, and he reached his hand toward her. "Get up, Anna. Come with me."

She shook her head. "I cannot. If it pleases you, kill me, too. But I cannot marry you."

Thedric dropped his hand and took a step forward. "You refuse to honor your vow?"

"I am sorry, Thedric. I intended to honor my word. Surely you can understand why I cannot board the ship with you now . . . like this."

"Aye," he snarled. He raked his gaze across Peter. "Keep her. But I'll not take the blame for this. If anyone questions me about the old woman, I shall swear you did it. 'Tis your dagger."

"What happened?" Willem rushed toward them in giant strides. Peter suddenly felt dizzy. Willem knelt on one knee over the dead woman. "Rosmunda?" He looked up at Peter. " 'Tis your dagger, Peter. Who did this?"

Peter pointed to the figure of a man just bounding up the ship's gangplank. As he did so, he noticed the oozing blood on his hand and pressed it against his tunic.

"Thedric?"

"We must take Rosmunda to her sister," Anna said. Then she glanced up at Peter. "You are bleeding!"

Willem looked frantically around, then focused steely eyes on Peter. "Can you make it to *de Lowlander*?" Peter nodded. "Then take Anna. At once!"

Peter's dizziness subsided, and he felt a surge of strength. He twisted his tunic over his wounded hand and grabbed Anna's arm with the other. "Come. Hurry."

"Nay." Anna's eyes were round with disbelief. "We cannot just leave her."

"Go! I will handle this," Willem insisted. "Peter, get Anna aboard. Tell my first mate I gave you the order to weigh anchor. I shall meet you in the harbor with the dinghy before nightfall. Go!"

Peter tugged Anna's arm. "Anna! If you have ever needed to obey, the time is now."

She stumbled to her feet. "Wait!" She felt around in her pocket and plucked out one of her papa's seashells. She placed it in her brother's palm and said, "Give this to Berta. She will understand." Then she turned to face Peter. "I am ready."

He snatched her hand and pulled her along. Neither of them spoke. The only sound was their panting breath and the faint din from the quayside. By the time they boarded the gangway to Willem's ship, *de Lowlander,* they were both breathless. The first mate recognized Anna and took the master's orders to heart.

"Break out the anchor! We get underway!"

Peter had addressed the first mate, but he had not spoken another word to Anna, who trembled against him. When the ship began to ease slowly through the water, Peter wrenched his hand away from hers. Ignoring her, he stumbled forward to the ship's rail. A series of dry heaves wracked his body. When he was spent, he laid his head on his folded arms, his forehead pressed against the rail.

"Peter?" Anna inched forward. The raw pain on his face lingered in her mind, and she felt ashamed. It was all her fault—everything. While they had been running for the ship, she had seen the haunted expression on Peter's ashen face and was afraid he would never forgive himself.

As Peter hunched over the railing, Anna felt sick herself. Timidly, she stroked his arm. "Oh, Peter. I am so sorry."

Slowly he straightened and turned toward her. His eyes were glassy and distant. "I killed her."

"Nay, *I* killed her." Peter looked at her, and she cried,

" 'Twas my fault! If I had not refused to forgive her, and schemed to marry Thedric . . ."

His eyes narrowed. "Why did you?"

"We made a deal. He would get you and Guido released from the donjon. In return, I would marry him." Anna hung her head. "I betrayed my love for you. Then I betrayed my word to Thedric. I am a disgrace to my Lord . . . to everyone."

Peter's brown eyes softened momentarily. "Your Lord? What you told Rosmunda about Jesus . . . it was true?"

"Aye. But I have ruined everyone's life. How can Jesus forgive that?"

"Rosmunda was a perfect example of Jesus. Her sacrifice." Then Peter's eyes hardened. "I wish to God I had never seen that dagger." He looked out over the water, his face set grimly.

In silence they watched the shoreline diminish. His body was close enough to touch, but Anna had never felt so distant from the man next to her.

"Peter?"

"Aye." His voice was flat.

"We need to get your hand bandaged."

He lifted his hand and stared at it as if the wound were a foreign, repugnant thing. Was it Rosmunda's blood? Or his?

"Come." Anna tugged on his tunic. He dropped his hand and went with her to the ship's surgeon.

After Peter's hand was stitched and bandaged, he and Anna again took their dismal place at the rail. They stared at the perpetual procession of waves and the ever-darkening horizon. When the air grew chilly and Anna shivered, Peter drew her against his side and sheltered her loosely with his arm. Anna could see, though, that he was lost in thought. In mere hours his handsome, strong face had aged. His expression was inscrutable. He had closed himself off from her as surely as if he had closed and latched a massive wooden door.

"There they are!" Peter disengaged his arm and pointed

toward a dark, little shape bobbing in the waves. Anna squinted into the twilight. It was a dinghy! And indeed, Willem and her mother were aboard, waving their arms.

"Thank the Lord," Anna breathed.

The crew had also spotted the dinghy, and the sailors scurried to bring their master aboard. Willem held Mariel tight while rigging was lowered, and they were hoisted up into the ship. Soon the able crew had retrieved the dinghy, too.

Safely on deck, Mariel rushed over to embrace Anna. Willem gave instructions to his first mate, then led everyone inside to his cabin.

He leaned against the bulkhead in his cramped quarters. "Sit and rest, Mam, Anna."

The women sat down on Willem's cot. Peter remained standing.

"We took Rosmunda's body to her sister," Willem reported. "The authorities are questioning everyone who was in the area, but, thankfully, no one knows what happened. The believers report that the bailiff thinks Menno Simons is still in the area. But, in truth, he is long gone. It seems we have made good our escape. It is over. I would like for us to thank the Lord right now for his protection. And for Rosmunda's sacrifice."

Anna knelt alongside the others, confessing and placing herself in the Lord's mercy. When they rose from their knees, she knew that Christ had forgiven her.

But she still grieved over all that had happened, especially the events that resulted from her own misdeeds. Willem insisted that she and Mam try to get some sleep. And he and Peter left them alone in the tiny compartment.

Chapter 36

 The next day, after discussing things with her mother and receiving her encouragement, Anna went in search of Peter. She now felt sure of God's forgiveness, but she also longed for Peter's. She found him on the main deck, by the starboard rail.

He looked up, gave a brief smile, and nodded. "Rested?"

"Aye. And you?"

He shrugged and looked away.

She moved next to him and looked out across the water. Mere words could not express the regret she felt, yet she had to try before she lost her courage. "Peter," she said gently, "I release you from all the things you once said. I do not expect you to ever care for me again the way you did."

Peter turned and faced her. "Anna, do not say these things. I am not ready to think about all that."

She raised her hand. "Please, let me finish. Then I shall leave you alone."

He raised an eyebrow and leaned against the railing, looking directly at her. "Do I have your word?"

Anna colored at his mocking tone and turned to leave. Peter grabbed her arm. "I am sorry. That was unkind. I will listen to you, Anna."

Anna took a deep, quavering breath. It was hard to rise above the humiliation of her mistakes, but she was determined to do it. "I was completely wrong about Papa and about God. I allowed fear to rule me. That night at the meeting,

I felt God's presence, and since then, I have come to understand his saving grace. Even though I made every mistake, Christ still lives in me. And it is enough. I grieve over all my losses, over the mistakes I have made, yet his peace and his love are enough."

Peter's expression softened. "I have made mistakes, too. And I have learned some things. But right now I hurt."

"There is more," Anna went on. "Where my heart is concerned, I have been a fool. If I could only turn back time, I would marry you without hesitating. I still love you so much. That is how I am able to release you now. But I want to ask, even if you reject my love, will you at least try to forgive me for how I have treated you?"

"I want to," he said wistfully, "someday. I will try. If you are patient."

Anna nodded, but she could not hold back her sorrow that he was not yet able to forgive her. She gave a ragged sob and covered her face, weeping.

After a moment, Peter tilted her chin upwards. "Anna . . ." She let her hands fall to her side and looked up at him through wet lashes. His earnest brown eyes looked into her blue ones. "I've not stopped loving you, Anna, but we have a lot to mend—to forget. I still feel the pain of what happened to Rosmunda. I feel so heavy in my heart right now, I may never feel the carefree, reckless love I once felt for you." He shrugged. "Perhaps what I feel now is even deeper. I still care, but I think you do not understand how angry I was with you, how betrayed I still feel." He lifted his face and stared straight ahead, his jaw clenched.

Slowly, Anna slid her arms around his rigid body and squeezed him tight, speaking into the fabric of his tunic. "Oh, Peter. I am sorry for the pain I caused you. I love you so. I always have. But I will wait! I shall try to be patient and good and . . ."

"Shh," Peter whispered, gently pushing her away, his lips brushing her forehead before he released her. "Shush. All in time, all in time."

Anna drew back and gazed into the brown eyes she so loved. "You are right." Gently, she touched his cheek. "The Lord is keeper of my heart now. He and you can take all the time you deem fit. But there are two things I must do as soon as possible."

Peter clasped her hand tenderly in his bandaged one. "What things?"

"I must be baptized, and I must find Menno Simons and ask his forgiveness."

"And someday I must find Rosmunda's sister and . . ." his voice broke.

"We shall go together."

He cocked his eyebrow at her. "I know not what is in store for me. I am now a fugitive for the Lord's sake, which you have always abhorred. And do you so easily forget that the emperor despises our kind? His dukes would gleefully send their bailiffs to track me down for murder. I cannot go home yet. The first place they will look for me is Visserswert."

"Best you stay in Antwerp?"

"They could be looking for me there, if Thedric talks."

Anna suddenly straightened and blinked her eyes. "I am not afraid. For the first time in a long while, I feel confident about the future, even though I know not what it holds."

Her sincere words began to melt Peter's anger. "Confident?" he asked. "Even in death? Imprisonment?"

"With the Lord's help. Like Papa. Like Rosmunda."

They were silent, and Peter remembered Willem's words to him, *Gird yourself with the Lord instead of that blade.* Grandfather's dagger had not helped him to become a man that suited his name: *Peter, the rock.* Christ was the solid rock. It was time he put aside his pride and did what Willem had advised—gird himself with the Lord.

"There is a place that might be safe," he said. "Menno Simons has been talking about going to the territory of Holstein, east and north of Hamburg, along the Baltic seacoast." He glanced down at Anna, then continued. " 'Tis far from family and friends, but it would only be for a time."

"Oh, Peter, take me with you," she pleaded.

He held back a smile and pretended to be angry. "Now you are determined to go. And if I refuse, you will stow away. And then you will cause all sorts of trouble."

Anna shook her head in earnest determination. "Nay, but I shall not stow away! I promise to be patient and good and . . ."

Peter's face broke into a wide smile. "Come here." He pulled her close and squeezed her tight, burying his face in her hair, inhaling her sweet scent. When he spoke again, his voice was rough with emotion. "I forgive you. How could I not?"

"That is enough for now, Peter," she whispered back. Then Anna lifted her moist eyes over his shoulder toward the heavens, silently renewing her vow to trust the Lord with her heart, even her life.

Epilogue

Charles V, Holy Roman Emperor, stalked across the room and stared at the ornamental hourglass as if it were the enemy. Even if this glass contained all the sand from all the beaches of the world, it would not be possible to stop the spreading corruption of Christendom before it rent his kingdom in two. What would become of his kingdom?

Afterword

This novel was inspired by facts gathered from two historical events—one tragic, the other romantic. The tragic event was the martyrdom of a brave man from Visserswert. Not much is known about the man, only that he was a boatman from the hamlet of Visserswert who gave Menno Simons a ride down the Maas River to Roermond. This act, which took place during the time that Menno Simons preached in the area (around A.D. 1545), led to the man's execution.

The romantic event was the meeting of Kathrina and Martinus Luther. As told in this book, she did actually escape from the convent in a herring barrel, and Martinus Luther did take her and the other fugitive nuns under his protection.

The courageous faith of these people—and all martyrs for Christianity—moves me greatly and makes it my desire to encourage you in the hour when your faith is tested. The early martyrs knew nothing could separate them from the love of God, the *Keeper of Hearts*.

Historical Facts

When negotiations failed through the Council of Trent and other meetings between the church, Charles V, and the Protestant princes and cities, Charles V took military action. During the Schmalkaldic War of 1546-47, Elector John Frederick and Herman von Wied were captured and ejected. The Augsburg Diet treaty allowed German princes and cities the right to choose between Lutheranism and Catholicism. However, intolerance continued against the Jews and other "radical" reformers such as the Anabaptists. When Charles V died of malaria in 1558, his kingdom was split between his son, Philip II, and his brother, Emperor Ferdinand I.

Anabaptist Martyrdom

Pope Gregory IV, of the 11th century, organized the Inquisition, which became a terrible weapon during the Reformation. The popes had absolute power over life and death and used Titus 3:10— "that one who causes divisions should be avoided"—to justify execution, believing that this was the best way to carry out avoidance.

Under Charles V, some thousands were executed, most of them Anabaptists. Martin Luther supported capital punishment for the Anabaptists. The Diet of Speyer of 1529 advocated that "each and every Anabaptist and rebaptized man or woman of an age of understanding shall be judged and brought from life to death with fire and sword or the like according to the occasion without previous investigation by the clergy."

The Inquisition was gradually eliminated because of growing scruples against the death penalty for heretics and the obvious ineffectiveness of severe measures. One of the last formal executions was held in 1614 at Zurich. The last martyr in the Netherlands died in 1574 and the last in Belgium in 1597. But Christianity will always have its martyrs. Stephen, of the Bible, was the first recorded martyr and the book of Revelation speaks of martyrs. Martyrs are brave, faithful persons who know that nothing can separate them from the love of God.

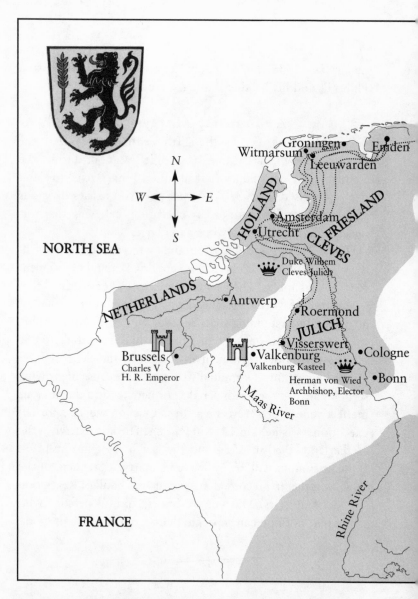

HOLY ROMAN EMPIRE (northern section), A.D. 1545

Europe was not divided into countries as we know them today. Instead, the empire was divided into large, hereditary land possessions held by noblemen and independent cities. The empire was governed by the emperor and his Diet. The Diet was made up of seven

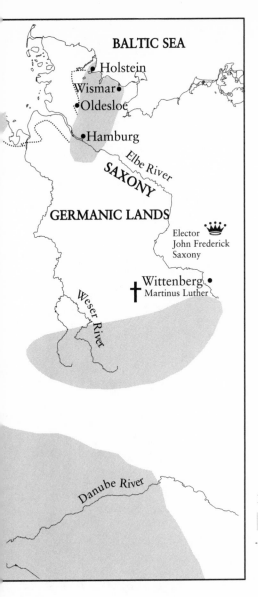

Anna's Political World
Holy Roman Empire

KEY

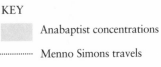

imperial electors, the imperial princes, and council
members of the free imperial cities.

Glossary

Anabaptists—Protestant sectarians of a radical movement that arose in the sixteenth century and advocated the baptism and church membership of adults believers only, as well as separation of church and state. Many were, and are, peace loving and nonresistant. The name means "rebaptizers" and was intended as a reproach. The name was not used by the group itself during that century, but has been embraced in later times.

Antwerp—wealthy Dutch (today Belgian) commercial and trading city on the Schelde River, near the North Sea

Archbishop Herman von Weid, Elector of Cologne—An archbishop in the bishopric of Cologne who had a tolerant policy and was favorable to the Reformation and Lutheranism. His Catholic enemies drove him out in 1546.

bailey—the space within the external wall of a castle

bailiff—court attendant with the power to execute writs, processes, and arrests

barbican—an outer defensive wall, surrounding a castle

beadle—law officer or church officer who assists the bailiff in enforcing law and order

brethren—name the Anabaptists called themselves as they tried to avoid any distinctive labels

burgher—member of the mercantile class of a medieval city

coat of arms—armor insignia, an arrangement of bearings usually depicted on a shield that indicates ancestry and distinctions, contains symbolic and ornamental figures that portray the history or character of an individual or family

donjon—or dungeon, a massive inner tower in a medieval castle, where prisoners were kept

drawbridge—a bridge designed to be raised up, let down, or drawn aside in order to permit or hinder passage, used over a castle moat

duchy—territory ruled by a duke

Duke of Cleves-Julich—one of the German princes (see "German princes," below). From 1391 until 1661, the Kasteel of Valkenburg was subject to the dukes of Cleves-Julich. Visserswert was also in the duke's domain.

dulcimer—a stringed instrument with wires of graduated lengths stretched over a sound box and played by striking two padded hammers or by plucking

Elector John Frederick—German prince and elector, supporter of Lutheranism and the Reformation, elector who protected Martin Luther from the emperor and the pope

escutcheon—a shield or shield-shaped emblem bearing a coat of arms

furlong—a unit of distance equal to 220 yards

German princes—noblemen of various hereditary ranks who ruled over independent kingdoms within the Holy Roman Empire. The emperor ruled over them and with them, and their votes and cooperation greatly influenced the emperor's power for good or bad.

guild—medieval organization to which professional men belonged. Guilds made rules for different branches of trade and crafts.

guilder—basic unit of currency used in Netherlands, coin

Holy Roman Empire—(800–1802) Its core was the kingdom of Germany, but included Czech-speaking Bohemia and Moravia, the Netherlands, Lorraine and Franche-Comte, the Swiss cantons, and much of northern Italy. The emperor was its high ruler, elected by seven electors. The estates within the empire were ruled by lesser princes, electors, and archbishops. There was no continuity or even common names for the leaders and systems within. There were even independent cities within the empire, governed by their own councils, but still subject to the emperor.

kasteel—old Dutch word for castle

lute—a stringed instrument with a body shaped like a pear sliced lengthwise and a neck with a fretted fingerboard, usually bent just below the tuning pegs

Mam—Dutch shortening of the word "mother"; an endearment

marlstone—a rock made up of a mixture of clay materials and calcium carbonate. Often contains kerogen, found in the Visserswert and Valkenburg area along the Rhine River.

Martinus (Martin) Luther—(1483-1546) German priest and reformer most responsible for the great Reformation and Lutheranism. Luther's views became widely known after he posted the "95 Theses" on the church door at Wittenberg. He translated the New Testament into German.

Menno Simons—(1496-1561) a former priest who visited the scattered Anabaptist groups of northern Europe and inspired them with his nighttime preaching. He was not the founder of the movement, but was their greatest leader. Later, some of the Anabaptists would be called Mennonites.

moat—deep, wide trench, usually filled with water, often surrounding a town, fortress, or castle as protection against assault.

nay—no

portcullis—iron grating hung over the gateway of a fortified place and lowered between grooves to prevent passage

principality—territory ruled by a prince

Reformation—sixteenth-century movement in Western Europe aimed at reforming some doctrines and practices of the Roman Catholic Church and resulting in the establishment of the Protestant churches

stonecutter—in medieval days, one who cut or carved stones for building or art projects

Valkenburg—early Dutch city for which recorded history begins in 1040; highest in elevation in the Netherlands, located south of Visserswert

van—meaning *from* or *of,* often affixed to Dutch surnames. Surnames were just originating in the fourteenth through sixteenth centuries. Many times these names were derived from places where the people lived.

Visserswert—a small hamlet on the Maas River in the present Dutch province of Limburg, which in the sixteenth century was in the territory of Valkenburg. Menno Simons preached in a pasture near Visserswert in 1545, and from Visserswert went by boat to Roermond.

whetstone—a stone used to sharpen edge tools

Wittenberg—German city in the Holy Roman Empire, under the jurisdiction of elector John Frederick. Luther resided here and carried on much of his reform.

The Author

Dianne Christner is a full-time writer whose fascination with church history and genealogy prompted her to write about the Reformation and early Anabaptists. Her Mennonite background, research of the Rhineland area, and experience in leading Bible studies provided valuable insight for writing *Keeper of Hearts*. Christner and her husband, Jim, live in Arizona and are the parents of two grown children.